NIGHTBIRD

BY EDWARD DEE

Little Boy Blue
Bronx Angel
14 Peck Slip

NIGHTBIRD

EDWARD DEE

WARNER BOOKS

A Time Warner Company

Copyright © 1999 by Ed Dee
All rights reserved.

Warner Books, Inc., 1271 Avenue of the Americas, New York, NY 10020
Visit our Web site at www.warnerbooks.com

Ⓦ A Time Warner Company

Printed in the United States of America
First Printing: October 1999
10 9 8 7 6 5 4 3 2 1

Library of Congress Cataloging-in-Publication Data

Dee, Ed.
    Nightbird / Edward Dee.
      p.   cm.
    ISBN 0-446-52039-X
    I. Title.
  PS3554.E32N54   1999
  813'.54—dc21
                                                        99-14591
                                                          CIP

For my mother and father,
Ethel and Edward Dee Sr.,
who patrol the bookstores of south Florida
and move their son's work to the best-seller rack
with love

ACKNOWLEDGMENTS

Thanks to my editor, Susan Sandler, and to Jackie Joiner, for their skill and honesty in muscling this story into a novel; Jimmy Franco, Harvey-Jane Kowal, and everyone at Warner Books; and especially Maureen Mahon Egen, for creating an atmosphere where a writer can grow and still feel at home.

To my guardian angels: my agent, Gail Hochman; and Sona Vogel for the fourth time, somehow managing to make sense out of the scribbled notes of an ex-cop.

To my friend Larry Sheaf, for the theater trivia; to Bobby Doyle, for the phone info; Red McGrath, for the circus material; and Terry McCorry, for the weight of old cash.

To the usual suspects for the war stories, the laughs, the drinks, and those wonderful cop voices: you know who you are.

To my lovely researchers: my daughters, Brenda and Patti; and my wife, Nancy, for her insight and patience.

NIGHTBIRD

1

It was one A.M. when a figure in white plummeted through the incandescent Times Square sky and slammed onto the roof of a parked Ford van. Bits of broken glass danced gracefully across the luminous pavement in one of those silent, slow-motion moments that occur when the world stops. Stunned. As if even God were taken by surprise.

"Jumper," Detective Joe Gregory said.

Gregory and his longtime partner, Detective Anthony Ryan, were stuck in traffic across the street, in the short block near the TKTS booth on West Forty-seventh Street.

"You *saw* someone jump?" Ryan said.

"I saw white falling. A woman in white."

"From where?"

"Those terraces above the billboard. The white caught my eye. White nightgown. Young woman."

Within seconds downtown traffic backed up past David Letterman's marquee, and the horns began. Ryan rolled down the window of their unmarked, radioless Buick.

"How do you know she's young?" Ryan said.

"Because I'm a trained investigator."

"What's her zodiac sign?"

"Go ahead, mock me," Gregory said, peering up as if he could see the phosphorous trail of her flight. "But I'll lay odds she's under thirty. Distraught over a lover's quarrel. Ten bucks says we find a tearstained note on her pillow."

A few minutes earlier the veteran detectives had decided to call it a night, take a slow cruise downtown to Brady's Bar. Sip a gin and tonic, tell a few war stories. Now that nightcap would have to wait, because fifty yards away a crowd gathered as dust rose above the crushed roof of a van like incense in the glare of neon.

"Where the hell are all these young foot cops when you need them?" Ryan said as he waved his hand in a futile attempt to part traffic. "You see any uniforms anywhere?"

The NYPD's senior homicide investigators were accustomed to arriving when the scene was framed in yellow tape, blood already dry on the pavement. Gregory blew the horn long and angrily at a cabbie in a skullcap who acted as if the Buick's front bumper were not really inches away from his cab's side door.

"How do you say 'asshole' in Urdu?" Gregory said.

"Asshole," Ryan answered, and he opened the car door.

"Stay in the car, pally," Gregory said, grabbing his arm. "We'll get there soon enough."

But Ryan knew exactly why his mother-hen partner wanted him to stay put; they'd been reenacting this same scene . . . with every young victim . . . ever since the death of Ryan's son eleven months ago. Anthony Ryan Jr., known as Rip to his friends, died in a Utah hang-gliding accident. In the cruelest confirmation of their brotherhood, Ryan and Gregory had both joined the league of men who'd lost their only sons. Across the street the crowds began to spill into the roadway.

"Someone has to get over there," Ryan said, pulling away.

He slammed the car door behind him, then rapped his knuckles on the hood of the Buick to let Gregory know he'd be just fine. He tapped out the shave-and-a-haircut knock he'd heard his partner inflict on apartment doors for three decades. He'd be just fine. Then he shoved his leather shield case into his breast pocket, the gold badge hanging outside, and weaved through the jumble of cars jamming the intersection. The warm night air was moist and heavy, the pavement soft underfoot. The smell of sewer gas spiked the air.

The woman in white had landed on a dingy white Ford Econoline. Hand-painted on the side was "Times Square Ark of Salvation." A halo of loose dirt ringed the pavement beneath the van, jolted from the undercarriage by the force of the falling body. On the sidewalk in front of the van stood a tiny black man in a white shirt and black bow tie, holding a microphone in his trembling hands.

"Sweet Jesus," the street preacher kept saying. "Oh, sweet Jesus."

Ryan elbowed his way through the crowd as a familiar queasiness came over him. It was a feeling he remembered from his days as a young uniformed cop, when a sudden scream ricocheted off the buildings. Everyone looks right at the uniform; you cannot hide in the color blue in this city. John Q. Citizen demands that the monster be dealt with quickly, shoved back under the bed. And that shove was the street cop's stock-in-trade.

"Where did she come from?" Ryan said.

"From the Lord," the preacher said.

Ryan couldn't remember how long it had been since he'd felt the jitters that came with being the first cop on an ugly scene. But the standing rule of the first cop was, "Take control." The crowd calms when a uniform appears. The first cop plays all the roles. He's the doctor: he takes a pulse, checks for breathing, performs CPR, fakes CPR, fakes something, anything. Then he plays cop: covers the body, talks into his radio, barks at the crowd, yells, "Move back . . . give her some air!"

But he "takes control." No matter how wildly his stomach is doing back flips.

"I mean what building did she come from?" Ryan said, the thunderous boom of the falling body still ringing in his ears.

"From the house of the good Lord Jesus," the preacher said.

The woman lay curled on the swayed roof of the van, her head tucked awkwardly under her left shoulder. Long reddish brown hair covered her bloodied face. Ryan's legs trembled as he stepped up onto one of the preacher's wooden speakers. He leaned across the van's roof and adjusted the white garment to cover her bare thighs. The material felt thick and coarse between his fingers. It was *not* a nightgown, but a dress, pleated and full skirted. Old-fashioned, like something you saw on *American Bandstand* in the fifties.

Ryan took a deep breath and tried to detach, to keep his mind calm and think of this simply as a freak occurrence . . . not his life . . . not his problem. He looked around for his partner, then thought, Where the hell are the sirens?

He took another deep breath, and he was doing just fine . . . until he saw the pearl white shard of bone jutting through the skin at the base of her skull, and he saw his own gentle, funny son and shivered at the thought of his body shattering as it struck the floor of a bleak desert canyon.

"Someone call 911," Ryan said to the crowd, his voice hoarse. "Anyone, please." Someone had to have a cell phone: a hooker, a tourist, a drug dealer.

Ryan looked for Gregory, but the faces in the crowd were blurred and hazy. He tried to focus on something else. From its billboard perch across the street, the red Eight O'Clock Coffee cup steamed endlessly into the sultry night air.

Then he heard something.

Sounds. Coming from the woman in white. Like words . . . whispered in a moan or grunt. In that instant his senses exploded and he was aware of everything. Images of air and light went large and floated in slow motion. He moved closer to her face, trying to hear or feel the slightest hint of a breath or twitch. He could smell her hair, a fruity shampoo.

The Ark of Salvation groaned under Ryan's weight as he climbed onto the roof of the van. Creases in the metal cut into his shins; sweat ran down his sides. He cleared the woman's hair away, and white beads from a broken necklace fell, tinkling onto the tin. At first he thought pearls, but then he found the crucifix of a rosary. He placed his hand on her shattered ribs. She felt like a bag of broken glass.

Ryan curved his body until his cheek touched warm metal. He opened her mouth. He could feel her blood on his face. Wet. As were her lips . . . warm and moist.

He didn't know how long he'd stayed up there or exactly what he'd done. But a cop on horseback pulled at his jacket, saying that it was enough. Next thing Ryan was back on the sidewalk, where a uniformed cop half his age said, "I've been in this precinct five years, champ. This is the last place in the world I'd be giving anybody mouth-to-mouth. Know what I mean?"

Amid the lights swirling, radios squawking, car doors slamming, Joe Gregory handed his partner a wet cloth that reeked of disinfectant.

"You know that was stupid," Gregory said softly. "I don't have to tell you that, right?"

Ryan wiped blood from his face and felt a slight stickiness on his upper lip. A tacky sensation he'd first noticed when he was trying to breathe for her. Maybe she'd creamed her face, or it was some residue of makeup remover.

"I thought she might be alive," he said.

"Are you nuts, or what?" Gregory said, not softly this time. He looked around to see if anyone had heard him. It was private business, between partners.

"You gotta let go, pally," Gregory said. "You're gonna make yourself sick like this, the way you're going."

Horns honked, cars rode by slowly in the warm electric night. Some guy yelled to a cop, asking if it was a movie set, looking around as if he expected to see Schwarzenegger or Bruce Willis.

"Who is she?" Ryan asked.

"Some actress, they think," Gregory said, pointing up. "From this building here. The Broadway Arms. It's a co-op for theater people."

The pace of the street had risen to near normal again. Act one to curtain in a New York minute.

"Do we know her name yet?" Ryan said.

"Gillian something. Nobody I ever heard of. The squad's canvassing the building as we speak. But I'm having second thoughts about the jumping."

Ryan himself had wondered why someone would cream her face, then choose to die. But he'd seen enough strange suicide rituals, from donning a tuxedo to complete nakedness, the latter being the most common. He folded the damp cloth carefully and put it into his pocket with the broken rosary beads.

"Just come over here with me for a second," Gregory said, his big paw on Ryan's shoulder. "I got something to show you."

Ryan followed his partner around to the back of the van. A uniformed cop had covered the body with a red-checked tablecloth, a souvenir from the closing of Mama Leone's. Gregory held the tablecloth in the air and pointed to her feet.

"Check this out," he said. "She's barefoot."

"I see that," Ryan said, shrugging.

"And her feet are clean," Gregory added emphatically, still holding the tablecloth in the air. "How the hell did she walk across a terrace in this city without getting dirt or soot on her feet?"

Maybe the terrace was newly carpeted, Ryan thought, or she'd kicked off her shoes at the last minute, then stood on a chair. Maybe her shoes came off in the fall. There were logical explanations. Almost always.

"She said something to me," Ryan said, and instantly re-gretted it.

On the sidewalk, a black midget in an ornate blue-and-gold doorman's uniform hawked the stragglers and out-of-towners. Yanking them toward the entrance to a tacky nightclub on the second floor.

"Said what?" Gregory asked.

"I couldn't understand it."

The rolling lights of the ITT Building announced, "Swel-tering! 95 degrees high. Yanks 1, Tigers 3."

"This woman was dead before you got there," Gregory said. "What you heard was expelled gas. The body expels gas after death. You know that. She didn't say a freaking word."

Maybe he's right, Ryan thought. With all the street noise, the sirens, everybody yelling. Who knows? He tried to recall the moment, to hear the sounds again, but it was like trying to snatch a puff of smoke from the air.

"You're probably right."

"Freakin' A I'm right," Gregory said.

Ryan was well aware that in moments like this you stuck with what you knew for sure. Two things were definite: He could still feel the stickiness on his lips; and he could not pos-sibly have saved her. The words she spoke, the words he thought he'd heard, were the spoken testimony of nightmares, not courtrooms. He would now go about the business of try-ing to put them out of his mind. After all, it didn't make sense, not even to him. It was just a whisper. He was being weird again, he knew that. But it had sounded as though she'd said, "I love you."

2

The late city final edition of the *New York Post* identified the Times Square jumper as Gillian Stone, a young actress only weeks away from opening in a chorus role in a superhyped revival of *West Side Story.* It was topic A on all the morning talk shows. Danny Eumont reread page three of the paper, editing the story, as he leaned against the warm stone wall of the Mid-Town North Precinct.

Three reporters shared the byline of the piece, which was well written considering the short deadline. As a journalist himself, Danny knew he had to write a far different West Side story. One with a personal subplot buried between the lines. He circled a reference to unnamed police sources who stated that the preliminary investigation indicated suicide. He knew that was false.

Angled shafts of sunlight formed geometric patterns on the brownstone across the street. A beat-up Honda sat directly in front of the hydrant, the windshield full of PBA cards, two baby seats in the back. A new bumper sticker stood out on the car's fading blue paint: "New York City Cops Deserve More." Just above the left brake light, another warned: "If You're Not a Hemorrhoid, Get Off My Ass."

Although he had press credentials Danny decided to wait outside rather than give the beleaguered desk officer an opportunity to break his balls. His most recent piece in *Manhattan* magazine painted one of the boys in blue as much less than New York's Finest. The welcome mat is never out for snakes in the media grass. Danny checked his watch; another two minutes had passed. Patience was not his virtue. He sipped coffee from a Starbucks double cup and stared at the front door, watching for his uncle, First Grade Detective Anthony Ryan.

Shifts were changing at the precinct, the day tour relieving the midnight watch. Armed people in baggy shorts and tight T-shirts bullshitted at the curb, the exchange of priceless parking spots in full swing. The late-tour cops looked grubby and exhausted, as if they could not possibly stay awake long enough to survive the LIE or the Palisades Parkway; as if they'd nod off long before the first breath of salty air in East Cupcake, Long Island, or the sharp scent of Rockland County pine.

Many of them never got home, for one reason or another. If they were lucky, however, a shower awaited—wash off the soot of midtown. Then fall into bed, hopefully make love to the good woman waiting there, still warm and funky from the night, sleep until five P.M., awaken to meat loaf and mashed potatoes, kiss the kids good night, drive to Manhattan. Do it all again. It was a tough life. One his uncle had told him to avoid.

Anthony and Leigh Ryan had practically raised Danny. After his father split, he and his mother, Nancy, moved in with the Ryans. That first night at the Ryans' they stayed up all night, unpacking boxes and talking. Danny remembered sitting in his cousin Rip's bedroom, crying as Rip furiously shoved furniture around, making room, making plans. Rip was a year older and seemed infinitely wiser. This is gonna be great, he kept saying. And he made it great. Leigh and Nancy were sisters who got along well enough to share the same household for four years. After four years in that tiny room Rip and Danny were brothers for life. He still couldn't believe he'd never see him again. When Danny and his mother finally moved to their own place, it was to an apartment less than a block away from the Ryans.

From the open station-house window Danny could hear the madhouse that was morning in Mid-Town North. A convoy of pissed-off hookers shuffled past the desk, heading for the front door. The smell of cheap perfume infused the air as the gang-chained hookers yanked each other sideways down the three front steps. They knew the drill and moved directly across the sidewalk, stepping up into the waiting wagon.

"Y'all waiting for me, sugah?" said a tall black girl in thigh-high boots and a red leather micro-mini. The line slowed as those with the highest heels and tightest skirts carefully negotiated the stretch up onto the van's metal steps. "You gorgeous baby, you stay right there till I get back. You hear me?"

Danny set his coffee on the window ledge and stared at his paper.

"Ain't that lovable, he's blushing," the woman said. "When I get back I'm going suck that pretty boy's dick until he screams, 'Lu Ann, Lu Ann, I love you!' I am, sugah baby, I am. You wait right there."

Danny ignored her and kept his eyes glued to the newspaper. The front page consisted of two pictures, side by side, underneath the headline. One picture was a studio head shot of the beautiful Gillian; the other was a long-range photo of the Broadway Arms. A curving arrow, superimposed on the eighteen-story building, traced the path of Gillian's descent. From a terrace on the top floor she traveled past a billboard of an immense sweating navel—an ad for suntan products—past the marquee of a shuttered porn theater—to the roof of a preacher's van.

Suddenly the paper flew out of Danny's hands and he was spun around, almost yanked out of his loafers by the force of two meaty hands. Blood drained from his face as he was spread-eagled against the wall, his hands yanked behind his back. The metal teeth of handcuffs clicked through their ratchets.

"We got a collar here, pally," Joe Gregory said. "Lewd and lascivious leering at an official New York City hospitality hostess. Wadda ya got to say for yourself, Romeo?"

This can't be legit, Danny thought as the Egg McMuffin he'd wolfed down earlier returned for a bitter encore in his throat. Maybe they got their wires crossed. He hadn't quite heard what Gregory said. It happened so fast. He turned his face away from the wall, far enough to see his uncle standing on the sidewalk, hands in his pockets . . . smiling. Anthony Ryan wouldn't be smiling if this were legit. Then he winked at Danny. It definitely wasn't legit. Just Joe Gregory's sick idea of fun. Danny caught his breath and in that instant went from frightened to angry. He twisted around to face Gregory.

"What the hell's wrong with you, asshole?" Danny yelled. He appealed to his uncle. "Please call this lunatic off."

"I never interfere with due process," Anthony Ryan said.

"This is my neighborhood, for Christ's sake. I live here."

Danny actually lived two blocks from the precinct, on West Fifty-sixth, in a studio with a broken Murphy bed.

"Taking the Lord's name in vain in proximity to an official police station," Gregory said. "The charges continue to mount."

The hookers begged Gregory to put Danny into their van. Cops on the sidewalk offered their opinions as to where he should go.

"Why don't we just let him ride to Central Booking in the van," Ryan said. "I hear he's quite the ladies' man."

"Yeah," Gregory said. "But then the *media* might criticize us. That might be sexual harassment, or some kind of ethical faux pas."

"Right," Ryan said. "We wouldn't want an ethical faux pas on our records."

Joe Gregory steered Danny by the back of his shirt all the way to Ninth Avenue. Apparently not satisfied that Danny was handcuffed behind his back in broad daylight, Gregory would jostle him every few steps so that he wobbled drunkenly. Danny never understood what his uncle saw in an idiot like Joe Gregory. And they'd been partners forever. Go figure.

"Okay, joke's over," Danny said. "Let's act like adults now."

"Oh, this guy deserves a beating, pally," Gregory said. "Just say the word. It would make my day."

"Great," Danny said. "Now he thinks he's Dirty Harry."

"I'd eat Dirty Harry for breakfast," Gregory said. "By the way, how soon can I expect to see this police brutality story in *Manhattan* magazine?"

"Soon as you find someone who can read it to you," Danny snapped.

"Maybe you can pick me up some comp copies," Gregory continued, pulling his handcuff key from his pocket. "I'd like one for my brutality scrapbook, one for my false arrest scrapbook. Couple others . . . send to my loved ones. They'll be so proud."

When they reached Ryan's car Danny felt the handcuffs fall away. His wrists ached from just that short time of steel against bone. He understood why more civilian complaints were filed over too tight handcuffs than any other police act.

"See . . . you . . . there, pally," Gregory said, pointing to his eyes, then to Ryan. Cops used signals, shrugs, and nods like a private language, their business not meant for the ears of civilians, especially reporters.

Joe Gregory tousled Danny's hair, then walked away north on Ninth Avenue. Gregory was a big meaty guy, the definition of burly. Pedestrians swung wide around him as he lumbered up the hill, arms hanging, the backs of his huge hands facing forward. *Planet of the Apes,* Danny thought. Pure Neanderthal. Only once, when he reached the corner, did Joe Gregory turn around to flash his red-faced, shit-eating grin.

"Funny guy, your partner," Danny said, rubbing his wrists. "He have an overwhelming need to be an asshole, or what?"

"Actually, he likes you."

"He's got some way of showing affection. I bet women are lining up to go out with that guy."

"He was just kidding with you, Danny."

"No, he wasn't. It's the Todd Walker story. That's what that shit was all about. Because I wrote a negative piece about a cop. Gregory's letting me know I've stepped over the thin blue line."

"Don't overanalyze him, please."

"I'm not. I don't care what he thinks. I'm proud of that story. Todd Walker was a bad cop. He should have been convicted, and you know it. He beat that kid for no reason, pure and simple. Beat him half to death. For what . . . because the kid called him a fag in Spanish?"

"Todd Walker was a dirtbag," Ryan said. "And most cops, including Joe Gregory, think he got off way too light. My partner just has a thing about seeing our dirty laundry in public."

"Yeah, and I'll bet he has a pile of his own dirty laundry."

Ryan gave Danny a look. A look he knew meant "Don't be a wiseass, nobody likes a wiseass." It was his pet peeve with Danny, who claimed he was haunted by the ghost of Groucho Marx whispering wiseass comments in his ear.

"How did you know I was here?" Ryan said.

"I called Aunt Leigh. Are you assigned to this case?"

"It's officially a Mid-Town North investigation, but it's high profile, so the chief of detectives wants us to keep a hand in. Plus we were first on the scene."

Anthony Ryan stood on the edge of the curb and turned to face foot traffic on Ninth; cops hated to leave their backs exposed. He leaned against his blue Oldsmobile Ninety-eight. The car was a 1990, but new to Ryan. He'd been driving Rip's

1975 olive green Volvo, but after Rip's death, he gave it to Danny. The car was such an ugly color, it was simple to find in any parking lot. Rip had nicknamed the car "the olive" and said all he needed was the martini.

"What were you guys doing in Times Square last night, anyway?" Danny said.

"Fighting the forces of evil."

"No, seriously."

"If you must know, we were schmoozing. Gregory was collecting money for the boat ride for Project Children."

"Project Children," Danny said. "Isn't that the charity that brings delinquents from Northern Ireland over here so they can swap notes with our delinquents?"

Ryan smiled. Danny knew he could never be angry with him for long. That was the smile he remembered whenever he and Rip got in trouble. The smile and the calmness.

"Okay, what is it, Danny?" he said. "What's going on?"

"It's about Gillian Stone."

"Information *from* the press. That's a switch."

The smell of baking bread wafted up from an ancient brick oven in the basement beneath the Laundromat. An old woman in a checked raincoat stood in the sun outside the OTB, chin tilted upward, studying a racing tout sheet.

"The *Post* says Gillian was wearing a long white nightgown," Danny said. "Is that accurate?"

"What if it is?"

"Gillian Stone never wore a nightgown that I know of. Go through her clothes, I bet you don't find one. She slept in panties and T-shirt. If anything at all."

"You slept with her?"

"Gillian and I went together for almost a year. We broke up about six months ago."

"Did I know this?" Ryan said.

"You kidding—tell the family? You know how they are. 'When are you getting married?' When this, when that. It's all I would hear."

"But the bottom line is you haven't seen her in months, right?"

"Until last night. I was with her last night."

"Jesus Christ," Ryan said, and he looked up at the sky. "That's why you freaked out when Gregory cuffed you. Jesus Christ. Get in the car, Danny."

"It's not what you think."

"Don't say another word, please," Ryan said. "Just get in the goddamned car."

3

Anthony Ryan made a hard right off Ninth Avenue and drove toward the river. He wanted no part of the streets around the precinct; too many cops were coming and going, observing, overhearing. He knew all the clichés about cop paranoia, but still he'd move the conversation to a safer venue. Never take chances with your own. He'd lost a son, he wasn't about to lose Danny. His mind raced in a thousand directions, exploring elaborate escape routes legal and otherwise. Just in case.

"Start from the beginning," he said as he backed the Olds against the piling that stopped it from rolling into the Hudson. He cut the engine and faced his nephew. Fifty yards to their left tourists boarded the Circle Line ferry.

"You mean when I first met her?" Danny said.

"No, let's focus on last night."

"I want to help out on this. Anything I can do, please. Let me help."

"Last night, Danny. Did you run into her somewhere? Was it a phone call? Stick to the specifics of last night."

"Okay, last night. Well, I hadn't even talked to her in maybe four months. Not a word. Last night my phone rings about seven-fifteen, seven-thirty. It's Gillian, and she's upset. Wants to see me."

"She called you from where?"

"Home, I guess. I don't know for sure."

Ryan pulled a small leather case out of his jacket pocket—his personal notebook, containing index cards, not the official NYPD notebook. He wasn't ready for anything written that might become public record. He set a stack of three-by-five cards on the seat and motioned for Danny to continue. He'd check the LUDs, get the exact time on all local calls from Gillian's phone.

"She said she wanted me to meet her in Caramanica's," Danny said. "It's a bar on Third Avenue."

"Why Third Avenue when you both live on the West Side?"

"The *Cheers* syndrome. She liked to be in a place where everyone knew her name. She used to live around the corner from the place. Models, jocks, yuppies, wannabes, rich assholes."

"We don't have time to editorialize, Danny. Please. Who arrived first?"

"I got there about eight-twenty, she was already there."

"What was her mood?"

"Angry, but not foaming at the mouth. More of a quiet anger; subdued, actually. Sad may be a better word. She looked tired, too."

Danny said they talked for more than an hour, Gillian doing almost all of it. Whispering, with an agitated, husky intensity. She left alone, shortly after ten P.M. Grabbed a cab outside as Danny watched through the window.

"Did you notice anything on the cab?" Ryan said.

"Don't you want to know why she called me?"

"A medallion number would be nice," Ryan said, ignoring him. Checking his watch.

"It was yellow, that's all I know."

"Did you see or hear from Gillian after that?"

"No," Danny said softly. "Not until I heard her name on the radio this morning."

A sudden crash made Danny jump. A UPS truck rear-ended a baby Mercedes whose driver had stopped in the middle of Twelfth Avenue to gawk at the USS *Intrepid.*

"You need to call that in or something?" Danny said, pointing at the instant traffic jam.

"Nobody's hurt. The Mercedes has a phone if he wants help."

"I thought maybe you had some official duty here. Some regulation to follow, rule eighteen point five or something."

"Let's concentrate on this right now. Was Caramanica's crowded?"

"Jammed. All the beautiful people du jour. Sorry, editorializing."

"It's okay," Ryan said, starting to relax a little. "I can see there's no stopping you." He rolled down the car window. Water slapped against the pilings beneath them. "So then some of those beautiful people saw Gillian leave alone. And beautiful witnesses can verify that you stayed behind?"

"Absolutely. I stayed to watch the last inning of the Mets game. Maybe another twenty minutes."

"Did you go straight home after that?"

"Absolutely."

"How?"

"Cabbed it. All by my lonesome. Got home in time to catch the news at eleven."

"What were you catching at one A.M.?"

"Nothing but zees. Snug in my bed."

"All by your lonesome?"

"Don't sound so surprised. It happens."

"Yeah, but for once it's not a good thing."

"Am I a suspect?"

"No suspects, Danny. It's a suicide, remember."

"Then why the third degree?"

"To make sure you're out from under."

"Out from under what?"

Ryan didn't know exactly *what*. Probably nothing. It was too complicated to explain. Just an instinctive reaction to protect someone he loved.

"There's more to this, isn't there," Danny said. "It's not a suicide, is it."

"I thought you came here today to *give* information."

"The minute you finish your interrogation, I'll be glad to give you everything."

"It's not an interrogation. I want you to understand that another detective will be running the show."

"I thought you said you were working this?"

"Not after what you just told me. So if you need me to do anything for you, let me know immediately. While there's still time to maneuver."

"I have nothing to hide," Danny said, wondering what his uncle could possibly do if he was involved. What maneuvering room could there be?

"Good," Ryan said. "Good."

"I can give you a solid suspect in this case. This producer, Trey Winters. He's a big mucky-muck on Broadway."

"I know who he is," Ryan said, putting the car in gear.

"That scumbag had something to do with this, Uncle Anthony. I know it."

"Save it for a few minutes. We're going up to her apartment."

With the window open Ryan could feel heat rising from the blacktop, warning that the day would be another scorcher. He knew his nephew wasn't finished talking. He hoped he wouldn't complicate things any further.

"Last night," Danny said, "I couldn't get her out of my mind. I remembered her smell, stupid jokes she'd told me. I kept thinking, She could have called anybody . . . but she called me. That means something to me. Then, this morning . . ."

Danny Eumont had his mother Nancy's good looks, her deep brown eyes and fair skin. The same coloring as her sister, Ryan's wife, Leigh. And their son.

"Why did you break up with her?" Ryan asked.

"She dumped me, that's why. It wasn't my idea. She dumped me for a part in *West Side Story*. Her almighty career. She knew taking the role and that apartment had strings."

As he waited for the light, Ryan tapped his index cards against the steering wheel. Behind them a jackhammer beat a steady rat-a-tat, breaking concrete to make way for the bright new, user-friendly waterfront. He longed for the old dark, dangerous waterfront and the huge swinging nets filled with crates of Scotch being dropped on traitorous longshoremen; of fights to the death with curved box hooks; of tarantulas lurking in a ton of bananas. It was a less complicated city then, a less complicated time. A time when all Detective Anthony Ryan's family knew about dark, dangerous places were the things he told them.

4

At the corner of Broadway and West Forty-seventh a pair of female uniformed cops from Mid-Town North stood outside the yellow tape that encircled a van with a crushed roof. The body of the young actress had been removed to the morgue hours earlier, but investigators from the Crime Scene Unit were still going through the paces of their particular specialties. Although a uniformed cop's only job was to secure the scene and protect the evidence, midtown cops knew the moment they set foot on the street in uniform that they became walking information booths: Where is Broadway? "You're on it." Where can I find a cheap place to eat? "Jersey."

The two attractive rookies were also accustomed to being gawked at by men, particularly foreign men. At the edge of the curb a dark, muscular man carrying a large blue duffel bag inched closer to them, straining to make eye contact. He wore a tight white turtleneck shirt, accentuating wide shoulders and a narrow waist. His black hair and copper brown skin shone as if oiled and polished. The cops ignored him, figuring he'd be gone when the light changed.

"Another Latin lover to contend with," one cop said.

"That's the juggler," the other said. "Thinks he's God's gift."

The light changed and the juggler moved away gracefully despite the heavy bag. When he reached the center island he found his performing partner sprawled against the statue of George M. Cohan, snoring peacefully in the morning sun. He let the duffel bag slip from his shoulder. The bag contained his juggling props, including three bowling balls, and weighed almost seventy pounds. It hit the sidewalk like a clap of thunder.

"Bastard," the man yelped. "What is wrong with you? I thought it was bombs."

"Russian bombs, Pinto," the juggler said, laughing. "Your own people's bombs. Who else would bomb New York?"

"Bomb is joke to you?" Pinto, the Russian said, squinting into the sunlight. "Scaring people to heart attack is joke. Everything big joke."

Pinto was a baggy pants clown who specialized in magic. Time and vodka had dulled his skills, but he could still work a crowd. His given name was Nickolai Timoshenko. A skin condition, called vitiligo, had earned him the nickname Pinto when he worked the one-ring Mexican circuses. That was where he'd first met the juggler Victor Nuñez, twenty years ago. Only eight years old then, Victor Nuñez was already a vital part of his family's trapeze act, which was on its way to becoming the premier trapeze act in all the world.

Victor flattened his back against the cool base of the statue. He shoved Pinto over and they sat shoulder to shoulder in a spot they called the best seat on Broadway.

"Your head should be examined," Pinto said, peeking around to check the lines.

The lines for the TKTS booth behind them were already past the statue of Father Duffy, the doughboy priest. The booth carried half-priced tickets for that day's non-sold-out theater performances. On matinee days like today they opened at ten A.M. In a few minutes the lines would stretch all the way back to where they sat, back to the statue of the Yankee Doodle Dandy. Hours of waiting, a bored crowd. It was a street performer's dream.

"So, last night where was the Mexican stud horse?" Pinto said. "Performing between whose legs?"

"You wish you were between someone's legs, you jealous Russkie."

"Tell me jealous when I visit you in the AIDS ward. I have enough to worry with living in the same house with you."

"If you saw this *chica,* ooh, baby. You should be jealous."

"I should get another roommate, that's what I should. You chase too much pussy. I boil the forks after you eat."

The pair had worked the New York theater district for many years. They knew where to find every back door, open bathroom, free meal, and loose woman in a ten-block radius. They appeared only in the hot months, Memorial Day to Labor Day, then went south. They loved the big city's money but hated the cold weather, Victor especially. Jack Frost strummed cruel tunes on his arthritic joints.

"We'll have a crowd today, my friend," Pinto said. And the day did look promising: plenty of young, well-dressed Europeans with money to burn. "I can smell the shekels already."

"Shut up, Russkie. Don't talk about work, talk about women."

On Wednesdays they did two shows: one for the matinee line, one for the evening ticket seekers. Matinee days were always a strain on Victor Nuñez; he'd hurt tomorrow. But today was different; he could feel the adrenaline rush, an excitement that had nothing to do with juggling. He needed to calm down.

Victor closed his eyes and turned his face to the sun. The sun was important to him; his bronzed skin made him stand out in any crowd. Every day he rubbed baby oil into his face. A man needed lubrication to keep his skin young. Especially a man who worshiped the sun. And getting sun in this city was not an easy task. A bare sliver of morning sun sliced between the buildings. Noon was the best time, when the sun stood directly overhead. Two hours either way and the narrow floor of the canyon turned dark enough for vampires. In front of them a steady stream of tourists crossed the small concrete island that separated Broadway from Seventh Avenue.

"We need the bucks today," Pinto said. "To pay the blood money in the parking lot."

"Why do you bring the stupid car? Take the subway. Leave the car in the Bronx."

"With this bag to carry? Besides, too many spics in the subway."

Pinto had his own bag of props containing the tools of prestidigitation. He'd learned his craft in the Moscow Circus, but the lure of easy rubles in con games and the pickpocket trade won him over, and he wound up having to do a disappearing act . . . to America. For eighteen years he'd plied magic in every flea-bitten circus and side show this side of the Atlantic. At least those desperate enough to hire him.

Victor's part of the act ran about twenty-five minutes depending on crowd banter. But banter, as long as it was gentle and funny, established rapport, and that was Pinto's most valuable contribution. Victor with his dark good looks zeroed in on the ladies. Always the ladies. And that drew more cash than any artistry. On days like today, with the weather warm, Pinto worked the kids, while Victor did his entire routine—the pins, the bowling balls, then finishing with the torches. The bowling balls were the hardest part, ravaging his elbows and shoulders, but fire was the big ending. Guaranteed to open wallets. They liked to finish at the exact moment the ticket booth opened. Moods changed at that moment, people sensed movement, progress, and happy people were generous people.

"The woman from the Big Apple Circus could come today," Pinto said.

"Forget the Big Apple Circus, Pinto. They don't want us,

and I don't want them. This summer is my last in this city. *Finito.*"

"Oh, I forgot. The man with big plans. *El patrón,* strutting around his fancy restaurant in his white suit. Fucking all the little waitresses."

"*Silencio, por favor.* Your bad breath is making dark clouds."

Victor angled his body so he could watch the flow of detectives coming in and out of the Broadway Arms. He could tell the detectives by the way they walked. Cocky little bastards, strutting around as if they owned the city. Pale, paunchy guys in cheap suits, hair sprouting from their ears. Cops didn't frighten him at all. He'd already buried one in a tropical swamp.

"Show time," Pinto said. "Grease the crowd for the star . . . the Mexican stud horse. Maybe some rich lady is here who will buy restaurant for you. All you have to do is fuck her five times a day. Right, my friend?"

"Find her and tell her it's a deal."

Victor heard the laughter as Pinto began. He worked the back of the crowd slowly, pretending they weren't there, like Emmett Kelly sweeping away the spotlight. Then the scarf trick; he blew his nose in the last one. Bodily functions were guaranteed laughs.

Across the street, cops on the eighteenth floor of the Broadway Arms lined up on the terrace. All doing the same thing: looking down. As if that would somehow reveal the answer. Their heads lined up along the rail like painted coconuts on the cart of a Juarez street vendor. If he had an M-16, he could pick them off one by one. Splat, splat, splat.

On the sidewalk, under the green canopy of the Broadway Arms, the big red-faced detective flailed his arms at the doorman. Victor wondered where the other one was, the thin one. The one who had climbed onto the roof of the van.

Victor reached into his bag and took out his performing gloves. Right on top for a change. He pushed his hands into the tight leather fingers. He rolled his shoulders back toward the statue and heard the pop of cartilage. The sounds of his body grew louder every day, crying out to him that enough was enough. The family curse of rheumatoid arthritis had not skipped his generation. But he could sense change in the air, the life he'd dreamed of, a life he could almost taste.

Opportunity knocked, and he had answered. The days of passing the hat were numbered, days of sunshine promised to be endless. He could pull it off. It was like the trapeze. The critical moment in trapeze was the moment you left the platform. The timing had to be perfect, and his was flawless. The courage to push off . . . he'd always had that. Victor Nuñez was fearless. It was the most exhilarating feeling in the world, the rush of danger. Off into the darkness. Without a net. No turning back. He was airborne.

5

Everybody in my family sneezes twelve times," Detective Joe Gregory said, the back of his hand up to his nose. "Exactly twelve. Physically impossible for any of us to quit before twelve sneezes."

He was sitting on Gillian Stone's bed, recovering from sneeze number six, surrounded by delicate lacy bras and French-cut bikini panties in shimmering Jell-O colors.

"Maybe you're allergic to perfume," Danny Eumont said.

"It ain't perfume I'm allergic to, kid," he said. "Trust me on that one."

Danny told Gregory the same story he'd told his uncle: the time sequence they were so worried about. Gregory added that the Broadway Arms night doorman said Gillian got out of a cab a little before ten-thirty. They both seemed to think this backed up Danny's story.

"Do you still have a key to this place?" Gregory said.

"I never *had* a key to this place."

Gregory registered sneeze number seven. Ryan excused

himself, saying he was going to see what the Crime Scene Unit had done on the terrace. A male uniformed cop from the precinct sat in the living room, reading magazines.

"You're sure you never had a key," Gregory said. "Young stud like you might have so many keys he forgets which is which."

"I was never even *in* this place before. When I was going out with her she lived on the East Side. And I never had a key to that place, either."

Danny had overheard Gregory saying that detectives responding from the Mid-Town North Precinct found Gillian's door locked—dead-bolted. It was one of those locks where the dead bolt could be engaged by a thumb switch from the inside but needed a key to be locked from the outside. Gillian Stone's house keys had been found in her purse.

"Who, to your knowledge, might have a key to this place?" Gregory said.

"Trey Winters, of course."

"The squad interviewed him in the precinct this morning. Anybody else?"

"Maybe her sister, only other one I can think of."

"Faye Boudreau," Gregory said. "One hundred eighty-five East Sixty-fourth Street, apartment three-K."

"Gillian's old apartment. I've been in that one."

"Faye surrendered a key to detectives at the morgue this morning. What's your take on the sister? Little wifty, isn't she?"

"I met her three or four times," Danny said, wondering what "wifty" meant. "Hardly opened her mouth. Hello, good-bye."

"This morning at Bellevue," Gregory said, "she came off as a bit of a space cadet. Wouldn't even set foot in the viewing room. Now we have to wait for the parents to fly in from Arizona to make the official ID."

That's one for my book on cops, Danny Eumont thought. The fact that Joe Gregory found it strange that Faye Boudreau was unable to look at the body of her sister. It was another piece of irrefutable evidence that cops, like the rich, were different from the rest of the world.

"I gotta tell ya," Gregory said. "The thing that bothers me about all this is *you*. Why call *you?* You say your relationship ended six months ago. Now she's involved with someone else. But . . . out of the blue, when she's upset, she calls you."

"I've been trying to explain that. The reason she called me . . . and why she was so upset . . . was that she was afraid she might be getting dropped from the show. Her producer, Trey Winters, trumped up this phony rumor that she had a substance abuse problem."

"So she calls you for a shoulder to cry on."

"She couldn't exactly cry on Trey Winters's shoulder, could she?"

My bombshell, Danny thought, and Joe Gregory didn't even look up. As if he'd heard it all before. He continued to pick his way through her underwear, nonchalantly, enjoying it.

"Still seems strange," Gregory said, "she calls *you*. Seems to me she'd have to have a damn good reason to call a boyfriend she dumped six months ago. You think maybe it was because you're a magazine writer, and she's thinking—"

"*She* didn't bring that up. *I* asked *her* if she wanted me to write a story."

"Are you writing this story? Let's get that out on the table right now."

"No, I'm not writing this story," Danny said. "But you're missing the point. The point is that there was no drug problem in the first place."

"Winters made it all up."

"Exactly. That's what needs to be looked at. Not what happened six months ago."

Gregory's Charlie Chan style of questioning was beginning to get on Danny's nerves. His uncle had told him that interrogation was becoming a lost art. He said that some detectives got so used to easy cases, or "ground balls," that they forgot that sometimes they actually had to solve one.

"According to Winters," Gregory said, "Gillian's drug problem has been an ongoing issue for over a month. If so, what set her off last night?"

"Winters did. He called her last night and insisted she had to be tested by a lab of his choosing."

Gregory changed the focus of the questioning to Gillian's family. Danny told him the little he knew. Gillian was Arizona born and raised. Gillian's mother, Lynnette, was active in theater groups around their home in Scottsdale. Her father, Evan, was a high-profile investor and developer, known mostly for extravagant shopping malls in the Southwest. On the dresser was a picture of a smiling Evan Stone arm in arm with Barry Goldwater, both wearing cowboy hats and bolo ties.

"So what's the bottom line here, Danny? Was she doing drugs or not? Toxicology will eventually settle the issue, but it might take a while."

"Let me put it like this: I went with her for almost a year, and we were very close. Very, very close. I'd know if she was doing drugs, believe me."

"Then why was she so upset about the test?"

"Because Winters had her trapped. Once the word got around, no matter what the outcome, her reputation on Broadway would be damaged. People would remember the fact she was tested, not the results."

"You buy that?"

"Yeah. Broadway is a small town."

"What kind of shape was she in when she left the bar last night?"

"She had a buzz going," Danny said. "A minor buzz."

"Slurring her words, according to the bartender. Wobbly on her feet, according to the doorman. After only three drinks."

"She only weighed about one oh five. It doesn't take many drinks at one oh five."

"But she was drunk, right?"

"Maybe she didn't eat; I don't know."

"See, now that bothers me," Gregory said, looking up from a stack of Broadway show T-shirts. "She's someone you care for, and you admit she had half a load on. Yet you didn't even offer to see her safely home?"

"See her safely home? What century are you from? For your information, I *did* ask her if she wanted me to take her home. She said no. End of story."

"Number eight," Joe Gregory said, and sneezed into a camisole.

Anthony Ryan stood on the terrace, looking down onto Times Square and wondering what it would be like to fall upside down in the wind, your last glimpses of life confined to fleeting glances into the windows of the neighbors below . . . seventeen sad scenes . . . a flickering stack of Hopper paintings, subtly hinting that everyone was lonely and desperate, the rest of us only one disappointment away from going off a terrace ourselves.

A few floors below, a large-winged bird floated in the murky heat. It was odd watching a bird from above. A hawk, maybe. Ryan had read there were hawks in the city. He didn't know anything about birds. But he did know about his son, who had flown through the canyons of immense western states on nylon wings that failed. He couldn't stop seeing his son falling through space, the sound of collision suddenly so catastrophic that the mere thought sucked the breath from him. He clutched the railing as his legs buckled and his knees banged against the opaque panel.

Ryan had always been terrified of heights, but with the death of his son all fear of death evaporated. What difference did it make? *Death will come, sure as shit it will, but we'll all be together again. How bad is that?* He'd lost all patience for people who complained about niggling crap. At night he'd sit in front of the TV and watch people complaining about taxes, traffic, politics, prices, about every stupid thing. How shallow were the lives of these people to get worked up over such inconsequential bullshit. Try losing a child. See what's important then.

The hawk flew closer. Ryan spoke his son's name aloud, and the hawk floated toward him. Anthony Ryan was angry with himself for not having been a better father. But he was comforted by the thought that his son was no longer falling.

Did you know Trey Winters owns this apartment?" Gregory said.

"I figured he did," Danny said. "A lot of the production companies own apartments. They use them to lure big-time stars. It's a major perk, especially in New York."

"But Gillian's small potatoes in this show. Doesn't a major perk like this apartment sound a little generous to you?"

"I know exactly what you're driving at," Danny said. "And I couldn't agree with you more."

"Did she actually say they were having an affair?"

"Not in so many words. But the point I got was that this trumped-up drug charge was Winters's way of insulating himself from any accusations she might make."

"You got all that from 'not in so many words,'" Gregory said. "Did Gillian tell you that she expected Winters to visit her last night? Here in this apartment?"

"No, she didn't," Danny said.

He was aware that Gregory was staring at him, trying to gauge his reaction. It was surprise. Genuine surprise.

"Well, he was here," Gregory said. "Apparently the last person to see her alive."

"She didn't say anything about it to me," Danny said, and he wondered if it would be too nervy to take out his own notebook. "Maybe he dropped by unexpectedly."

"And by the way," Gregory said, reaching into a dresser drawer, "contrary to your prediction, we found these three nightgowns."

"I swear to God, I never saw her wear one before."

"Did you know Gillian was the understudy for the role of Maria?"

"No," Danny said.

"I guess she forgot to tell you that, too. Yeah. Actually, what she was wearing when she died was a costume, not a nightgown. It was a dress from the show's wardrobe, for the 'I Feel Pretty' number. A costume Trey Winters brought over last night for her to try on."

"I had no idea," Danny said. "He brought her a costume to try on?"

"That doesn't sound like someone who is about to be dropped from a show, does it?"

"Why would he bring a costume at that time of night?"

"That was my next question, kid."

On the terrace, Anthony Ryan went through Gillian's motions again. He always walked in the victim's footsteps. Only two steps: door to hassock. The hassock was short and wide with small, round wooden legs. Her white ballet shoes had been found, side by side, next to the hassock. Apparently she'd stepped out of the shoes, then up onto the hassock, thus destroying Joe Gregory's "clean feet" theory.

He tried to imagine the young woman in the white dress moving from the glass door to the hassock. Barefoot, Ryan stepped up onto the cushiony hassock. The covering felt like rough wool, the pattern varied red and beige squares and circles. His jacket whipped and snapped in the blast furnace of a breeze. The top of the metal rail was now even with his knees. He put one foot on the rail. For the five six Gillian the rail would have been at midthigh. Still easy to step over. Fall over. Be pushed over.

He wobbled on the hassock as he glanced down at the chaos of Times Square. A haze of smog and dust had turned the scene surreal. He wondered what indescribable pain could cause a beautiful young woman to step over the metal rail and fall into space. To fall and fall, for a length of time his mind would not let him consider. He'd heard that people fainted, passed out, before they hit bottom. He hoped so. He hoped with all his heart. My God, he hoped his child hadn't suffered.

Gregory looked up when the squat, uniformed cop appeared in the bedroom doorway, a copy of *Variety* in his hand.

"I'm outta here," the cop said, pointing to his watch. "It's my meal hour, and the house informs me that no personnel is available for relief. So fuck it, you're on your own."

Danny took the opportunity to look around the apartment, try to photograph it with his mind. Nail the detail.

"Give us a few more minutes, kid," Gregory said.

"I don't think so," the cop said. "You guys are dragging this out like I got all day."

"Ask my partner to watch the door for a while," Gregory said.

"You mean the guy out on the terrace in deep conversation with himself."

The cop made a gesture, flipping his thumb toward his mouth, as if to let Gregory know that he was so streetwise, he knew Ryan was a drunk. Gregory rose from the bed, one of Gillian's T-shirts in his hand, a black one from *Les Misérables*.

"Get back in the hallway, Officer," he said. "And plant your ass out there until I tell you to leave."

"Hey, don't get your balls in an uproar with me," the cop said. "But I'm not holding the bag if that oiler falls off the fucking terrace. You don't believe me, go look yourself. Walking tightrope on the rail, whatever the fuck he's doing out there."

"I don't have to look," Gregory said, shutting his notebook and slipping it into his jacket pocket. Anthony Ryan had told Danny that Gregory had a special little pocket sewn into all his suit jackets, to hold his shield. It was something he'd learned from the Mob guys, who had the pocket made for their cigarettes.

"I know exactly what he's doing," Gregory said. "He's walking in the victim's shoes; reconstructing her last acts, trying to get inside her head. It's called detective work, hoople. And the fact you didn't know that illuminates the reason why he's a first-grade detective and you're up here guarding furniture."

"Hey, the man is placing himself in a dangerous position. Consider yourself duly notified. I wash my hands of this matter."

Gregory mumbled something, then turned to Danny, his face crimson. "We got an appointment. We'll continue this later."

He walked to the terrace door. But he didn't step outside.

"Hey, Spiderman," he said. "Get your shoes on and let's get going. We have to meet the Stones. I don't want to keep those people waiting."

"Now?" Ryan said as he stepped out of the sunlight. Gregory didn't answer him. Ryan's hair was windblown, his pupils dilated, as he stepped into the darkened apartment, giving him an oddly confused look. "What time are we supposed to be there?" he said.

Again Gregory didn't answer; this time he was too busy sneezing.

"How many is that?" Ryan said.

"I lost count," Gregory said, still clutching Gillian's shirt. The sketch of the dark-eyed waif Cosette stared out from under his meaty fist. "I'll complete the sneeze cycle in the car."

"Where are you meeting them?" Danny asked.

"At a prearranged location," Gregory said.

"Am I going with you?" Danny said.

"*You're* going wherever you go," Gregory said. "Not with us."

"Which hotel are they staying in?" Danny said, looking

directly at his uncle. "Might as well tell me. I can find out through other sources."

"Then that's how you should do it," Gregory said.

6

Danny Eumont strode furiously up Ninth Avenue, crossing streets against moving traffic, banging into everything and everyone in his path. Curses and car horns littered his wake. Fuck Joe Gregory, he thought. He'd tried to make him look foolish, ambushed him, let him say his piece, and then sprung information he'd held back. Like he was Mike fucking Wallace.

How the hell was Danny supposed to know Gillian was in costume? And that understudy shit, what was that all about? Gillian would have told him if she was the understudy for the lead role. Was Gregory too stupid to see that? Trey Winters was selling a bogus story, painting Gillian as some out-of-control junkie, trying to make himself look like the good guy. It was too late, too obvious. Gregory may have bought into it, but not him. Danny wasn't going to let Trey Winters skate on this. The hell with Gregory, he'd write this story. He owed it to Gillian.

When he arrived at his apartment, the fresh baguette he'd picked up at the baker was still warm, but in two pieces from

Danny squeezing it in the center. He tossed it on the kitchen counter and snapped on his computer. Then he put his baby to bed for a short nap. His baby was a 525-page manuscript, his first novel, one he'd been working on since college. It was an NYPD story about a renegade gang of brutal cops.

He dropped the novel into a fireproof box in the closet, then he called his mother. His mother would never forgive him if she had to hear this news from Aunt Leigh first. He'd call so she'd be able to say those all-important words: "I already know."

Danny's phone and his computer sat on an old maple butcher block–style table near the apartment's lone window, the monitor raised by the Manhattan Yellow Pages. The table had once resided in the kitchen of his boyhood. It was a gift from Mom, intended for dining, but Danny's culinary conflicts were rare.

His mother seemed to know more than he expected. Her long silences during his phoned-in confession were the worst penance he'd ever received. On the wall directly above the computer screen were pictures of his heroes: Hemingway, Fitzgerald, Jimmy Breslin, Pete Hamill, Groucho Marx, and Rip Ryan. To his left: the window. Danny liked working near the window; he could watch all the other budding writers walking the street, and he knew he was pounding out more pages than they. Plus he could see over the small park adjacent to a luxury high-rise, across Fifty-seventh Street, keep an eye on the front window of Kennedy's. Many nights he heard the siren call of neon. Finally Danny told his mother someone was at the door.

He began writing the minute he hung up. He knew he had to jump on the story while the images were still fresh. Get words on paper when the fire was burning. Write in the wild flames of passion, edit in the cool blue afterglow. Starting with Gillian's bedroom: family pictures in silver frames, mostly people in shorts and T-shirts; a cactus garden in a red clay pot; the head of an American Indian carved out of a chunk of solid turquoise the size of a peach; the smell of perfumes and powders; a gold tassel slung across a framed theater program, the Arizona State University production of *Oklahoma!* at Gammage Auditorium, a building Gillian had once told him was designed by Frank Lloyd Wright.

On Gillian's nightstand sat a familiar music box that Danny knew played "Oh, What a Beautiful Morning," a gift from Evan Stone. It was engraved, "To my shining star, From Daddy." The gift from Daddy was the key detail. Soften the reader with a universal tug of the heart, then snap them back into real life. Describe the black fingerprint powder swirled on glasses and tabletops. The fat asshole detective sitting on the bed among tiny lacy underwear. Juxtaposition.

Danny typed for three full hours before he realized he was starved. The act of banging the keys had calmed him. He went into the kitchen, barely wide enough for one slender adult standing sideways. Technically his apartment was a studio, but a previous tenant had built a wall to create a tiny bedroom. The wall lacked electrical outlets, and the bedroom lacked a door. Only a landlord could imagine it as a junior three.

He flicked on the small portable TV that took up too much of his kitchen counter space. The news at six. The teaser hinted at new information on the dead actress.

Danny started a pot of water heating on the stove. He had a small repertoire of meals, most of them centered around pasta. Yesterday rigatoni, today . . . rigatoni. From the refrigerator he took the leftover canned asparagus. And the butter, real butter, let it melt a little for the baguette. Then he poured a glass of wine from the box in the refrigerator. Chillable red, five liters for eight bucks, you couldn't beat it. He was set. A man with cheap wine and a mission.

On the TV screen Evan Stone, with perfect white hair and a desert tan, pushed through cameramen hustling backward through the crowds at JFK airport. A woman, probably Gillian's mom, walked head down, her face buried in an upturned collar. They were moving fast toward the departing gates, leaving reporters breathless in the pursuit of a sound bite.

It was this kind of banzai journalism that gave the business a bad name. Not his style. He knew exactly how he was going to get his story, the old-fashioned way: digging it out detail by detail. Danny scooped out a rigatoni noodle and tasted it cautiously. It was still a beat away from al dente.

Danny knew that the broken hearts in this story resided not only in the lights of Broadway, but also in the Arizona desert, where the tale began. He planned to make airline reservations as soon as the funeral date was announced. He'd talk to Gillian's friends. Visit her high school, her drama professors at ASU. Her parents. Maybe see her room. He'd ask to see a pink blanket she'd told him about, one she'd carried as a child, worn so thin that light shone through it. A writer knew that heartbreak's permanent home was in the small, personal details.

He tried to recall Gillian's face last night, the way she'd acted. Had he missed something? She'd seemed stressed and more subdued than he remembered, but that was understandable; she'd said she'd been betrayed by someone she loved. She'd been a little drunk, not bombed, not staggering sloppy. Joe Gregory had implied Danny should have been more observant; he should have seen a girl in trouble. He kept replaying the evening over and over in his mind. Had he been so concerned about himself that he'd missed something? The one thing Danny swore he'd never be was a self-centered man, a man like his father, who found it so easy to walk away from a wife and son.

Cameras zoomed in on the tired face of Evan Stone. The couple slowed up at the security checkpoint. Reporters kept pushing, wouldn't take no for an answer. Danny poured another chillable red as a security guard stepped in and ordered the TV crews back. About time.

Safely through the checkpoint, Evan Stone snatched his carry-on from the short conveyor belt beyond the X-ray machine. His wife faded into the distance, walking quickly out of camera range. He turned to the cameras.

"Do something about your city," he said.

Danny held up his glass, toasting the TV. "I'll make it right, Mr. Stone. I'll bring that bastard to his knees."

This is a damn shame," Leigh Ryan said as her detective husband walked through the door of their aging Cape Cod in Yonkers. Leigh sat cross-legged on the floor in front of the TV, dozens of theater *Playbills* scattered around her. She was watching the news, Evan and Lynnette Stone fighting their way through a handful of reporters at JFK. "Why didn't someone go to the airport with them, Anthony?"

"Because Evan Stone told us they were staying overnight," Ryan said, lowering himself next to her. "They must have checked out right after we left."

"We need a hands-off rule," Leigh said, waving at the TV. "A forty-eight-hour grief moratorium, something like that."

Anthony Ryan focused on Evan Stone, his arm around his wife, whose face was hidden in her jacket. Ryan saw the anger boiling in him, and he understood. At that moment he wanted to be at JFK with them, to lay his hands on someone, to shove a cameraman, to knock some goddamned reporter on his or her ass.

"The mother looks terrible," Leigh said.

"She was heavily sedated."

For all the deaths he'd seen as a cop, he'd never understood the shock that enveloped people on the unexpected death of a loved one. Now he did. It was a good thing, a state of grace, a protective sac. A state of floating disbelief that God wrapped us in as he slammed us against the bare stone walls of grief. Especially the waves of bottomless grief that followed the bewildering deaths of the young.

"Danny called his mother a little while ago," Leigh said. "Told her all about Gillian."

"I'm glad to hear that. I was hoping I didn't have to break the news."

"You don't, but Nancy wants to talk to you anyway. I told her we'd take her to dinner."

"Why?" Ryan said, sighing. "I'm sure Danny told her everything."

"She just wants reassurance."

"Dinner with Nancy, and a cross-examination? I don't know. Tell her he's not in any trouble. Nothing to worry about. I'll call her tomorrow."

"He's her son," Leigh said, and knew she didn't have to say anything else. "Besides, she probably knows more about this than you do."

"According to Danny she doesn't have a clue about his love life."

"Is that what Danny told you? Nancy knew it long ago. It was obvious. All of a sudden he develops this big interest in theater, going to more plays than a critic. Who else but a woman could drag Danny Eumont to Off Broadway? One day Nancy asked him about the Gillian on his speed dial, and he almost wet himself lying. We put it all together this morning, when he called looking for you."

Leigh shuffled *Playbills* around the floor, looking for something in particular. She had saved them since the first play she went to with her young husband, both of them awed by live theater.

"We saw Gillian Stone in *A Chorus Line,*" she said, handing him one of the programs folded over to the cast page. "The last time we saw it, just before it closed. She played Sheila."

Leigh and Anthony Ryan had tried to expose their kids, Margaret and Rip, to all the wonders of N.Y.C.: plays, concerts, restaurants, parades, exhibits, museums, ball games. Rip loved Yankee Stadium, a place he roamed like an explorer; he made a point of sitting in every single section for at least one at bat. Their daughter, Margaret, always told them she missed the theater. Margaret and their granddaughter, Katie, were living in Dublin for the year, unearthing the family roots.

"Was it definitely suicide?" Leigh said, lacing up a pair of Reeboks that were the same exact model she'd worn for twenty years. She had to scour the outlets and discount stores to find them now. Then she bought every pair in her size.

"Suicide is the early consensus," Ryan said.

"Had she been depressed?"

"Not according to her father. But he also denied she had a drug problem. No problems whatsoever."

"Gillian had been away from home for a long time," Leigh said. "So maybe Mom doesn't know, either. One of the TV reporters said there were rumors she was going to be fired from this show. Maybe she was more brittle than anyone realized. She gets the first bad news of her life and snaps."

"Danny doesn't think so."

"Men do not notice subtle changes. Ask a woman."

Ryan wondered if Evan Stone noticed the identification room in Bellevue morgue. Would he remember its fake leather couches and low tables? Did he read the religious pamphlets or notice the boxes of tissues, the pitcher of water and two glasses? Would he recall the glass partition that separated the room from the one next door? The dark blue curtain that covered the partition? The bright light that came on when the curtain slid back? The single gurney covered by a blue sheet? The attendant in blue scrubs who pulled back the sheet?

"People handle bad times differently," Leigh said, standing over him and putting on her linen blazer. "Gillian might have been one of those who just couldn't deal with it."

"If she was that fragile, somebody should have been looking out for her. I'd like to know who."

"What would that accomplish, Anthony?"

"Whoever it was should be called on it."

A TV reporter stood in front of the Broadway Arms, explaining how Gillian Stone fell to her death. Ryan put his face between his knees. Leigh wrapped both arms around her husband. "Come on, we're not going to mope tonight." She reached for the clicker. "I can't watch this anymore."

The images faded to black. But the image unerased was the one in Anthony Ryan's mind: of himself as he listened to the Utah Public Safety officer explain how their son, Rip, had died.

The official Utah verdict was called PIO, pilot-induced oscillation. Pilot error. The police had ascertained from witnesses that young Rip Ryan, in his inexperience, was unable to make his final turn into a turbulent wind. He hit the ground at approximately fifty miles an hour. In the state-of-the-art morgue of a western state, Ryan listened to the drone of official words as he silently begged God to let him change places with the broken body being caressed by his wife. Never in his life had Ryan felt so helpless, so useless. Leigh whispering hoarsely to their son, as if crooning a lullaby.

"Maybe nobody is responsible," Leigh said as she stacked the *Playbills* back in the box. "I'm going to call my sister, tell her we'll pick her up in five minutes."

Somebody is always responsible, he thought. Who would tell the Stones that no one was responsible? He thought about them in the Bellevue morgue this morning. Did they think their daughter was only sleeping? He'd noticed that it always took an oddly long time for parents to react in the morgue. He didn't know if it was the familiarity of the closed eyes or the absolute stillness. Or merely a few extra seconds of hope. How easy it was for parents to convince themselves, for those few seconds, that their child was only sleeping.

"Enough dwelling," Leigh said. "Dwelling is not good for anybody."

She grabbed his wrist and tried to pull him to his feet. He sat there looking up as she yanked. "On your feet, pally. Let someone else worry about who's responsible. The only thing you have to worry about is where you're taking us for dinner."

The weight of being up for over twenty-four hours had descended on Anthony Ryan. Fatigue had left his emotions too close to the surface. He buried his face in his arm. He wanted to stay in this room where he knew the stories behind every framed picture, every souvenir and knickknack, every odd creak and groan.

"I need to be fed, Officer," Leigh said, still pulling. "Something Italian and fattening as hell. Maybe a nice bottle of wine. A big bottle. We'll all get stoned on that Day-Glo red you half Italians drink."

"Dago red," he corrected, and had to smile because his southern girl had said it the same way for over thirty years. "It's called dago red."

She yanked with both hands, grunting, as if pulling him out of jungle quicksand. Her back was almost parallel with the floor, head thrown back recklessly, gray hair flying. Ryan got up slowly, holding tight; he had to or else she would have fallen backward. When he was up, she wrapped her arms around his waist.

"Dago, Day-Glo, whatever," she said. "We'll get two bottles."

7

The borough of Queens was named after Catherine of Braganza, the queen of King Charles II. She could have it back as far as Danny Eumont was concerned. On Thursday morning road crews had funneled Fifty-ninth Street Bridge traffic into one eastbound lane; it took Danny two hours to drive the olive green Volvo from home to his office.

Manhattan magazine, despite the facade of a P.O. box and a telephone exchange indicating Manhattan, was actually located in a fading industrial section of Long Island City, Queens. For a quarter of the price of Manhattan square footage, the fledgling journal rented the entire top floor of a two-story concrete block structure only two subway stops east of the East River.

Danny jogged up the steep and narrow stairway to the second floor. An auto body shop occupied the ground floor of the kind of building his uncle called a "taxpayer." The magazine's main office was empty, nine A.M. being too early for real journalists. The floor plan consisted of one long room, with private offices at the far end. Only editors and bean counters rated private offices. Danny's desk sat in the big room, near a back window, overlooking a pyramid of used tires and a vicious one-eared mongrel restrained by an anchor chain. The only time he'd brought Gillian to the office, she'd gone out and actually petted the greasy, psychotic beast.

Ball-peen hammers *ping*ed and air compressors *whoosh*ed as Danny opened and slammed his desk drawers, looking for his tape recorder. The recorder was the only reason he'd made the trip in the first place. He rarely used it, but this time he wanted verification of the impromptu interview he was about to spring on Trey Winters. Verification was the right word. Verification, because he didn't trust Trey Winters. Not for evidence. Danny wasn't in the evidence business. He wanted to set things straight for Gillian, tell her story. And after all, it was he she had called, nobody else. His uncle always said that life was a series of loyalty tests. He wasn't going to start flunking them.

He found the recorder under a menu for Chinese takeout. The batteries seemed strong. He popped in a fresh microcassette. Then he checked his messages: nothing pressing. He did have three new letters he assumed were from cops. Most of his recent correspondence were reactions to his Todd Walker police brutality story. Usually he opened them with a carving knife, turning his face away in case of a malicious surprise. But no time for that now; he was running late for his own surprise. He decided it would be quicker to leave the olive parked here and take the N train back to Times Square. The smell of burned toast wafted out from the coffee room. He shoved the recorder into his pocket.

No more two shows on Wednesday," Pinto said. "One show, we quit. Go home. You did too much yesterday, showing off for those Swedish bitches. It's no good for you. Then you take too many pills, and that's no good."

Pinto had rubbed the entire tube of cream into Victor's neck, arms, and back, and when the Russian wouldn't massage hard enough Victor took over himself, his fingers pressing deeply into his flesh, kneading the muscle, digging underneath his shoulder bones, trying to squeeze the nerve endings themselves. The spasms were visible, the muscles almost jumping through the skin.

"Shot of cortisone straighten you right out," Pinto said. "I'll drive you to the accident ward. One shot you'll be old self."

"I have things to do."

"People to see," Pinto said. "I know all about it."

"You know nothing; what do you know?"

"I know something with you is always up. Trouble is coming, that's what I know."

Pinto helped him get his shirt on. Victor wore a starched white shirt with a high collar. White shirts accentuated his tan, lit his face. He believed that a man with good skin should wear white, high around his face, especially turtlenecks. Victor could feel the warmth of the cream tingling on his skin, as if itching from a wool sweater.

"I'm sorry about the act today, Pinto."

"Just go. Go to your important business. Thursday's not so busy anyway. I'll do a solo today. Not to worry."

The bone-deep pain returned in full before the D train left the Bronx. By the time he got to Times Square Victor was desperate, his white shirt soaked with sweat. He'd taken only one pill before he'd left home, thinking it would be enough. The pain had returned too quickly.

He bought six little red pills from a pregnant woman in a doorway on Thirty-ninth Street and took three immediately. They weren't his usual muscle pills, but by the time he got to the overhang of the hotel he was breathing easier.

Victor realized that he'd caused his own problems yesterday, starting his act without warming up. Then he'd overdone it. From the beginning he was too keyed up, too jazzed from the events of the night before. He'd put everything into the performance, showing off for the crowd, tossing the bowling balls higher than it was wise to do. Showing them what a former Barnum & Bailey headliner could do. The women, he'd heard the women squealing with pleasure. They should have seen him in his trapeze days.

Yesterday brought back the old days, and as always, he fed off the spotlight. But it was the end for him. Not even if a miracle took the pain away would he ever again beg an unappreciative street audience for loose change from their pockets. For their crumbs. *No más.*

In his hand Victor held the second installment of his golden egg. It was an envelope containing great discomfort for a very rich man. A man rich enough to spend a little to buy his own peace of mind. Victor had no desire to hurt this man. But they could ease each other's discomfort. It was a simple business deal; he'd said as much in the note. Simple business. Done every day in this city. No worse than the stock market or General Motors. In fact, much less greedy. Mr. Trey Winters would see that his request was reasonable.

Victor felt better with each passing minute. Everything coming up rosy, as his friend Pinto always said. He almost smiled as Trey Winters came down the steps of his office. Victor knew that Winters met business associates every day at this time in the hotel coffee shop. Winters was right on time. Everything coming up rosy. Victor pulled the hat down tight on his head and adjusted the dark glasses. He planned to follow him into the hotel, hand him the envelope, and walk out the front door onto Broadway. Disappear into the crowd, just like last time at the Mexican restaurant.

Winters stopped at the rear entrance of the hotel. A young man had caught him as he was about to enter the revolving door. Winters appeared startled. The young man shuffled his feet and gestured with his hands. Victor wondered who he was. Then, Winters stormed into the hotel, an angry look on his face. Victor waited, the envelope that would change his life still in his hands. He felt his own fury erupting.

Danny Eumont's timing was impeccable. Just as he came around the corner he spotted Winters walking into the driveway underpass of the Merrimac Marquis. He sprinted to catch the tall, lanky Broadway producer. Winters spun around and did a half pirouette.

"Sorry, Mr. Winters," Danny said. "Didn't mean to scare you."

"You did a damn good job of it."

Winters patted his long fingers against his chest. His theater-trained voice boomed with amplified resonance under the hotel. Danny had no doubt his tape recorder would pick it up easily. He handed his business card to Winters.

"I'm doing a story on Gillian Stone," he said. "I wonder if I could talk to you for a few minutes."

"I'd be glad to. Call my office and make an appointment."

Except for a meat truck and one taxi, they were alone in the block-long underpass that was created to let vehicles pick up and drop off hotel guests without interfering with traffic on Broadway. Danny stepped out of the path of the departing taxi.

"I'll call for an appointment," Danny said. "But just a few short questions. I'll be quick."

"I'm running late right now."

"About the rumors that Gillian was taking drugs, everybody I talk to seems to think that they're false."

"Whom did you speak to?"

"People close to her. Very close."

"They couldn't be that close. What magazine did you say you were from?"

"*Manhattan.* It's on the card. Mr. Winters, I also have information from that same reliable source that you were sleeping with Gillian Stone. Could you comment on that?"

"That's a rude, insulting question. Who the hell are you?"

"My source swears you were sleeping with her."

"Your source and you can both go to hell."

Winters turned gracefully and moved toward the revolving door.

"Don't you want to know who my source is?" Danny yelled.

Not much of an interview, Danny thought as Winters disappeared through the *whumpf, whumpf* of the revolving door. He'd taken a shot, hoping Winters would be vulnerable so soon after Gillian's death. It was a long shot, but he'd thought maybe Winters might lose it, say something stupid. His uncle always said the most truth was gathered in the hours immediately after the crime. The longer you waited, the more everyone hardened up, lawyered up. Stories got set in stone.

Danny walked along the sidewalk that edged the hotel side of the underpass. He stopped at the top of a stairway leading under the hotel, where the driver of a refrigerated truck had been sliding boxes of filet mignon down a metal chute. Danny used the truck for cover in case Winters came back out. He began playing back the tape. Danny's voice sounded small in comparison with that of Winters. The conversation was short. He played it again.

The first thing Danny felt was the man's wetness against his back, the heat from his body. Then the arm around his throat. He grabbed the tape recorder out of Danny's hands. And shoved. Danny flew headfirst, reaching for anything, clutching only air. His left knee slammed down on the metal chute, his right knee missed the chute, and he spun right and tumbled down the steps, twisting as he grabbed a pipe with his right arm and heard the pop. He came to rest on the stacks of filet mignon, his right shoulder directly under his chin. He closed his eyes.

8

"How's Ryan's nephew?" Chief of Detectives Paddy "Roses" Ferguson said without looking up. He'd heard Joe Gregory's signature knock on his open door.

"Feeling no pain," Gregory said. "They didn't admit him. We brought him home from the emergency room, put him to bed. I told him he was lucky, his first mugging and all he lost was a tape recorder."

The Chief, known to his old friends as Paddy Roses, shoved a file in his bottom desk drawer, then waved them in, pointing to the chairs.

"The kid's pretty banged up," Ryan said. "Dislocated shoulder is painful."

"I coulda fixed that myself," Gregory said, raising his own arm to demonstrate. "I watched the surgeon at St. Luke's. Nothing to it. All he did was pick his arm up and twist, then he snapped it in. Like this. Rolled it back . . . then *craaaack!* Sounded like a gunshot in an alley."

Ryan and Gregory belonged to a small cadre of experienced

detectives personally assigned to the Chief's office. They handled high-profile homicides and crimes that lingered on the front page. Informally they were referred to as the "Political Response Team."

"The mugging thing is a little hinky," Ryan said. "The guy didn't take his cash, just the tape recorder. Danny had just finished interviewing Trey Winters, and like a dope, walks ten feet and starts playing the conversation back. The guy comes up behind him, grabs the tape recorder, and shoves him down into the cellar."

"I've seen rookie undercover cops do that," the Chief said. "They can't wait to hear their own voices on tape."

"So waddaya figure, pally, Winters's bodyguard sees it and coldcocks him?"

"Makes more sense than a mugging."

"Find out if he has a bodyguard," the Chief said. "We'll throw the prick in a lineup."

"The kid didn't see shit, Paddy," Gregory said. "All Danny knows is the guy was strong and smelled like Vicks VapoRub."

"Vicks VapoRub?"

"That's what he says," Gregory said. "I say, mugger or not, you gotta admire the work ethic. Chest congestion, bad cold and all, he's out there hustling."

"I was just hoping some cop didn't do it," the Chief said.

Longtime New York City cops refer to the people with whom they started their careers by saying, "We were cops together." It's a specific identification of a specific time: the rookie years in uniform. Chief Paddy Ferguson and Joe Gregory were "cops together" in Brooklyn, where the Chief earned his nickname because his preferred drink was a lower-shelf whiskey called Four Roses with a water chaser. In the days when foot cops drank free and freely in uniform, Paddy, after first checking his post for Internal Affairs spies called "shooflys," would back into local bars, in a Rockaway version of the moonwalk, while knowing customers crooned, "Roses and water, roses and water."

"How about this actress thing?" the Chief said. "We closing that one?"

"Just a couple of loose ends away," Gregory said.

"I hate that phrase, 'loose ends.' Is it still classified a suicide, or am I out of the loop, as usual?"

"Apparent suicide," Gregory said. "Until we can explain the sticky substance we found on her mouth."

"What sticky substance? Licorice, Jujubes, what?"

"Stickier," Gregory said. "We can't rule out the possibility it's glue residue from tape. Somebody could have taped her mouth."

"What's wrong with that?" the Chief said. "I put tape over my old lady's mouth all the time."

"But you don't toss her from eighteen stories up."

"That's because we live in a split-level."

When relaxed with old friends, the Chief was Paddy Roses, the cigar-chomping street cop. But on cue, the handsome Irishman could transform himself into the very model of a modern major police executive: the leader of the largest metropolitan detective force in the world . . . Chief Patrick Ferguson. Informed, articulate, suave, positively elegant.

"I don't want a big Hollywood production made out of this case," the Chief said. "The news gets a whiff something's wrong here, they'll start making shit up. What's the story on this drug thing? Was she a user or wasn't she?"

"I read the interviews of Gillian's friends in the show," Ryan said. "None of them mentioned anything about drugs. One woman says she had mood swing problems. Nothing stronger. They all say she was a doll to work with."

"That's what friends are supposed to say," the Chief said. "When I die I expect you guys to say I was an Irish American saint."

"She didn't have any needle marks," Gregory said, shrugging. "No drugs found in the apartment. We're waiting on toxicology."

"Toxicology takes two weeks," the Chief said. "We ain't waiting two weeks to close this."

Paddy Roses' fortunes changed when he was "kidnapped" from a Rockaway gin mill by Monsignor Dunn's AA crew. They delivered him directly to the NYPD's secret dry-out farm upstate. After six months of picking apples he returned a healthy man, with an appreciation for his mind as well as his liver.

"I found these around her neck," Ryan said, handing the Chief the broken rosary he'd taken from Gillian. Inscribed on the back of the silver crucifix was the word *FAITH*. The loose white beads had pooled in the bottom of the plastic evidence bag. "I'm going to voucher them separately. In case we get a rash of confessors."

"So now we have a possible junkie who says her beads," the Chief said, examining the broken rosary. "And who may or may not have had her mouth taped."

Paddy Roses started studying for boss after he "dried out." He made number four on the sergeant's list and was in the top ten for lieutenant and captain. As a test taker Paddy Roses was pure genius. On the wall behind him was a plaque that read, "God Bless Multiple Choice."

"In the meantime, what do I tell Hizzoner, that bastard," the Chief said. "He tells me he's getting worried calls from the Mouse in Hollywood. The Mouse is worried about bad publicity for his new Shangri-la on Forty-second Street."

"Tell him we got a plan," Gregory said.

"And what will that plan be?"

"To conduct a thorough and tireless investigation," Gregory said. "We will not sleep until we get at the truth, and if necessary bring the alleged perpetrator to justice."

"And after I extract the phone from my ass, what will I tell him next?"

"Tell him to go fuck himself if he can't take a joke," Gregory said.

The Chief leaned forward, almost halfway across his desk, and fixed his blue eyes on his two senior investigators.

"We're having fun, aren't we," he said.

"All we need is a bottle a booze and a coupla broads," Gregory said.

"Fun's over," the Chief said as he slapped his palm on his desk. "The deal is this: Was she alone in the apartment at the time of death, or wasn't she? It's as simple as that. I'll let you guys work on this for two days, understand? Two days. As long as we keep it on the QT. The official word is we're tying up loose ends."

"We gotta confirm the glue thing," Gregory said.

"Fine, what else?"

"My nephew thinks Trey Winters, the show's producer, has something to do with her death," Ryan said.

"That's a writer's opinion," the Chief said. "You know what writers are in this town, don't you? Writers are actors who're too lazy to work in a restaurant."

"Gillian told my nephew she was sleeping with Winters. And he was the last one to see her alive."

"What time was that?"

"He popped in around eleven-fifteen," Gregory said. "Stayed approximately twenty minutes. Left alone."

"Eleven-fifteen's a little late for a pop-in," the Chief said. "Who is this Winters? Why is that name familiar?"

"He's married to Darcy Jacobs, daughter of Marty Jacobs, the developer."

"Mother a God," the Chief said, smacking his forehead with the back of his hand. "Ever since Marty Jacobs died that outfit has been a major pain in my ass."

"We ran a name check on Winters," Gregory said. "He doesn't have a record. Plus he has solid alibi witnesses. The Broadway Arms doorman says he was only up in her apartment about fifteen minutes. His own doorman and his wife confirm he was home before one."

"Thank God for doormen," the Chief said. "Reinterview

Winters anyway. Doormen, too. Thorough is my middle name."

"What about Mrs. Winters?" Ryan said.

"You don't need to talk to her," the Chief said, motioning for them to hurry up and finish.

"After Winters left," Gregory said, "Gillian made a phone call to her sister on the East Side. Next thing we know it's one A.M. and she's airborne."

"Guy like Winters is too rich to toss anybody off a balcony," the Chief said. "He'd hire a pro."

"That's what you said about O.J.," Gregory reminded him.

"Hey," the Chief said, jabbing his finger at Gregory. "You could be picking your Jockey shorts outta your ass on a foot post in Staten Island tomorrow. All it takes is a stroke of the pen, remember that. Now tell me about the apartment. Crime Scene find anything?"

"*Nada,*" Gregory said. "No physical evidence, no note, no signs of struggle or forced entry."

"If this is a homicide," the Chief said, "we'll need a god-damned crystal ball to solve it."

"Save that line for the press," Ryan said. "They'll love that one."

"You got the LUDs there, smart guy? Any other phone calls?"

"She made a total of three calls that evening. The one to my nephew, a two-minute call beginning at seven-fourteen. The second was to her sister, eleven oh-seven for three minutes. The third call, made after Winters left, lasted twenty-eight minutes, ending at eleven minutes after midnight. Apparently the sister was the last person she spoke to. We're going to interview her as soon as we leave here."

"I didn't think you could get length of time on local calls."

"You can since NYNEX went digital," Ryan said.

"Live and learn," the Chief said. "Talk to the sister again. What about the canvass?"

"Mid-Town North handled the canvass," Ryan said. "Covered the whole building and the one across the street. Less than seventy percent of the residents of the Broadway Arms were home at the time. Nobody heard or saw anything. Three apartments on Gillian's floor were out at the time and have still not been contacted."

"Where the hell are all these people at that time of night?"

"Broadway babies," Gregory said. "They don't say good night till early in the morning. Quite often the milkman's on his way."

"Who are you supposed to be, Cole fucking Porter?" the Chief said, checking his watch again, the hint to wrap it up. "You at least got a name for this case?"

"In keeping with the Broadway theme," Gregory said, "we're thinking of calling it 'Fiddler Off the Roof.'"

9

Anthony Ryan was surprised when Faye Boudreau answered the phone. He'd expected an answering machine. He'd expected the sister of Gillian Stone to be in Arizona with the family. She told him she'd explain when he got there.

"I hope we don't have a problem with Danny on this case," Joe Gregory said as they drove up FDR Drive, past the UN. "First he tells me he's not writing this story. Next day he turns around and interviews Winters."

"He's writing the story," Ryan said. "He says he owes it to Gillian. I'll keep an eye on him."

"Answer me this, pally. Why the hell would Winters's bodyguard go to that extreme? He coulda killed him."

"Maybe he didn't intend for Danny to fall down that chute."

"Yeah, and maybe it's just a garden-variety mugging. Wouldn't be the stupidest I ever heard of."

"That's true. But I figure Winters knows who Danny is; you always know the previous boyfriend. And he probably knows Gillian ran to him on the night she was murdered. Maybe he thinks she told Danny something."

"Like he was screwing her. I could see him worrying about that, but that's all, because he has an airtight alibi for one A.M."

"Nothing is airtight."

Out in the dark waters of the East River the rolling wake of a fast-moving tugboat rocked an immense sparkling sailboat.

"I'm gonna drop you off at the sister's place," Gregory said. "You don't need me for this. I'm gonna take a quick run up to the Bronx and turn this Project Children boat ride money over to the Duck before the worst happens. Carrying somebody else's cash around always makes me nervous."

"I thought the Duck retired to Florida," Ryan said.

"He did, for two months. Hated it. The day before his terminal leave was scheduled to end, the Duck gets up in the middle of the night . . . while the wife is still asleep . . . knows nothing. He sneaks outta the house in a T-shirt and a pair of shorts, drives all day and night, straight to One Police Plaza, drops to his knees, and kisses the ground. Goes upstairs, gets his shield back. They stick him in the Bronx. The Five Oh Precinct."

"What happened to his wife?"

"Who knows," Gregory said, shrugging emphatically as if that line of questioning were irrelevant.

"I'll give you thirty minutes," Ryan said. "I don't care what old buddy you run into. Just get your ass back here. I don't want to hear about traffic jams, and I definitely don't want to hear that you stopped in the Greentree Bar for a quick pop with the Duck or any of the board of directors. Or whatever you guys call yourselves."

"Pally," Gregory said, "I'm deeply wounded by that remark."

"You *will be* deeply wounded if you're not back to get me in thirty minutes."

Faye Boudreau lived on East Sixty-fourth Street off the corner of Third Avenue, on the third floor of a seven-story tan brick building. Ryan leaned on the buzzer until the imprint appeared on his thumb. Then he tried his own keys in the door. Sometimes the tumblers in the locks on outside apartment house doors were so worn down that any similar key would work. One did.

"Damn buzzer never works," Faye Boudreau said.

She wore only a black T-shirt, with the new logo of *West Side Story*. A black bra strap dangled midway down her upper arm. Her voice sounded thick, as if she'd been sleeping or crying.

Ryan's eyes adjusted to the darkness as he followed her down a short narrow hallway: closet on the right, bathroom on the left. The entire studio apartment had less floor space than the first-class cabin on a 737. Two steps past the bathroom was the kitchenette. Beyond that, one single square room so small, Patrick Ewing could have touched the two most distant walls simultaneously.

"I'm sorry about your sister," Ryan said, and he watched her mouth twist as she fought back tears. She was older, heavier, and darker than Gillian, but her legs were as long and cheekbones as pronounced. She was barefoot, bare-legged.

Faye sat on the edge of the unmade sofa bed, which took up most of the room. She folded her legs swami style and yanked her shirt down between her legs. Sheets and a blanket lay half on the floor. A heavy drape covered the lone window, behind her. In the front center of her right thigh was a small circular scar that looked like a cigarette burn.

"Tell me something about Gillian," Ryan asked softly. "Who was her favorite actress?"

"I don't know. She never said. Meryl Streep, maybe. She liked Meryl Streep."

Ryan lowered himself carefully onto a beanbag chair. The light from the lamp on top of the TV was less than dim. A pair of cutoff jeans lay on the floor next to his feet, white pockets turned inside out. A baseball bat leaned against the wall near the TV table.

"Everybody has said such wonderful things about Gillian," Ryan said. "Not one negative comment."

"She was moody, sometimes," Faye said. Then, gesturing to the unmade bed, the clothes on the floor: "But she was neater than me, that's for sure."

Ryan saw his opening and prodded Faye to admit that Gillian was the cleanest woman on earth, often staying up all night cleaning her apartment. She ironed everything she wore, flossed her teeth after every meal, and washed her bedspread at the Laundromat in December and May. Like clockwork.

"What kind of foods did she like?" Ryan asked.

"Anything tart, like things made with lemons and limes. And ginger snaps."

"Anything else?" Ryan said, meaning food.

But Faye misunderstood and said she was sorry, she really didn't know that much about Gillian. They'd missed so many years of growing up together.

"You didn't grow up together?"

"They just found me."

"Who just found you?"

Faye took a deep breath and pushed her hair from her face. "Our mother gave me up when I was born," she said. "She gave birth to me in Key West, and the next day she gave me to the nuns. Then she left Florida."

"Why?"

"Poor, scared, fifteen years old. I can understand that."

"How long have you known this?"

"First time I heard about my real mother was two years ago. Some private investigator came into the bar I worked at in Miami, asked a bunch of questions. Then a few days later Lynnette and Evan Stone flew in from Phoenix. Eight o'clock in the morning they knock on my door. 'I'm your mom,' Lynnette says."

"Knock, knock . . . we're your parents."

"Just my mother. Evan Stone isn't my father."

"Who is your father?"

"You are," she said, smiling for the first time. In the sliver
of light coming through the opening in the drapes, he could
see the whiteness of her teeth. "Just kidding. I don't know, and
it sounds like she don't, either. She named some guy in the
navy, but the private investigator couldn't find him in the
files."

"What made her decide to look for you?"

"Some shrink in Arizona said she had to confront her
past."

"And you were in Florida the whole time?"

"With the Boudreaus, mostly. They adopted me. French
Canadians. I grew up in Sarasota, Bradenton, around there. A
few different places. I did okay."

Faye's skin had a rough, blowsy look, as if weathered in
cigarette smoke and long nights. But her hair was a lustrous
black and shoulder length, her eyes dark brown and huge.
You could see an inherent beauty, but a squandered beauty. If
it had been nourished and cultivated, who knew?

"Then you met Gillian?" Ryan said.

"Me and Gillian hit it right off. She flew down to Miami
when she found out. Brought me here. This is her old apartment, the lease is still in her name."

"Call me if you have any problems getting it changed to
your name."

"Oh, I'm not staying. I'll go back to Florida."

"Why not Arizona?"

"Don't think so," she said, raising her eyebrows. "I'm too
low-class for Mother. I embarrass her."

"That's why you didn't attend the funeral."

Faye nodded, then stretched her arms above her head, lazy
and catlike. The room smelled like Gillian's apartment in the
Broadway Arms, delicate, powdery scents.

"Tell me about the last time you saw your sister," Ryan said.

"Sunday, she came over. She brought me that bat." Faye swung her legs off the bed and picked up the baseball bat near the TV. She handed it to Ryan. "It's a Bobby Bonilla model. She met him at the All-Star Cafe, I think, and got him to sign it for me. She knew I was a Marlins fan."

"My son was a big Baltimore Orioles fan," Ryan said. He gave the bat a short swing, all wrist, and wondered why he'd mentioned his son; he never did that. He asked Faye to finish telling about Sunday.

"We went to lunch. Around the corner to Caramanica's."

"What was Gillian's mood?"

"Laughing, joking around. That's what sucks."

"What sucks?"

"Like, all those years we missed. You know, like playing Barbies or dressing up, things like that. Talking about boyfriends, whatever. I'll never get that back now. Know what I mean?"

"Yes, I do," Ryan said. "Did you see Gillian or speak to her after Saturday?"

"Not till Tuesday night."

"The night she died?"

Faye nodded, but Ryan already knew it. It was in Faye's interview with Mid-Town North, plus Gillian's phone records. Two phone calls, the last one twenty-eight minutes, terminated less than fifty minutes before Gillian's fall.

"I read your statement, but tell me again about the phone calls. Did she seem depressed or despondent?"

"Try pissed off."

"About what?"

"The drug thing with Trey Winters. She knew it was bull-shit."

"So she didn't have a drug problem. Not even prescription drugs, painkillers, tranquilizers?"

"She drank a little. Gin and Mountain Dew. Tasted weird, like a high schooler's drink."

"She wasn't worried about the drug test?"

"If she was, she didn't say it to me."

Faye scratched at her legs unconsciously. She had long fingernails, black polish badly chipped.

"So what did you two girls talk about?"

"Everything. Everything in the world."

"And her mood was good."

"Except for being pissed."

"Did she talk much about Trey Winters?"

"Shit, yeah."

"Did she tell you about her affair with Trey Winters?"

"No, she never told me anything about that. First call she said he was coming over. The second one she told me that he just bullshitted about trying to help her and shit. She didn't believe him."

"But I didn't surprise you just now when I mentioned a relationship between them," Ryan said. "Did I?"

Faye gave an "I don't know" shrug. The sound of metal rattling caused Ryan to look toward the window . . . the fire escape. Ryan had been uneasy in apartments with fire escapes since his rookie years in the Bronx. Another burdensome piece of cop knowledge was that so many rapists and thugs slithered in through the fire escape window. Like most street cops, even off duty, he always scanned upward toward the fire escapes, watching for climbing predator scum. Faye seemed not to notice the noise. Maybe a neighbor's ritual: shaking a dust mop or watering a marijuana plant.

"I know you loved your sister, Faye."

"I would have done anything for her."

"Sisters have a special bond," he said. "My wife and her sister have an amazing connection. Spooky almost. Sometimes my wife says she has to call her sister, and that second the phone rings, and it's her. It's almost mystical. An understanding that goes beyond words."

"We were getting like that. Sometimes Gillian would say something, and it was exactly the thing I was thinking. We'd both go 'Wow.' "

He watched her fight for control again, biting the inside of her lips so hard, it had to bleed.

"The thing I can't understand," Ryan said, "is that she called you on that night and talked to you for twenty-eight minutes . . . hung up . . . and less than an hour later she took her own life. And you had *no idea* that anything was wrong."

"I knew she was upset."

"Upset. Of course. She'd just heard she might lose her role in the show. Her producers wanted her tested for drugs. Everything she worked for was being destroyed. I'd be nuts if that happened to me."

Faye tightened and coiled, as if trying to squeeze out some deep reserve of inner strength. She wasn't a cold woman; Ryan knew ice when he saw it.

"Don't you think I would have done something if I thought she was going to hurt herself? Called somebody?"

"Not necessarily. Maybe you didn't believe what she was saying. That's understandable. People say wild things when they're under stress. Crazy things, like they're going to kill themselves. Most people ignore them at a time like that. I would. If we reacted every time people threatened crazy things . . ."

He wanted to tell her to just go ahead and cry, for chrissakes. Let it loose. Blow the dam. She wrestled her demons in.

"She was a little drunk . . . just blowing off steam."

"I'm sure," Ryan said. "Probably exaggerating, talking stupidly. We all do it when we're mad."

"She said a few things. I didn't think she'd really do anything. Just blowing off steam."

"It wasn't your fault, Faye."

"Some big sister, right? Big help I was."

Anthony Ryan leaned over and touched her hand. He had

other questions, but he wouldn't ask them now. He'd made Faye Boudreau suffer enough for one day. She wrapped her arms around her chest, as if to physically hold herself together. A low moan slipped from her throat, escaped past the guards. She never cried.

10

Victor listened to Danny Eumont's tape on the subway ride home. He didn't see how questions about Gillian Stone's drug use and her affair with Trey Winters could affect his plan. In fact, the reporter's probing might encourage Winters to pay greater attention to him and settle the matter quickly. The only thing on the tape that worried Victor was the mention of a "source." No "source" was going to screw up his plan.

Back in the Bronx and too stiff to bend over, he kicked the reporter's tape recorder into the gutter and sent it clattering down a sewer. Then he walked around the corner, dropped the microcassette on the sidewalk, and smashed it under his heel. The pulverized tape went into another sewer directly in front of the wood-frame house on Echo Place in which he shared two rooms and a bath with Pinto the Russian clown.

Pinto's Chevy Nova was gone from its parking spot. Lazy Pinto always drove the car, although it was less than a block walk to the Grand Concourse, where you could catch the D train straight to Times Square. Every year Victor suggested they store the car for the summer, take the subway. Much cheaper in the long run.

But what the hell did he care now. Next year Pinto would be on his own, begging tourists for coins by himself. Next year he'd be a businessman, a man of wealth and respect. Basking in the warm breezes off the Sea of Cortés and the charms of beautiful women. Many beautiful women. As Pinto himself always said, more than anything else, it was money that made women horny.

Victor climbed the front steps, clutching the rail. The hallway smelled of fresh disinfectant. Their Jamaican-born landlady, the widow of a Puerto Rican subway motorman, had carved the house into five odd-shaped apartments, which she ran like a Nazi den mother, demanding order and cleanliness. Cleanliness at their price level was a rare commodity. That was why every year, as soon as the weather turned warm, Pinto and Victor tossed their belongings into Pinto's old Chevy and drove north, hoping she had a vacancy.

Though clean, the place came sparsely furnished: a couch, chair, two beds, dinette set, a few kitchen items. He'd brought his own sheets and towels; he wasn't going to sleep on the sheets of another. A TV and a weight bench were their only other furnishings.

Victor flicked on the TV and tossed his undelivered envelope on the dinette table. The envelope contained instructions for Trey Winters on how and when to deliver the money. It was a simple plan, and simple plans worked best. In light of the involvement of this reporter, he'd need to rethink his strategy.

He put on his gloves and took an old newspaper from the stack. He'd cut out a new message outlining his demands. Winters would see he was not greedy and jump at the deal. He leaned down to pick up the scissors off the floor.

A sharp pain flashed down Victor's lower back and down his right leg. The red pills were wearing off. They weren't as strong as his usual white ones. He dropped the scissors on the table and went into the bathroom. He took the remaining three red pills and washed them down with Pinto's vodka.

The French Connection was playing on TV, a movie he loved. He felt dirty and sweaty; he needed a shower, fresh clothes. He hated to feel this way. On the train home he'd promised himself a long, hot shower. But for the moment fatigue won out. He sprawled on the sofa. He'd watch the movie for a while, then clean up. His fingers had trouble working the remote control, trying to turn the volume louder.

Victor had gone downhill rapidly this past year, having more and more difficulty manipulating delicate objects. The simplest small movements of wrist and finger had become torturous, as if his hands were bound with twine. It was the way he'd seen his father start to deteriorate, the small motor skills first. The fingers, then the wrists, then spreading to the larger joints. On TV the Frenchman Alain Charnier outwitted the dumb cop Popeye Doyle, leaving him stranded on a subway platform.

Like his father, Victor had been one of the premier trapeze artists in South and Central America. Like his father, he had been in his late twenties when the first signs of the progressive disease had begun to plague him. Cruelly, for his father, the degeneration worsened just as he attained his lifetime dream, a chance to bring the family act under the big top. Less than three years after being signed by Ringling Brothers, his father could no longer perform safely. Both the family and the act fell apart. His father went back to Mazatlán, where he proceeded to drink himself to death.

Unlike his father, Victor would not let bad luck dictate his life. A man made his own luck. He would not wind up a peon, an object of ridicule. He was better than that. His mother said the Gypsies always told her she'd have a famous son. He was meant to be important, to live his life as a man of respect. Nothing was going to stop him.

On TV, Alan Charnier, a neat, elegant man, was head and shoulders above the poorly dressed and scatterbrained cops.

Charnier planned and used his mind. He made fools of the NYPD, defeating them in their own city. A warmth came over Victor as the pain subsided. Everything coming up rosy. He pulled off the tight gloves and closed his eyes.

11

Trey Winters's duplex had not one, but two top-dollar views: he faced west toward Central Park, and to the south you could see the afternoon sun glinting off the MetLife Building.

"You know somebody's rich when you can walk behind their furniture," Joe Gregory said, running his hand along the back of Trey Winters's leather sofa. "The rest of us got everything jammed up against the walls. Couches, chairs, lamps, everything. Up against the walls. Rich people, they got room to stroll behind their stuff."

Anthony Ryan had been quiet on the ride from Faye Boudreau's apartment. He couldn't get her out of his mind. Until he met Faye he'd thought that he was overwhelmed with grief. But she was consumed by it. To him she seemed childlike, a case of arrested development. A woman who knew only how to lead with her heart.

The maid abandoned Ryan and Gregory in a room paneled with a very dark reddish wood, the color of fallen chestnuts. She told them Mr. Winters would be with them in a moment.

"It must be in the rule book of the rich," Ryan said. "Make the little people wait in the library."

Tall bookshelves lined the room's interior walls, running close to the ceiling, ten feet up. Top-shelf tomes were accessible only by the sliding ladder. The ceiling appeared to be tin, hammered designs radiating out from the center in ever larger circles. An oriental rug big enough for the lobby in Carnegie Hall covered most of the floor. Floor lamps stood next to over-stuffed chairs.

Trey Winters entered the room as Ryan pulled *The Sun Also Rises* from a shelf. The actor was tall and lanky in baggy linen pants and a dull orange shirt buttoned up to the neck. He strode across the big oriental, all loosey-goosey.

"That's a first-edition Hemingway," Winters said, his voice resonating throughout the room. "My wife's father was an avid collector. I believe that's Hemingway's first novel."

"Second," Ryan said, replacing the book. "*The Torrents of Spring* was his first."

"I forgot that one," he said. "I suppose he wanted to as well."

Winters's hair was combed straight back, thinning but well disguised. The color was a too dark brown, a dull bottle tint that reminded Ryan of wet coffee grounds. He directed them to sit on the leather Chesterfield opposite him. The sofa was filled with decorative pillows. Gregory squirmed on the seat, trying to get comfortable with the pillows behind him.

"We appreciate your seeing us on such short notice," Gregory said.

"My lawyers aren't happy about it, but it's the least I can do. This has been a terrible tragedy for all concerned."

"Why would your lawyers object?" Ryan asked.

"Civil liability. I do own the apartment. Lawsuits, I'm sure, are looming down the road."

A young woman is dead and he's worried about money, Ryan thought. He waited for his partner to get comfortable; it was Gregory's show. One by one Joe Gregory stacked the decorative pillows on the floor. Finally, flush against the back of the sofa, he took out his notebook.

"Okay, Mr. Winters," Gregory said. "We've spoken to the doorman at the Broadway Arms and your doorman here. They confirm your times of arrival and departure. What we'd like to talk about is Gillian's drug use. When did you first become aware of it?"

"About six weeks ago. I began noticing some erratic behavior."

"What kind of erratic behavior?" Gregory said.

"Bursts of emotion. One extreme to the other. Some mornings she seemed exhausted, her eyes dull. Then suddenly she'd be sky high, couldn't stop talking."

"My ex-wife was high-strung," Gregory said.

"I'm not talking about personality traits, Detective. I've been around enough cocaine users to spot the symptoms."

"You been around a lotta coke heads?" Gregory said.

"Cocaine is hardly new to the entertainment industry."

Ryan hadn't observed Mid-Town North's interview of Winters on the morning after Gillian's death. But, unlike the case with Faye, this was definitely not someone grieving.

"When did you first confront Gillian about your suspicions?" Gregory said.

"We'd been discussing it for about a month. Futilely, I might add. Gillian was in complete denial. Finally, I decided to force the issue. I told her she'd have to take a drug test."

"When did you tell her this?" Gregory asked.

"About six-thirty, the evening she died. I called her from my office."

That call should bother him more, Ryan thought. It clearly upset her. After that call she'd contacted Danny.

"Why didn't you tell the officers in Mid-Town North about that six-thirty call?" Ryan asked.

"They didn't ask, and I assumed their main concern would be my later call and visit."

Winters crossed his legs and waited for the next volley. He

seemed completely relaxed, a guy with all the answers. He ran his fingers along the crease in his shirt, which was the same dull orange as a duck's feet. His socks matched his shirt.

"We know you made a second call to Gillian at ten forty-five P.M." Gregory said, reading from notes. "What did you do between those two calls?"

"I had dinner with Abigail Klass at El Bravado. I gave the other detectives all that information."

Ryan had just left a woman in such pain that she could hardly look at him. Winters seemed to be making a point of staring at them with each response.

"We just want to clarify some details about that," Gregory said. "She's an old family friend, apparently?"

"Abigail is a dear friend," he said. "She's the youngest sister of Paul Klass, who was my mentor and best friend in this business. Paul died from the complications of AIDS almost three years ago. Abigail is a well-known food writer. She was critiquing the restaurant, which was near my office, and she asked for my company. We were there for almost two hours. Then Abigail caught a cab, and I walked back to my office to call Gillian."

"I know you told the other detectives," Gregory said. "But let's go over the reasons why you made that second call to Gillian."

Winters retold his previous story with perfect diction, enunciating clearly, using his voice and hands to emphasize certain points. He said he'd decided he'd been too harsh with Gillian earlier. He'd try a new tack: positive reinforcement. He decided that some good news might turn her around. That was why he'd brought the dress. He was trying to show her what the future could hold for her.

"That seems like a major change of strategy," Ryan asked. "One moment you're ready to fire her, the next you're promoting her."

"I was never going to fire her."

"Unless she showed positive for drugs."

"I would have made my decision when and if that occurred. My only goal was to get help for her. I'm not the kind
of man who gives up on people."

"So she gets this good news," Anthony Ryan said, leaning
toward Winters. "This encouraging news. She puts the costume on and jumps off the terrace."

"I had no idea," he said. "I never would have left her alone
that night if I'd had any idea she was that despondent. When
I left she was wearing jeans and a gray silk blouse. She was
certainly not in that costume."

"What the hell happened to her, Mr. Winters?" Ryan said.
"You were the last one to see her alive."

"I have no idea what happened."

"How did you know the blouse was silk?" Gregory said.

"Because I gave it to her," he snapped.

Ryan and Gregory had decided earlier they wouldn't push
the relationship issue at this point. And Winters certainly
wasn't pining or vulnerable; he wouldn't crumble and admit to
love lost. But in Ryan's opinion, extramarital relationships
were not about love and seldom about sex. They were about
ego, and Winters had that in spades.

"How would you characterize her mood when you left?"
Gregory said.

"Hopeful, I thought."

"Did you notice she'd been drinking?" Ryan said.

"I told her I was not pleased with her drinking."

"You argued?" Ryan said.

"I was displeased with her. I suppose that was evident in my
tone."

"No matter how delicately you phrase it," Ryan said, "it
sounds like an argument to me."

"Your words, not mine," Winters said. "When I left her she
was not happy, I admit that. But she was not suicidal. And the
doorman, I'm certain, will verify my time of departure. Irish
Eddie will back up—"

"We already covered the doormen statements," Ryan said,

ending Winters's soliloquy before it started. He didn't want to let him get into the rhythm of prepared script. "But doesn't it seem strange to you that she kills herself after you left? Almost immediately after getting your good news?"

"With that question we end this interview," Winters said. He stood up quickly. "Gentlemen, I agreed to talk to you without legal representation, but if you're going to insist on taking an adversarial approach, I'm going to have to insist on a more formal arrangement from now on."

The detectives let him stand there. They sat, taking their time. In the quiet Ryan could hear a clock ticking in another room. Precious quiet in a noisy city. One of the advantages of living on a high floor, far above the sidewalk. Above car horns, sirens, and garbage trucks at dawn. Far above the screams of the street.

12

Still groggy from the morning's tumble, Danny Eumont wrestled open the front door of Brady's Bar with his one good arm. Brady's Bar stood directly behind New York City Police Headquarters at One Police Plaza and was unapologetically a cop's bar. Official business placards adorned the dashboard of every vehicle on the street. Stacks of empty beer boxes lined the curb. Inside, it smelled of stale beer and Old Spice.

"Danny Boy," Joe Gregory said, waving him over to his corner of the bar. "I thought you'd be laid up for a week."

"That little fall?" he said. "I do that all the time. This sling and the pained expression on my face mean nothing."

"Your uncle's across the street, finishing up paperwork," Gregory said. "He'll be over shortly."

Gregory introduced Danny to Shanahan and Sakin from Missing Persons. The two detectives finished paying Gregory for tickets to the Project Children boat ride, then he slid their drinks down the bar to make room for his partner's nephew.

Gregory wrapped a rubber band around the remaining tickets and shoved them into his jacket pocket.

"Trey Winters buy any tickets today?" Danny said. "He's got to be good for a few dozen."

"That's a good tactic," Gregory said. "Latch on to the subject at hand and lead it by the nose. Not bad at all."

"It was a simple question."

"No, it was an obvious ploy to get information on our interview with Winters. But there's nothing wrong with being obvious. The idea, though, if you really want the information, is to keep working on me until your persistence wears down my resistance."

"Then you'll tell me everything."

"Not a chance in hell," Gregory said.

The early sports guy on Channel 2 was lamenting the Yanks' loss of Bernie Williams, fifteen days on the DL, strained left hamstring. Pitcher Hideki Irabu was wearing long sleeves to cover tiny magnets that adorned his body to relieve tension and promote blood flow. A small cartoon lightning bolt in the corner of the screen warned of thunderstorms.

"In regards to Trey Winters," Gregory said. "His alibi checks out perfectly. The guy was long gone before Gillian took the header."

"So what does that mean, the investigation is finished?"

"It's at least up shit's creek without a paddle."

The lower edge of the bar's woodwork was ringed with Christmas lights that stayed up all year. Sinatra sang "Nancy with the Laughing Face." The night bartender came through the door to greetings all around.

"I never said that Winters killed her by himself," Danny said. "All I said was that he's involved. He had something to do with this. Something. And I don't know about you, but I don't intend to let him off the hook that easily."

"Maybe you need to get mugged again," Gregory said.

Then he broke into "Give My Regards to Broadway," the first line of the song. Gregory had a habit of bursting out in unprovoked song in a deep, operatic voice, his chin tucked down against his chest. Just one line of a song, two at the most. Show tunes, top forty, church hymns, Gilbert & Sullivan, nonsense songs, anything. One line. Then, just as suddenly, he'd stop and resume the conversation as if nothing had happened. It was like watching *Tourette's Syndrome: The Musical.*

"You find out anything new at all?" Danny said.

"Same story he told on the night of her death, kid. Same old shit, chapter and verse."

"Sounds like a wasted day."

"All's well that ends well," Gregory said, hoisting his glass. "This bar is in my will, you know. Three grand for a big party in my honor. Your uncle is my executor."

Danny knew all about Gregory's legendary will, which was a living will only in the sense that it never stopped growing. His uncle said he had shoeboxes at home stuffed with Gregory's codicils, written on cardboard coasters and cocktail napkins. Beneficiaries included bartenders, waitresses, coat check girls, cabbies, hookers, even the shoe shine guy in the subway station at Columbus Circle.

"What does my uncle think about Winters?"

"Your uncle, bless him, thinks he gave us too many details."

"What's wrong with that?"

"He says people who give too many details are usually trying to deflect attention away from something else."

"Like an affair. He was having an affair with Gillian. You agree with that?"

"Is the East River a river?" Gregory said.

"Actually, no," Danny said. "The East River is a saltwater estuary. A strait that connects upper New York Bay with the Long Island Sound."

"Well, it was a river when I was growing up," Gregory said. "And I do agree, Winters was screwing her."

Gregory reared back and sang, "They . . . tried . . . to sell us egg foo yung. . . ." Then quiet. He took a drink, then turned toward Danny. "One bitter cold night," he said, "about a dozen of us are sitting here. All guys from the job. December, January. It's late. The wind is howling outside, snow swirling. Everything is copasetic . . . when the door opens. This guy in a ski mask walks through the door. The place goes silent. The guy in the ski mask pauses at the end of the bar, right there. Looking around. He doesn't say a word. Then he reaches in his pocket. The whole thing took maybe fifteen seconds. When he looks up a dozen guns are pointing at him. The guy falls right out, smack on the floor. We look in his hand and he's got an address, around the corner. He wanted directions."

"A little bit of an overreaction," Danny said.

"No shit," Gregory said. "Who the hell faints, Marie Antoinette?"

Solitary drinkers did not visit Brady's Bar. Their isolation alone would make them suspect. Five small cliques made up the entire crowd, virtually all male huddles, except for two cop groupies humping the backs of the youngest group. Two women trying desperately to be discovered, laughing too loudly and rubbing up against men who'd rather hear war stories than love stories. But every time the door opened, every cop in the place, no matter how subtly, turned to check the door. They all went quiet when Anthony Ryan walked in.

"You two bonding?" Ryan said, touching his nephew's right shoulder.

"Your partner is giving me the benefit of his vast knowledge."

"That shouldn't take long," Ryan said.

Rank does not matter in a cop bar. No attention is paid to stripes, or bars, or gold eagles. It's all about respect. Danny had noticed long ago that although most cops treated both Ryan and Gregory with respect, there was a difference. Gregory they treated like a rough-and-tumble older brother. But Ryan was accorded a quiet reverence, as if he were a visiting cardinal.

"He's touched on every subject except the Winters interview," Danny said.

"I have something of interest," Ryan said as he dumped a bag of salted pretzels on the bar. "The lab called on the sticky substance on her lips."

"Should I leave?" Danny said.

"No . . . ," Gregory said. A hint of reluctance.

Ryan ordered a Jameson and water and frowned when he noticed Danny's beer on the bar. But Danny was only sipping, well aware of the brew's effects on his medication.

"Apparently, right before she died," Ryan said, "she put on some heavy stage makeup and lipstick. When it mixed with the blood it became sticky. That's what the lab thinks I noticed."

"Case closed," Gregory said.

"Not quite. They also found a trace amount of a viscous substance. Something pine based. They think it's rosin."

"Like the ballplayers use?" Gregory said.

"Coletti says it's used in some exercise and dance studios, too," Ryan said. "For grip, to prevent slipping. So we're going back into Gillian's apartment. He wants to check her ballet shoes. She might have put them on and touched her face. I made arrangements with Crime Scene for a second search, tomorrow."

"Tomorrow?" Gregory said. "Mid-Town already closed down the crime scene."

"I called Trey Winters and told him we needed the key back. We're also going to simulate her fall."

"That involves Emergency Services; that's a major operation, pally. You got something else up your sleeve."

"I've got this up my sleeve," Ryan said, and with his index finger pushed his nose to the side in the universal sign of the bent-nose Mafia thug.

The crowd in cop bars consists of various circles of men who alternate between raucous, backslapping laughter and solemnly whispered secrets. Anthony Ryan spoke so softly, both Danny and Gregory had to lean forward. He said he'd received the LUDs, the local calls, from Trey Winters's office phone. Besides calling Gillian on the night she died, he also made three calls to the Orpheus Lounge and one to the Pussycat Palace. The following day he called both locations again. Once each this time. Ryan looked around for eavesdroppers, then said both places were owned by Buster Scorza.

"Who's Buster Scorza?" Danny said, and they shushed him.

"Mobbed up big time," Gregory said. "At one time he owned over twenty massage parlors and peep show locations. He still owns half the real estate west of Times Square. And he got it the old-fashioned way. With muscle."

"You thinking Winters hired Scorza to have Gillian killed?" Danny said.

"That's a stretch," Gregory said.

Someone handed the bartender a newspaper. The back of *The Daily News* read, WEATHER HOT, IRABU COLD.

"Not for nothing," Gregory said. "But Scorza also has some connection to the stagehands union. It could be legit business. Just make sure you got the res gestae first."

Gregory moved away to sell tickets and glad-hand. The bar was packed with potential boat ride customers and guys who hadn't heard his entire repertoire of war stories. Danny wanted to take a few notes on the cryptic jargon that passed for conversation in a cop bar, but he knew better.

"What the hell is the res gestae?" Danny said.

"It means 'the thing,' in Latin. It means nothing here. He's just breaking my balls. Reminding me it's his case."

"The Pussycat is that big porn place on Eighth Avenue," Danny said. "It's a raging cash machine. Three floors of sex in every possible contortion."

"I don't want you going near Buster Scorza, Danny. Or Trey Winters. Understand? Even with two good arms."

"Where's the Orpheus Lounge?"

"Ninth Avenue. Years ago it was a hangout for Broadway musicians. Now it's a wrinkle room."

Danny knew that wrinkle room was shorthand for a bar that catered to aging gays. "Let me help out on this. I could approach it from a different angle. Not everybody wants to spill their guts to cops."

"Not Scorza," Ryan said. "We'll give you people to interview. Just don't go near Scorza."

"Give me somebody, please. I want to do something. I keep thinking I screwed up here. I should have noticed something was wrong with her. Maybe she'd still be alive today if I had something else on my mind besides getting laid."

"It's not your fault," Ryan said, and wondered how many times he was going to say it in this case. "Something happened earlier that night. Winters had made his mind up to have Gillian drug tested. Then he apparently changed it between six-thirty and eleven. All we know now is that during that time, he made phone calls to Scorza and had dinner with Abigail Klass."

"Abigail Klass the food writer? I can interview her."

"Winters says he had a change of heart and decided not to give up on Gillian. You believe that, Danny?"

"I think he was scared shitless his rich wife would find out about his affair with Gillian."

"Gillian's sister, Faye, spoke to her after Winters left, and said she was very upset, talking crazy. If we believe Trey Winters, she should have been happy."

"You think Winters is lying?"

"All the years I've been a cop," Ryan said, "I talked to a lot of liars. One thing they all do is rationalize. No matter how you push, accuse, insult . . . they give you a rational explanation. Today I pushed Trey Winters and he never got mad at me. Liars are never angry, Danny. Remember that."

13

Victor awoke to sirens, the music of the Bronx night. The apartment was dark, except for a sliver of light from under the bathroom door. Victor assumed he'd left it on when he took the red pills, earlier. He was slightly foggy, but the rest had helped. He pulled himself up to a sitting position, feeling the tug of his stomach muscles. A good tug, the pain less severe. The retribution from Wednesday's reckless performances was wearing off. He got to his feet as the bathroom door opened. Pinto stood framed in the doorway.

"I'm not good enough for you," Pinto said, his body a question mark in silhouette. "Not smart enough, or you don't trust me. Which is it?"

The envelope meant for Trey Winter was not on the table. It was in Pinto's hand.

"You have no answers, my friend," Pinto said, waving the note. "Before you always have answers."

"That note is none of your business, Pinto."

"It wasn't my business when I took you from your busboy

job and taught you to juggle. It wasn't my business when I taught you to work crowds."

"Give me that," Victor said.

"I should have let you waste yourself like your father."

"You don't understand."

"You found a way to strike it big, and fuck Pinto. I understand that."

"I thought it was too dangerous for you. A man your age."

"Oh, too dangerous for me, but not too dangerous for you, taking your pills like little candies."

"You never keep your mouth shut about anything, Pinto. What was I going to do?"

"You thought I would tell somebody? I had schemes in Russia make your scheme look like little potatoes. I didn't even tell myself things then, in case I talked in my sleep."

Pinto threw the letter on the table.

"See," Victor said. "You put your fingerprints on the letter. Sometimes you don't think."

"Blackmail needs two to work it right."

"I'm not blackmailing anyone. It's a simple business deal."

"That is why you cut words out of the newspapers. Because of a business deal. You think I'm stupid, that insult is worst."

Victor walked into the bathroom to wash his face. The water felt good. The smell of the soap invigorated him. Victor had inherited his father's looks, lady-killers, both of them. His mother always said that if his father prayed at all, he prayed to the Virgin Mary, because he believed he had a way with all women. Victor saw in the mirror a tired man, his skin losing the glow of health. He needed to get out of this city. He heard Pinto banging things around.

Victor dried his hands. He put his gloves on and took the scissors from the table. He walked into the bedroom. Both dresser drawers had been dumped on the bed. Pinto flung clothes into his old scarred trunk, a trunk they'd lugged for many miles in his Chevy. Victor knew he deserved better than this.

"We are ended," Pinto said. "No longer partners, no longer friends. I am driving to Florida in my car; you get your own car. Get your own limo. That's what you see about yourself. Big boss in the limo."

Victor plunged the scissors down into Pinto's back, but the blow lacked force, and his hand slipped off as the metal struck bone. Pinto jolted straight up, arching like an angry cat. The scissors loosened, dangling down toward the floor.

"What are you doing!" he bellowed, reaching behind him.

"What do you think, you dumb bastard," Victor said.

Pinto twisted away and ran for the door, scissors flopping, his legs kicking high like a startled deer. Victor grabbed a fistful of the Russian's hair and spun him around, and the scissors clattered to the floor. He slammed Pinto down on his back and fell on his chest, knees first, with all his weight. "Ooomph!" came out of the Russian. Victor sat on his chest, his knees pinning the Russian's arms as he wrapped his hands around Pinto's throat and squeezed with every ounce of strength. Victor's arms and hands were weakened, but the Russian was no match. Pinto kicked wildly behind him. Victor held the pressure steady.

A knock at the door sent a surge of adrenaline into Victor Nuñez and he squeezed harder on Pinto's skinny neck, the veins in his forearms popping like blue electric cords. The knock at the door became louder. "Everything all right?" the landlady said.

Pinto surged and tried to throw Victor off. He rocked him hard, bucking wildly. Thirty long seconds ticked off the clock as the kicking slowed, then stopped. The gurgling sounds came softer. She kept knocking. "What's going on in there?" she said. Pinto's breath stopped.

Victor rose and stripped off the bloody shirt and pants. Down to his underwear. He took off the gloves, picked up a dumbbell, and went to the door.

"What is going on in there?" the landlady said.

"Lifting weights," Victor said, still breathing hard. "Hurt my shoulder . . . muscle locked. It scared me and I yelled. Sorry I disturbed you."

"Do you need the ambulance?"

"No, I'm fine," he said. He opened the door enough to allow her to see he was dressed in his underwear, his chest soaked with sweat. She looked away.

"I don't know if I like any weight lifting on my floors. All the iron banging down on my hardwood."

"I'll be careful," he said, closing the door. "Very careful."

He leaned back against the door and breathed deeply. When he put the dumbbell back under the weight bench he could see blood on his forearm. He wondered if she had noticed.

It was after midnight when he finished cleaning the blood off the walls and floor. Nothing worked on the stained throw rug. He dragged Pinto's old trunk across the floor and set it on the rug. It covered the stain completely, in case the landlady decided to snoop. He knew she couldn't move the trunk with all that dead weight inside.

14

Anthony Ryan stood in his second-floor bedroom, looking down at the moonlight shining on his backyard. Spring rains had spawned a jungle of unknown foliage growing out of control along their back fence, a spot where they'd planted hedges years ago. Rip had named it the green monster after the left field wall in Fenway Park. Unpruned and untended, it turned untamable. A deflated basketball protruded from underneath. Rip's bike and all the sports equipment he was supposed to store in the garage found itself behind the green monster. Ryan had no idea what else they'd find back there.

"We have to do something about that backyard," Leigh said. "Before it swallows up the house."

"It doesn't look that bad."

"It looks terrible, Anthony. I'm going to get back there this week, take everything out. Plant some flowers along the fence."

Ryan looked back down at the old basketball. Rip had played with it so much, he'd worn off the pebble grain. It was as smooth as young skin. A few nights earlier he'd leaped from his bed, heart pounding, when he'd thought he heard the thump, thump of a basketball beneath his window. He'd been half-asleep and imagined it. Heard it because he wanted to. Like he'd heard the words of Gillian Stone. I love you.

"Everything just keeps growing, doesn't it?" he said.

"I still have that old landscaping plan you drew up. Want to take a look at it, see where you went wrong?"

"You never get tired of that old joke, do you?"

A platoon of fully grown trees surrounded the backyard. The Ryans had bought the trees from a mail-order nursery catalog over three decades ago. Twenty-eight trees, the price so cheap that he couldn't help himself. He'd expected a huge truck to make the delivery, two or three strapping workers, maybe a forklift to handle twenty-eight trees. So when the UPS man handed Anthony Ryan the package of twigs wrapped in a cardboard sleeve no bigger than a baseball bat, the look on his face sent Leigh Ryan into a fit of laughter the kids had talked about for years.

"How's Danny's shoulder?" she said.

"He's got his arm in a sling. The doctor gave him only one exercise to do: walking his fingers up the wall. Some heavy-duty aspirin, that's it."

"Youth is grand," Leigh said. "I couldn't believe he went downtown to meet you just a few hours after he left the hospital."

"Surprised me, too."

"It must have been very important to him."

Barefoot, in a short pink summer nightgown, she padded back and forth, folding socks and underwear, stacking them neatly in dresser drawers. Streaks of silver glittered in her hair, which had gone completely gray in her early forties. He loved her hair this color; it seemed to glow around her face. It was a good thing he loved it, because no amount of persuasion could ever convince her to color it.

"Did you see Katie's postcard?" she said.

"I did. I never thought our daughter and granddaughter would both get to Ireland before us."

"Nothing stopping us from going," she said. "You have enough vacation time to travel around the world a dozen times. You just have to take some of it."

"Maybe this fall."

"The sun is shining now."

Finished folding clothes, Leigh pulled back the bedcovers. She grabbed the hem of her nightgown and yanked it over her head. After all the years of their marriage he was still surprised at the size and fullness of her breasts. She dressed to disguise her breasts, not because of shyness, he thought, but because she loved the look on his face. Her magic trick. Voilà!

"You owe me a back scratch," she said, kicking her panties across the room.

He slid into bed and pulled her against him, face-to-face, both on their sides. She buried her face in her usual spot against his shoulder, her face tucked under his chin as she nibbled at his neck, murmuring about its softness. He wrapped both arms around her and slowly, in circles, he grazed her back gently with the tips of his fingernails. Her breath was warm and steady against his chest.

"Danny came to see you about Gillian Stone, didn't he," she said.

"He feels guilty. Thinks he should have helped her somehow."

"Now he's going to try to make up for it by helping you."

"He wants to do something, Leigh. I can understand that."

"But he's too close to this situation, Anthony. You wouldn't allow a cop to investigate the death of someone he cared for."

"He's not investigating anything. He just wants to write a story about her. I'll keep an eye on him."

Ryan knew that Leigh meant that he was too close as well. She was getting to him. Circling around. She would have made a great interrogator.

"Why don't you let someone else work this case?" she said,

directing his hands to a specific spot below her left shoulder. A spot she called her left wing. She sighed when he found it, as if he'd pulled a thorn from her back.

"Everyone in the office has as much work as we do. Or even more."

"Gregory can handle it alone. We'll fly to Ireland and surprise Katie and Margaret."

"The case won't last that long. Not more than a couple of days. We'll talk about it then."

Leigh had a natural intuition that Ryan couldn't fathom. She was a mixture of qualities dominated by strength of character and an unbending stubbornness. She was sweet and funny and was uninhibited sexually long before it was chic. But no one he'd ever met in his life held on to their beliefs as ferociously as she did. Ferocious was the right word. Angry, she could be fearsome.

"I hope you're not staying with this case for Danny's sake," she said.

"I wouldn't do that, Leigh."

"Maybe he needs to be dealing with someone who's not close to him. Someone more objective. If you weren't there, Joe Gregory would just tell him to butt out."

"Gregory might do that anyway."

She moved her hand between his legs. Stroking him gently, almost as an afterthought, knowing exactly how to touch, rub, withdraw, touch again. A touch so practiced and delicate, so knowing. The exact right pressure, the exact right time. She had complete mastery of his mind, his muscle, blood, and bone. And he reveled in it.

"Maybe I'll give him a call," she said. "See if he wants to have dinner with me tomorrow."

"Tomorrow night he's flying to Arizona for Gillian's funeral. You'll see him on the boat ride on Sunday."

"But then I won't be able to ask him personal questions."

"I'm sure he can't wait for that."

Ryan rolled over and got to his knees. It was the way he

reached her lower legs; she wanted to be touched all over. First one foot and he massaged it, kneading the rough skin of her heel, the tender instep, running his fingers between her toes. Then scratching again, back down her ankles, her calves. She reached up and took him in her hand. Her eyes focused intently on the fruits of her labor.

"I started cleaning Rip's bedroom today," she said. "I took down all those Cal Ripken posters. I'm going to change it to a girl's room. Katie can have her own room when she's here."

He nudged her over onto her back. He continued scratching, reaching down her thighs, while his tongue and lips alternated on the brown skin of her nipples.

"Is that okay with you?"

"Shut up," he said.

He entered her slowly, holding himself above her while he kissed her, pulling his head up, letting her reach for him with her lips. She put her arms around his neck and tried to pull him down, but he resisted, wanting his own pace. Wanting to feel each sensation of her body as he touched it.

"Go look at the room, Anthony."

"I will," he said, then she rolled him over. Easily. Her strength and agility in bed were still amazing. She kissed him, pushing her tongue into his mouth, grinding her pelvic bone against his. Then she pushed herself up to arm's length, and he knew she wanted her arms scratched, and her head, then her back, her shoulders, her legs, everything kissed, rubbed, fondled, massaged.

"You scratch," she said. "I'll shut up and fuck."

15

By the time Anthony Ryan arrived at the Broadway Arms on Friday morning, the corners had been squared with blue police barriers. The barriers, arranged in the same tried-and-true configuration the NYPD had used for thousands of demonstrations and parades, allowed the officers to control the flow of foot traffic. In this case they were protecting the entire corner, as Emergency Services cops yanked a huge canvas mat from a truck.

The cops closed the bus stop while they inflated the mat. Downtown traffic choked into two narrow lanes. Ryan waited under the Broadway Arms canopy while doorman Irish Eddie from Waterford whistled down a limo. With a courtly bow he whisked a woman in a scarlet turban and dark glasses into the backseat of a Lincoln Towncar.

Irish Eddie told Ryan that he rarely saw Trey Winters in the building. Then he scanned the list of uninterviewed tenants that the Mid-Town North squad had shrunk to seven. Irish Eddie was pleased to inform Ryan that five of those missing tenants were now available; the other two were still out of town. Only one of the newly available resided on Gillian's floor. Apartment 18L. Directly across the hall from Gillian's 18K. Ryan started there.

The listed occupant was Stella Grasso, a professional tutor, on the road with *Annie*. She came home often when her show was in an eastern city. Ryan knocked. From inside he heard the sounds of an afternoon TV talk show, the audience hooting, berating a guest. Heavy footsteps coming to the door. The thin metallic click of the peephole. He held his shield for viewing.

"What's going on downstairs?" she said, opening the door. "All those cops?"

"We're going to simulate Gillian Stone's accident," he said. "I was wondering if I could ask you a few questions."

"Come in, come in," she said, backing up. "It's like Carnegie Hall out here, the way voices carry."

Stella Grasso had brown shoulder-length hair, curled up in a flip popular in the fifties. He followed her into the living room as she spelled out her name.

"Grasso is my married name. A cop, the bastard. Tommy the cop. Tommy Blue Eyes. Know him? Tall redheaded guy. He had the post on Eighth Avenue. He's famous. Famous, I find out later, for banging anything wearing a skirt."

Ryan was convinced that everyone in the world knew at least one of the thirty-eight thousand New York City cops. And for some reason they assumed they all knew each other. Ryan said he didn't know him.

"If you say so. I have no idea why I married him. His dick was the only thing he ever loved, honored, and obeyed."

Stella said she came to the city as a dancer and appeared in three shows that made it to Broadway. She pointed to the framed posters on the wall. Her career ended shortly after she'd assumed the role of wife. But Tommy Blue Eyes thought his part was a walk-on, and he'd walked off.

"I got my kid," she said. "That's the one thing I can thank

that bastard for. She's teaching in the Women's Studies program in NYU. She lives in Stuyvesant Town, so I see her all the time."

Abandoned by both her dancer's body and her blue knight, Stella dusted off her teaching degree and wound up in junior high, the bloody trenches of public education. Every student jumping out of his or her skin, hormones in turbulence. She hated it, and her heart was still on Broadway. Then an old friend called and asked if she'd be interested in tutoring child actors in the road show of *Oliver*. She jumped. Connections bred connections, and that was how she got the apartment in the Broadway Arms.

"How well did you know Gillian Stone?" Ryan said.

"We moved in about the same time, but we weren't any Mary and Rhoda. Sometimes she was friendly, other times . . ."

"She was moody, I hear," Ryan said.

"Yeah, but she was a kid. She didn't know enough not to start screwing around with that guy Winters. It's enough to put anyone in a bitchy mood. Maybe Winters gave her the apartment, but sometimes you bargain with the devil and he wants your soul. I'm living proof of that."

"What do you mean, screwing around?"

"Screwing around screwing. What else? The guy thinks he's the Warren Beatty of Broadway. Throws women away like dirty tissues."

"Do you know that for sure?"

"Hell–ooo. I don't think they were playing Parcheesi in there."

Stella said that Winters was a regular in the building. In the time Gillian lived in 18K, Winters visited at least once a week.

"Were you home the night Gillian died?" Ryan said.

"Yeah, getting ready to leave for Pittsburgh the next morning."

"Did you happen to notice when Trey Winters arrived?"

"I was watching the news at eleven, hon. Listening for the

weather. I try to check the weather on the nights I'm traveling, and if it's shitty, I call a car to get me to the bus station.
If not, I wait downstairs for a cab. The weather guy was just
starting when I hear lover boy banging."

"About eleven-fifteen."

"Yeah. Banging. He never banged on the door before. This
time he's banging, holding this white dress over his shoulder."

"He usually didn't bang?"

"Always before a little tap, tap, tap. Very quiet. Very discreet.
You could hardly hear. Usually, the only way I knew he was
here was when I heard the stairway door squeak."

"He usually came up the stairway?"

"Yeah, gotta give him credit, right? After eighteen flights
sex would be the last thing on my mind. But I figured he took
the elevator to another floor to fool people. Then he just
walked up a few flights."

"But this night he doesn't take the stairway, and he's not tap-
tapping?"

"Right. So I heard the banging. You gotta look out for
yourself in this city. I had the portable in my hand, got the
nine and the one already dialed. But I see it's just himself."

"So he's banging on the door. Holding this white dress over
his shoulder."

"Right. The whole floor should have been awake the way
he was banging. But not long; she answered quick. I couldn't
get a good look at her face. She was behind the door, and
those peepholes, they're not worth shit. But it was her."

"Could you hear anything after the door closed?"

"I wish I had a nickel for every time he called her a fucking bitch. Not that I was snooping, but he was loud."

"What was she saying to him?"

"Never heard a peep. Ten, fifteen minutes later he storms
out."

"You saw him storm out?"

"I was peeking; so sue me."

"You never heard her yelling?"

"Not once."

"Did you hear anything after he left?"

"Nothing."

"What else do you remember?"

"After he left, I thought, Good riddance. Then I went to bed. I had to schlep to Pittsburgh in the morning."

"You heard nothing at all after he left?"

"I went to bed, hon. That was enough excitement for one night for me. Six in the morning I left for Steeltown. I had theater brats to teach. I didn't even know what happened until I saw the commotion outside the next morning."

"A police officer knocked on your door at three-fifteen in the morning," Ryan said, double-checking the sheets.

"At three-fifteen, I was zonked," she said. "I have a ritual. Whenever I have to travel the next day I take a Darvon, put on the white sound machine, the surf, I like the sound of the surf. Don't ask me why, I hate the beach. But the machine I can take. It's soothing. Then I put on my eye mask and say-onara."

Ryan handed her his card. "I'm going to be across the hall in eighteen-K," he said. "If you think of anything else, please get in touch with me. Today, tomorrow, anytime."

"I can think of something right now," she said.

"Whatever you remember is important."

"Damn right it is. If you see that Tommy Blue Eyes, tell him that every day I say a prayer he gets fucking cancer. The bastard. And tell him to call his daughter."

16

In Danny Eumont's eyes Joe Gregory and his uncle were blind to the fact that their century was almost over. The evidence they ignored was more than numbers on a calendar. The old Hubert Street Police Academy where they started their careers was long gone, turned to rubble by a wrecking ball. Most of the boys with whom they'd entered that building were either in Florida or under the turf. Even their old war stories seemed to be told in grainy black and white, voice-over by Robert Mitchum, the score sad Sinatra songs. No Dolby, no 3-D, no slo-mo, no FX.

Danny pictured them standing in fog, wearing trench coats and fedoras, newspapers blaring headlines of a foreign war. They were a walking period piece. That was why he'd first assumed that the theater district informant they'd asked him to interview, code name Mister W.W., was some play on the initials of the late Broadway gossip columnist Walter Winchell. He was wrong. His name was Wacky Walzak.

"Yul Brynner ate brown eggs only," Wacky Walzak said.

"The King and I, 1951. He'd scream if you tried to sneak in white eggs."

Joe Gregory had told Danny that Wacky would meet him after the lunch rush, in front of Vasili's Shoe Repair Shop on West Fifty-first. Danny had been there for an hour when he spotted Wacky coming out of the Gershwin Theater, looking exactly as they'd described him, snapping coins into his belt changer. He said he only had a few minutes, he'd forgotten an egg salad sandwich and some road-show Olivier had thrown a hissy fit.

"When Brynner went on the road," Wacky said, pointing vaguely west, "he always had them paint each dressing room the same color as the one in the St. James. I first met him in the Plymouth Theatre, 1946. *The Lute Song,* his big break. He played Mary Martin's husband."

Wacky Walzak had run coffee and sandwiches around the theater district since he was a child. But he was clearly a few fries short of a Happy Meal.

"I'm working on a story about Gillian Stone," Danny said. "I suppose my uncle told you that."

"You're supposed to buy lunch," Wacky yelled. "Detective Joe Gregory said anywhere I want to go. Money is no object."

"If that's what Gregory said, it's fine with me."

"Too bad I don't have time today. Such an attractive young man. Have you considered acting?"

Wacky Walzak was a character Dick Tracy would have called "Mushface." His flattened features were set in the fattest cheeks Danny had ever seen, his eyes barely visible. His hair, dyed a coppery red, contrasted with his pale complexion and thick purple lips. Short arms hung at belt level, pudgy hands dangling, as if ready to begin typing. His belly peeked out from under a black T-shirt that read, "Who died and left you boss?"

"When did you first meet Gillian Stone?" Danny said.

"When she was a swing girl in *Cats.*"

"What's a swing girl?"

"A swing girl replaces any girl dancer in the chorus out for any reason, illness, death in the family, time of the month, et cetera, et cetera."

"What was your impression of her?" Danny said.

"I don't do impressions," Wacky said, and did a laughing pirouette. He was unable to stand still for ten seconds. He'd talk and turn, re-turn and then pirouette, often finishing a sentence with his back to Danny.

"Did you ever have a conversation with her?"

"Tuna on toast, she said to me," Wacky Walzak said. "Rye toast. No wheat, no white. Sprite, Mountain Dew, or Seven-Up. No diets, no Pepsi. The girl hated colas."

"Was that the extent of your relationship with her?"

"Va-va-va-voom," Wacky said, shaking his little hands in front of his chest. "I only wish our relationship had an extent. The lady was stacked. She looked like Judy Tyler, remember her? In *Pipe Dream,* Shubert Theatre, 1955. Stacked like her. Judy was Princess Summerfall Winterspring on the *Howdy Doody* show. Poor dear was killed in a car crash the year after *Pipe Dream* closed. Bill Johnson, the male lead, died of a heart attack the same year. Strange co-inky-dink, don't you think?"

Wacky arched his dyed eyebrows and gave a half turn.

"I know what she looked like," Danny said. He decided he'd better be more specific. "Did you hear any rumors about Gillian doing drugs?"

"I heard she was partying hardy. Some days she growled, some days she glowed."

"Where did you hear that?"

"On the street, here and there," Wacky said. "Speaking of Mary Martin. *South Pacific,* 1949. Wash that man right outta my hair." He smiled and aped the hair-washing motion. "She was supposed to use a bar of soap, but the soap wouldn't lather fast enough. So they sent me out to buy shampoo. I bought Prell."

"Were people surprised she took her own life?" Danny said.

"Mary Martin?" Wacky said, eyebrows ascending.

"Gillian Stone," Danny said.

"Ooo, shocked," he said. "Disbelief not suspended. She was a star in the making."

"But you heard nothing specific about drugs?" Danny said.

"Not my area of expertise," he said.

"What do you know about Trey Winters?"

"Did a turn in *Barefoot in the Park,* 1983. Espresso drinker, lousy tipper. At that time I had to schlep up to Sixth Avenue to get espresso. Marousek's Deli. It's gone now. They moved to Florida. And please tell Detective Ryan, please, pretty please, take a look over near the TKTS booth. Charlatans are selling pilfered tickets before the booth opens. Ripping people off and giving the theater a bad name. I told Mid-Town North, but they have bigger fish, apparently."

"I'll tell him," Danny said. "Were there any rumors of a romance between Gillian and Winters?"

"Whispers, whispers, whispers," Wacky hissed, baring his chewed-off fingernails.

"What were they saying?"

"The man is a swordsman," he said, pulling an imaginary rapier from his waistband. "Like Errol Flynn, he's always in."

"Anything more specific you can tell me about Winters?" Danny wanted to address him by name but felt funny calling him Wacky.

"Looks nine, talent three, class zero," Wacky said. "Mark it down. Without the wife's money he'd be working the ticket window. The only thing show biz about him was his Ethel Merman temper."

"What about his temper?"

"Kate Hepburn wouldn't put up with his shit. Threw him out of a run-through for *Coco.* Mark Hellinger Theatre, 1969."

"Threw him out why?"

"Late, he was always late. Union rules state you must be in the theater thirty minutes before curtain. Then she caught him bragging about his summer stock turn as Macbeth. Kate said he knew less about the theater than Clive Barnes's cat."

"What does that have to do with his temper?"

"It's bad luck to say the name 'Macbeth' backstage."

"But what does that have to do with his temper?" Danny said. "Wacky, listen to me. I really want to know what makes Trey Winters tick today, not twenty years ago."

"Women make him tick, young, pretty ones."

"Any current girlfriends?"

"Not since Gillian." He made a gesture with his hands like a wobbly aircraft fluttering to the ground.

"You have any proof they were having an affair? Did you see anything? Or know anyone who saw anything?"

"There is one witness," he said.

"Who?"

"Paul Klass."

"Paul Klass is dead."

"Don't remind me. AIDS, the plague. Empty chairs and empty tables. Empty apartments. Empty theaters."

Wacky rocked back and forth; Danny figured he was acting out a ticking clock. "What does Paul Klass have to do with anything?" he asked.

Wacky spun around, his eyes wide, incredulous. "One of the greatest people in the history of Broadway. Choreographer, performer, director. God rest his talented soul."

"With this case," Danny said. "What does he have to do with this case?"

"Paul Klass was pretty-boy Winters's mentor when he arrived here from Wyoming or Kansas. One of those big square states."

"And he witnessed Gillian's death?"

"His ghost saw it all. That was his apartment, eighteen-K. Paul Klass owned that apartment before Winters. He died there and tears flowed into the street. His spirit haunts that apartment, and the Morosco. Maybe the Royale."

"I'm confused," Danny said.

"So was everyone else," Wacky said. "No one knows what he saw in Trey Winters. I think he didn't have the heart to tell him he lacked talent. Too nice a man. No balls. His one failing."

He rolled his eyes in a complete circle, then pointed to Vasili's Shoe Repair. The window was filled with dozens of autographed pictures of stars. Sly Stallone . . . "To Sam, my pal, thanks for everything." Liza Minnelli, Glenn Close, Meryl Streep, Katharine Hepburn, all apparently counted themselves in Sam's circle of close friends. Danny couldn't remember the last time he'd been in a shoemaker's shop. He wondered why movie stars seemed to have more problems with their footwear than the average citizen.

"Kate Hepburn," Wacky said. "She has balls. One night she stopped the opening number of *Coco* and threw a woman out of the audience, a paying customer who took a picture of her entrance. Then she made them start the show all over again."

"Wacky," Danny said, pointing to his watch, "it's been marvelous, but I'm due back on the planet Earth."

Danny's Groucho Marx voice was humming the theme to *Twilight Zone*.

"Would it make it easier if I told you how Winters got into the building unseen?" Wacky said.

"The ghost of Paul Klass beamed him up?"

"Funny, but nooo . . . through the back door. I saw him do it a few weeks ago."

"Cops checked the back door," Danny said. "It's through the basement, and it was locked."

"I bet they didn't check the old back door," Wacky said, again displaying his exaggerated eyebrow arch. "Remember March 23, 1982?"

"I was in grade school that day," Danny said. "That whole year, in fact."

"Blackest day in the history of Broadway," Wacky said, clapping his hand over his heart. "Five theaters torn down. The Morosco, the Astor, the Victoria, the Bijou, and the Helen Hayes. We were all there, swaying, arm in arm. Like the barricade scene in *Les Miz*. We sang 'God Bless America' and

'Give My Regards to Broadway.' Voices of angels. And people in your uncle's profession arrested Colleen Dewhurst, Estelle Parsons—"

"What about the old back door?"

Wacky seemed annoyed at being stopped from ticking off the entire list of those arrested. He spun around twice, then drummed on his coin changer.

"The old stars," he said. "The ones who built this street. Before the no-talent pretty faces and the bean counters. They had a back door from the Broadway Arms into the alley behind these theaters."

"I bet they closed it up when they built the Merrimac Hotel," Danny said.

"You'd be wrong," Wacky said.

In his lifetime Wacky Walzak had seen more minutes of live theater than any human being. Every show on Broadway for half a century. But according to Anthony Ryan he'd never seen a single play beginning to end in one sitting. He'd catch the first act of this, the last act of that. He was antsy now, his Air Jordans wanting to fly down the boulevard.

"I have other eggs to fry," Wacky said, and feigned illness. "A television actor yelled at me, believe it? A regular soap opera Barrymore."

"We'll talk again, when you have more time," Danny said.

"Any day except Sunday," Wacky said. "I never work Sundays."

"*Never on Sunday*?" Danny said, smiling.

"I don't work on Sundays," he said. "But I do have sex on Sunday."

And then, like a cellulite Peter Pan, he exited across Fifty-first Street without so much as a single curtain call.

17

By the time Ryan left Stella Grasso and crossed the hall to apartment 18K, Joe Gregory's hands were already under the dress. He squeezed her hips tightly as he waited for the breeze to wane. Gently he leaned forward until her thighs touched the rail, with her light brown feet still atop the woolen hassock. He took a burlesque bite at her ass. Then, on cue from below, he let gravity take the upper body, and the 109-pound hand-sewn canvas likeness of Gillian Stone tumbled eighteen stories into the center of a huge air mattress surrounded by Emergency Services cops and a few hundred gawkers.

"If this was an Olympic event," Gregory said, "that would be a gold medal half-gainer."

The air mattress had been placed at the curb. A red sheet, cut to the exact dimensions of the roof of a 1984 Ford Econoline, had been taped to the top of the mattress in the exact spot occupied by the van registered to the Times Square Ark of Salvation. The mannequin scored a bull's-eye.

"This is what they should do here on New Year's Eve, instead of dropping the ball," suggested one of the Crime Scene techs. "A falling blonde has much more inherent drama than a lighted ball."

"I'll call Dick Clark," Gregory said. "Maybe he can sign Madonna for the millennium."

Down below, autos and pedestrians held up for the doll drop resumed the traffic dance. Emergency Services cops hauled the mannequin from the heaving air mattress and commenced the deflation process. On the balcony of the eighteenth floor cops from Crime Scene Unit filed back into the apartment to finish the room-by-room search. Anthony Ryan walked toward the door.

"Don't go away mad," Joe Gregory said.

"Who's mad?" Ryan said. "I'm going down to the car to get a couple of DD fives. Write up the interview I did this morning with the woman across the hall."

Ryan filled Gregory in on his earlier canvass of the Broadway Arms, including his talk with Stella Grasso. He recounted how Ms. Grasso observed Trey Winters using the stairs on a regular basis to sneak up to Gillian's apartment. Tap-tap-tapping on her apartment door. But on Tuesday night, during the eleven-fifteen P.M. weather report, he didn't use the stairs. And he was angry. Bang-bang-banging.

"I never doubted he was lying about screwing her," Gregory said. "But I definitely don't see his coming here pissed off as a major contradiction. He told us he was pissed."

"No, he said he was coming up here to smooth things out."

"Maybe he *intended* to come here peacefully, but when he heard her voice on the phone he knew she was sloshed. Got himself worked up on the way over. Still, pally, the guy went home."

The heavy slap of wooden police barriers being thrown into an open truck echoed throughout the canyon. The rolling lights around the ITT building predicted a high of ninety-three, a low of seventy, slightly less humid.

"What the hell is it going to take to convince you, anyway?" Gregory said, gesturing down. "Didn't that help?"

"That test? That didn't prove anything."

"Come on, pally. It proves she wasn't tossed off. You saw me. I let her fall under her own weight."

"We proved that's exactly what happened," Ryan said. "I believe that test. I don't think it was a big shove, maybe not a shove at all. But somebody did this to her."

"Like a guru, you mean? Hypnotized her."

"Anything is possible."

"No, it isn't," Gregory said.

Detective Armand Coletti rumbled across the white Berber carpet and appeared in the open terrace doorway. The partners ended their conversation; their disagreements were their private business. Under his breath Gregory said, "Speaking of gurus."

Coletti was the rotund poster boy of the Crime Scene Unit. Always on the news with information on the latest big case. Within the whispered world of cops he was known more for his dress than his expertise. White linen suits and Borsolino hats. The terrace trembled when his full weight settled on it.

"We're wrapping it up," he said, looking over the rail. "We found traces of a substance that appears to be resin on her ballet shoes. We got a few prints, a coupla fibers. Nothing to get excited about. Nothing from the balcony at all."

"Anything in the safe?" Ryan said.

Detectives had found a small built-in safe in the closet. Ryan called Trey Winters, who declined to come to the apartment but gave him the combination over the phone.

"Empty, except forrrr," Coletti said, as if expecting a drumroll. "A little Bolivian marching powder."

"The safe was locked," Ryan said. "I doubt Gillian knew the combination. The coke could have been there for years."

"Ko-kane is ko-kane to me. It's your job to find out who, where, and when."

"How do you know it's cocaine?" Ryan said.

Coletti held up a plastic bag. Inside was a small tube from a test kit. It looked as though it had been tie-dyed dark blue. Positive for coke.

"Remind me why we hate him, Joe," Ryan said, turning to his partner.

"We don't hate Armand, pally. We hate his brother, Louie. Armand we just don't care for."

"Who the fuck are you two to hate anybody? Two old fucks hanging on by the skin of your teeth."

Ryan grabbed Coletti by the tie and yanked him forward, pulling his face over the rail. Opaque panels shook like cheap windows in a storm. A button flew off the tech man's shirt, pinged off the rail, and sailed into space.

"See down there, Armand?" Ryan said. "A girl named Gillian fell from here. Could've been your wife, your sister, your daughter. That's how you should be thinking. Of Gillian. Now I want you to wait for the bloodwork from the lab before you go shooting off your mouth to the press. Allow Gillian that much dignity."

"My partner's talking to you," Gregory said. The ITT sign reported, "Yanks 11–Whitesox 3, Martinez is one-man show, hits two homers." "He can't answer when you're choking him, pally."

"We don't want to read this in the paper," Ryan said, releasing his hold on the chunky technician.

"You're fucking nuts, you two," Coletti said, readjusting his tie and collar. He waddled away quickly, up the step into the apartment.

"You gotta relax here, pally," Gregory said. "You're starting to scare me."

"He needed that, Joe. It'll make him a better person."

"I think Armand's just become the Coletti who hates us. And we can't hate Louie no more, he's gonna be handicapped."

"That's right, his lifelong dream," Ryan said.

Armand's older brother, Lou Coletti, was the kind of sleazy and underhanded cop who wasn't aware how sleazy he was.

He was the kind of cop that cops talked about among themselves but never mentioned to any civilian. Lou Coletti was a useless cop whose only goal in the police department was to acquire a line-of-duty injury so he could retire on three-quarters pay, tax-free, for the rest of his life. It was no secret. Louie said it was like winning the lottery. But he wanted the perfect injury, one that wouldn't interfere with his lifestyle or cause him any pain.

Louie's first attempt was a back injury from a minor radio car accident. He spent a fortune in orthopedists, but his attempt failed. Then he tried to get out on the heart bill, citing all the pressure from a six-month stint in Narcotics. But it backfired. Word was, he took so many stress tests on the treadmills of a dozen heart specialists that he inadvertently worked himself into fairly decent shape. Rejected again, Louie was bitterly disappointed, swore he was going to give up the chase.

But about a month ago Gregory saw Louie in headquarters. He said he'd just been transferred to the outdoor pistol firing range. Innocently Gregory asked him why the hell he wanted that assignment. Louie put his hand up to his ear and yelled, "To get deaf, Joey. To get deaf."

As they left the apartment, Gregory kept repeating the line in Louie Coletti's gravelly Brooklynese. He had Ryan smiling despite himself. He was still smiling when he opened the apartment door and ran into Danny Eumont.

"You taking us to lunch?" Gregory said.

"I'm taking you to the basement," Danny replied.

18

Winters knew about this entrance," Anthony Ryan said, his voice echoing. "No doubt in my mind."

The door Wacky Walzak had described to Danny led to a twelve-by-twelve outdoor space between the Broadway Arms and the Merrimac Hotel. Cluttered and claustrophobic, it was like being at the base of four sheer cliffs. Most of the ground space was occupied by generators, electrical boxes, and other metal containers that hid the mystery machines that made skyscrapers work. An immense aluminum air-conditioning duct, wide enough to be an on-ramp to the Jersey Turnpike, curved across the ground and up. The airspace above their heads ended in blue sky.

"Didn't that woman across the hall tell you Winters used the elevator the night of the murder?" Gregory said.

"Right, and he made a big show of it. Talking to the doorman on the way out."

"So he leaves Gillian, says hello to the doorman to set up the alibis. Then sneaks back, climbs seventeen stories."

"No, maybe this is where the Scorza connection comes in. Anyone could come through that service door in the Merrimac Hotel and get into the Broadway Arms this way."

"Provided it was open," Gregory said.

"It was open just now," Ryan said.

The three of them were standing at the foot of the metal stairs leading up to an entrance to the Broadway Arms known only to air-conditioning mechanics and a dozen living Ziegfeld girls. Cigarette butts, crushed Styrofoam cups, and soda and beer cans littered the concrete. On the other side of the courtyard was a back entrance to the Merrimac Hotel.

"See?" Gregory said. "You're taking little bits and pieces and making a case in your head."

"That's what we do, Joe. Put little bits and pieces together. What's your plan? Pack it in? Go play golf?"

"I hate golf."

"You don't even like grass, for chrissakes," Ryan said.

"Your voices are echoing," Danny warned.

"Maybe we just tread water a little," Gregory said, his voice lower. "Mark it closed pending further information. We can come back to it when we get some real evidence."

Danny, who once thought himself immortal, felt unusually vulnerable. Gregory and his uncle seemed unconcerned about dangers from above. They were an easy target for someone near a window to dump his stale coffee, hock a loogie, or toss out a half-eaten salami sandwich. Airmail garbage express. And he was the schlemiel it would surely splat down on. Or was the victim the schlemazel? He kept peeking up, hoping nothing lethal would fall: a loose air conditioner, a brick, a piano, a safe. He regretted watching all those Saturday morning cartoons as a kid.

"I don't see Gillian as a coke head," Ryan said. "She was too intent on her career. And you don't handle a schedule like she had with your nose full of powder. Beside, coke is not as big a deal as it was in the eighties."

"That's not true," Danny said. They both looked over at

Danny as if they'd forgotten he was there. "Powder coke is big-ger than ever. They've done studies: whenever the economy is booming, so does the cocaine business. Stock market rises, everybody gets high."

"He's right," Gregory said.

Danny felt like a traitor, but he was surprised at his uncle, who was usually up on drug trends. Cocaine was king again, thanks to Dow Jones and Colombian efficiency in manufac-ture and distribution. The kilo price was only twenty grand, half what it was in the eighties. It was cheaper than pot. Any bozo could score a three-and-a-half-gram eight-ball for thirty bucks a gram. It was the in drug with the cocktail culture. The three C's: cocktails, Cubans, and coke.

"Where did she get it?" Ryan said.

"Anywhere," Danny said. "It's easy."

Danny knew a hundred people who bought coke. People who didn't even have the street smarts to find a cheap black box to unscramble cable TV. You could score it in mailrooms on Wall Street, oyster bars in the Hamptons, unisex bathrooms in SoHo or Chelsea. Or if you were too lazy to go out, bike messengers delivered it to your home, as did limo drivers.

"So what are you saying, Danny?" Ryan said. "That you think Gillian was using cocaine?"

"No. Just that it's easy to get."

"Give the kid a break," Gregory said. "He's just starting to see the logic in this."

"What logic? And when exactly did you decide this case was closed?"

"Yesterday at two forty-five," Gregory said, then his voice got higher, imploring. "I don't know when, pally. I just don't see this guy getting himself in a jam where he has to kill somebody."

"Shh," Danny said, pointing up.

Whispering, Gregory said, "You're the guy who's always preaching to put yourself in everybody's shoes. What I figure, when I get in Winters's shoes, is that he isn't stupid enough to try to dump her by creating this whole scenario. This is a guy who's convinced he's slick. He'd find a different way, a simpler, safer way. Buy her off, something like that. Not freaking kill her."

Ryan stepped back. Danny knew he was thinking hard by the way his eyes moved. All his life he'd watched his uncle think things through as if he were reading a scroll, his eyes moving up and down. Then Gregory whispered to Ryan, so low that Danny could hardly hear it.

"I ain't against you here," Gregory said. "I'm just thinking we're getting real close to stepping on our cocks. Maybe it's time we go get a drink and talk about it. All this whispering is making me thirsty."

"I don't know about the drugs," Danny said. "But I don't think she committed suicide. And I think Winters is in on this. If he didn't do it himself, he hired somebody."

"We need to find the connection between Scorza and Winters," Ryan said.

"Send Danny Boy over to the Orifice Lounge."

"Orpheus, Joe," Ryan said. "It's the Orpheus Lounge."

"It should be Orifice," Gregory said. "Let Danny go in and ask them about the correct pronunciation. He can ask around how Scorza and Winters know each other."

A pair of pigeons fluttered above their heads, then disappeared into an immense metal air duct.

"No, we'll deal with Scorza," Ryan said.

"I'll do whatever you want me to," Danny said. "Just let me know."

"See if you can find out why you never see any baby pigeons," Gregory said. "I've lived in this city all my life, never saw a single baby pigeon."

"Now it's time for that drink," Ryan said.

19

Later that evening Danny Eumont experienced an epiphany in Morley's Bar. It happened when Leigh Ryan walked in. She paused in the doorway, looking for him. All his life Danny had heard people talk about her beauty; he finally understood. She wore a simple white blouse, open at the neck, and a black rayon skirt covered with gray orchids. She stood there against the window, in the bar's smoky haze. The light of the setting sun behind her. Aunt Leigh. Elegant and glowing.

"You act as if you don't recognize me," she said. "You probably don't. It's been what, months?"

"More like weeks. I figured I'd see you on the boat ride Sunday night."

"Oh, I have to come to Manhattan to see you, is that it? Now you're a big magazine writer, too good for our raggedy old neighborhood."

Leigh Ryan had a natural beauty. Her face was the sum of perfect, even features, big brown eyes, and a man-killer smile.

She even seemed to be turning age into an asset. That stunning, silver hair.

"So are you all packed for the desert?" she said. "Toothbrush, clean underwear?"

"Who needs that stuff? It's an overnighter, out and back. I'm just going for the funeral. I'll be home Sunday."

Morley's Bar was a place Danny had visited every Sunday after church since he was an infant. Then called the Emerald Isle, it dominated the top of a green mount called Hog's Hill in a residential section of the old industrial city. But, sick and dying were the three-story wooden frame buildings that had housed Irish immigrants since the turn of the century. The Irish, many from County Waterford on Ireland's rocky east coast, walked directly from ship's steerage to this hill, carrying everything they owned. A few decades later their sons and daughters drove away in BMWs.

"Do you know any of Gillian's family?" she said.

"I met her half-sister, Faye, a few times. That's it."

They sat at a table opposite the horseshoe bar, both comfortable up front. Aunt Leigh waved to Billy Harrington, the bartender, who told her he thought it was a movie star coming through the door. Deuce Doran, a high school pal of Anthony Ryan's, asked where her reprobate husband was. Almost all the stools were inhabited by men whom his uncle had grown up with. The bulk of them were alumni of Gorton or Sacred Heart High School.

"So tell me everything," she said. "Any new girlfriends?"

"You kidding? I hardly have time to visit my sainted mother and my glamorous aunt."

"Oh, my God. You've become a first-class Irish bullshitter. There must be something in the water up on this hill."

Danny wondered why Aunt Leigh had asked him to meet her in Morley's. It wasn't to discuss his love life. He was sure she knew all about the parts of that he was willing to make public.

"I can't imagine a handsome man like you doesn't have the girls falling all over him."

"Oh, I'm a babe magnet. I attract nuts, and I bolt."

Aunt Leigh approached touchy subjects cautiously, like a cat stalking a bird. He figured this came from her southern background. She was the exact opposite of the blunt, cut-to-the-chase New York women he knew. He preferred the forthright New York approach. Say it, get it over with.

"Your mom is a little worried about you, Danny."

"Tell her not to worry, Aunt Leigh. I'm fine."

"Just like your uncle. He keeps telling me he's fine."

"I am fine, honest."

"Your mom thinks you were more in love with Gillian Stone than you'd like to admit."

"I was, but I've had six months to get over it."

Leigh ordered the potato soup and a salad. Danny took the corned beef on rye, although the waitress was laughing so hard that she could hardly write. The Blarney Boys were holding court on the other side of the bar, giving an impromptu preview of some of their new material. The Blarney Boys were a pair of retired Con Ed meter readers who did stand-up Irish comedy in the local hospitals and nursing homes. Always a captive audience.

"I could understand it if you were upset," she said. "You had just been with Gillian a few hours before she died."

"It stirred up some old feelings."

"She must have had some old feelings herself, Danny. She called you when she was in trouble. Maybe going out to Arizona will help you reach closure."

"I have reached closure, Aunt Leigh. This is just something I want to do. Pay my respects to the family. Tell them how much I thought of her."

From the corner came the bells and boops of an electronic tote board. Two old-timers tried to outgame each other on the shuffleboard machine, playing for fifty-cent drafts. The metal puck clickety-clacked over the counters and slammed against the back of the machine.

"Remember the old shuffleboard?" Leigh said. "The long one? You and your cousin used to play it for hours. Your sweater sleeves would be covered with sawdust."

"We had to stand on chairs when we first started playing."

The old shuffleboard had taken up the length of the room in those days. No electronics, no coins required, just a gentle touch and the ability to keep score in your head. The sound of voices had dominated the place then, the musical Irish voices, telling stories and laughing. Some of the old-timers, in their beards and caps, would bet on Rip or Danny, calling them "the lads." They'd exhort them in those soft brogues as the green metal puck slid across the endless expanse of hardwood, striking the red puck with a delicate click.

"I miss Rip's sense of humor," Danny said. "God, he could make me laugh."

"I used to think he got the nickname Rip because he was such a rip. Then I found out about Cal Ripken. I should have known, all those baseball posters on the wall."

"The kid was flat-out crazy. Some of the stuff he dreamed up."

The TV was on, but silent, above Billy Harrington's head. Those who preferred the company of an idiot box could read the dialogue on the closed captioning flashing across the screen. Billy said the empty chatter of the TV should not interfere with good conversation.

"Does your uncle ever talk about Rip?" she said.

"He's a very private guy, Aunt Leigh."

"He keeps things bottled up."

"I'm sure he talks to Joe Gregory. A lot of private exchanges go on between the two of them."

"You know, I used to be a little jealous of the closeness between them. After all, he's probably spent more time with Joe than with me over the past thirty years. But when Rip died . . .

I don't know what either of us would have done without Joe. And him just losing a son himself."

Danny almost started to tell her a story he'd heard Gregory tell. He changed his mind; it was not for her ears. One St. Patrick's Day during their heavy drinking years the two of them hooked up with a midget in a Kelly green dress. They toured their old haunts, drinking free as the tiny raucous woman they called their leprechaun danced her jigs on the bar tops of Manhattan. True or not, Gregory's rendition had Ryan laughing out loud.

"A few months after Gregory's son died," Danny said, "I asked him how he was doing. He says, 'You pick yourself up, dust yourself off, and get back in the race.' I know Uncle Anthony loves him and all, but you have to wonder about a guy whose entire philosophy of life is spelled out in Sinatra songs."

Aunt Leigh laughed. Gregory seemed to have that ability to make them laugh. At least he's good for something, Danny thought.

"It's a wonderful thing for men to have close friends," Leigh said. "I can remember you and Rip on the phone for hours, talking about this girl and that girl."

"He thought he was the Ann Landers of Yonkers. But we talked about a lot of other things. Things just between us."

"Who do you talk to now, Danny?"

Danny shrugged and looked out through the Guinness sign in the window. The area around Morley's had changed since Danny was a boy. Now blacks, Hispanics, Asians, and Middle Easterners squeezed into the sad former digs of the McSpedons, the McGeans, the Sullivans, and the Coughlins, whose aging children returned to Morley's Bar every now and then to reminisce about their childhood in the last outpost of the endangered Irish hilltopper.

"I used to tell Gillian all those old stories," he said. "About Rip. Crazy stuff we did when we were kids."

"Was she easy to talk to?"

"Oh, Christ, yes. I could say anything to her. Anything.

That was the great thing about her. No pretensions. I could run around unshaven, in my underwear."

"It's nice, that kind of relationship, isn't it."

Danny pushed his glass around in circles. The truth was, that kind of relationship scared the hell out of him. He didn't know whether he was the type of man who could handle the forever part of it. One person for the rest of your life. They become your life. His uncle always said the price of love is grief. Maybe the price was too steep for him.

"I keep thinking that maybe I missed something that night, Aunt Leigh. Maybe there was some way I could have prevented all this. Maybe she was trying to tell me something. A cry for help, I don't know. And there I am all wrapped up in my act, showing off the wonderfulness of myself."

"If Gillian asked for your help that night, you would have heard it. She didn't. Go to Arizona, then put it all behind you."

"I'd just hate to think . . ."

"Hate to think what?" she said.

"Skip it."

"You are nothing like your father, if that's what you were going to say. Nothing at all, believe me."

They ate mostly in silence, exchanging bits and pieces of news and local gossip. Who married who, who was divorcing who. They didn't talk about death again.

20

Two candles flickered in the tiny apartment of Faye Boudreau. She led Anthony Ryan down the darkened hall as their shadows swarmed over the walls. It was six in the evening on Friday, and she wore an old black slip, the lace top frazzled, the material translucent from wear. The room was warm. It smelled sickly sweet, like decaying fruit.

"Your air-conditioning broken?" Ryan said.

"I got chilled with it on."

"Open a window."

"I don't like the windows open. Not in this city."

Ryan noticed that the clock on the microwave was the only evidence of electricity in the room. The air conditioner had to have been off for hours.

"I hoped you'd come," she said. Her face was puffy; it looked as though she'd been crying.

"How are you feeling?"

"Like caca," she said.

As his eyes adjusted, he watched her stop short, just before the unmade bed.

"I'm thirsty," she said, going back into the kitchenette. "Want something cold to drink?"

He could feel the heat off her body as she squeezed past him. A can of Café Bustelo sat on the kitchen counter.

"I want to go over your last conversation with Gillian," Ryan said.

"Why are you still doing this?"

"I thought you'd want to find out the truth."

"She's dead. That's the truth."

Faye took two bottles of Corona from the refrigerator and placed them on the counter. She held the door open with one leg while she searched for an opener. The stretch to the refrigerator door flexed the muscles in her thighs. Black silk clung to the curves of her ass.

"I know it's not easy," he said.

"It hurts like hell."

"But we have to know."

"So ask God when you see him."

In the light of the open refrigerator he watched her slice a lime with a bartender's practiced hand. As she raised her arm the weight of her breasts shifted within the flimsy black slip.

"We were just talking that night," she said. "We just talked."

"Twenty-eight minutes, Faye. You 'just talked' for twenty-eight minutes. You told me she was saying crazy things. What kind of crazy things?"

She pushed the lime slices down into the neck of the bottles and handed one to him. He found the beanbag chair and sat, although he knew Faye intended for him to sit on the bed, next to her.

"She told me she put her dress on," Faye said. "The costume. And she had an argument with Mr. Winters, and other shit I don't remember."

"Was Trey Winters there when she put the dress on?"

"She said he was there earlier, and he left. That's all I know."

"Did she say he might be coming back?"

"She said he was a prick."

Faye raised the beer bottle to her mouth. She didn't hold the top of the bottle against her upper lip, as he'd seen many women do; she put it entirely in her mouth. Head back, she drank. It was not a dainty sip.

Ryan said, "Did she ever say that there was anything sexual between them?"

"I didn't mean a prick that way."

"I know that. I was just thinking that maybe she confided in you. Sisters tell each other about their love lives, don't they?"

"Some, I guess," she said, and touched the bottle against her forehead, as if seeking relief from a fever.

"But not you two."

"Blame that on our mother. Maybe if we had grown up to-gether, we could have talked like that."

"We have a witness who says she saw Winters sneaking into her apartment on a regular basis."

"There you have it. You don't need me."

"You're not helping, acting like this."

"I thought you came here to see me. I thought we were simpatico."

"We are," he said. The beer tasted creamy smooth going down his throat, better than any beer he could remember. His taste buds were wired, seemingly intense enough to delineate the malt from the hops.

"You have no idea how I feel," she said.

"Don't be so sure."

"Of what, your deep hurt? Your pooch got hit by a car?" Then, after a deep, resigned sigh, she said, "I'm sorry, I didn't mean that."

Ryan ignored her. "Gillian argued with Winters before she called you, we know that."

"She said he was supposed to be on her side, but he wasn't.

She said he was a prick because he was making her take a drug test, and she didn't trust what was going on."

"I thought you said she wasn't worried?"

"She wasn't. She said it was an insult."

"Somebody is lying, Faye. They found cocaine in her apartment today."

Ryan waited; the air was stale and difficult to breathe.

"No!" she screamed, and threw the bottle at Ryan. It smashed against the far wall. "No, no, no! That's a fucking lie."

Faye swung her fist at him, and he caught it as he was getting up from the chair. She pulled away, then flopped on the bed and rolled onto her side.

"I agree with you," Ryan said softly.

She lay there quietly, rubbing her right wrist, her black hair across her face. He remembered the first time he saw her sister, her face was covered by her hair. Ryan sat back down.

"You have to talk about it," he said. "Talking about it will make it easier."

Faye was still. Except for the deep contractions of her chest she could have been dead.

"Then you start," she said, her voice muffled. "You say what hurts you."

The smell of spilled beer rose from the carpet. Ryan wondered if there was air enough for the grief of two.

"My son died a year ago," he said with surprising ease to this woman he hardly knew.

"Oh, Jesus," Faye said. She got off the bed and knelt in front of Ryan. She folded her arms across his thighs and leaned in until she was inches away from his face. "I'm sorry. So sorry. Tell me what happened, please."

He tried to lift her by her elbows.

"Please, please," she said, pushing his hands away. "Please, help me. I don't know how to deal with this. Just tell me I'm not a freak."

She smelled of cigarettes and a perfume that seemed astringent, more chemical than natural.

"You're not a freak," he said. "My son died in a hang-gliding accident in Utah last year. It still eats me up inside."

"Oh, God," she said. "Did you hurt him? Was he mad? Not speaking, or something?"

"No. We got along fine."

"Then why do you feel so bad?"

"Like you said about your sister. It's about the things I missed. He missed. The things I didn't say or do. I feel guilty about that."

"But you didn't hurt him. You were a good father to him, right?"

"Not as good as I should have been."

She leaned into him, and Ryan had to hold her to keep from falling backward. Her hair smelled of a fruity shampoo, the same as her sister.

"Like what?" she said. "How were you bad to him?"

He didn't have to think hard; he was a nightmare multiplex, a dozen horrors playing at all times. He told her about a Sunday morning when his son was eight years old and getting ready for his first mass as an altar boy. Ryan had stopped going to church years before, but he was dressed and ready to go this day. Then the phone rang. He answered it in the upstairs bedroom. It was Joe Gregory, hot on the trail of something he couldn't even remember anymore. What he did remember was pushing aside the bedroom curtains and looking down into the backyard. His son was looking up at the window, his hair slicked down, his face so shiny it glowed. He stood there, waiting. Looking up. Holding his black cassock and starched white surplice high, so it wouldn't touch the ground. With those skinny arms. Those big brown eyes. He saw those eyes in his sleep now. Hopeful, imploring, frightened, but still loving him without condition.

"But that's nothing," Faye said. "He forgave you, right? He knew you really loved him."

"When I got home that night he ran outside and jumped into my arms. Telling me all about it. When I put him down he kept holding on to my leg. Hugging it, really squeezing. I looked down at him, and he had his eyes closed. That's the way he always hugged, even when he grew up, with his eyes closed."

She put her head against Ryan's chest and closed her eyes.

"Gillian made me promise not ever to tell this," she said. "It was our secret. She told me that Trey Winters was her lover. I didn't want to betray her."

"You didn't betray anything," Ryan said.

"Do you have a picture of your son?" she said.

He took the picture from his wallet. Rip about twelve, wearing a Baltimore Orioles warm-up jacket, the impish smile, winking into the camera, his mouth full of the bubble gum he called his "chew."

"He looks happy," she said. "The big baseball player."

"Biggest Oriole fan in New York."

"You miss that, right?" she said. "Doing all the dad things, like I missed the sister things. I bet you played catch, stuff like that."

"Even when he was older. We shot baskets. Played golf. Went to ball games."

Faye jumped up and ran into the kitchen. He heard her behind him, opening cabinet doors. She came back and stood in front of him, holding a half-empty loaf of Wonder bread, the open end tied in a knot. She handed the bread to Ryan, then picked up the signed Bobby Bonilla baseball bat. With one big step she bounded onto the unmade bed and faced him, swinging the bat.

"Pitch it," she said.

"No, Faye. Don't. You'll break something in here."

"I don't care."

"This is thoughtful, really," Ryan said, getting to his feet. "I know what you're trying to do."

He reached out for the bat and took it as carefully as if it were a loaded gun. He put it against the wall. She jumped down and snatched the bread from his hands, then she walked backward, stumbling over the covers on the floor. When she got as far as the window she threw the bread. He caught it and held it.

"Wait," he said.

"No, no," she said, clapping her hands together. "Please don't stop. This is good for both of us. Play catch with me."

Ryan threw the half-empty bag of bread back to her. She caught it with her hands way out in front and threw it back with a big, roundhouse motion. At first he thought it was silly, then he decided he would go along, because it would stop her from questioning him about his son. Stop her from breaking his heart. It felt strangely good. A simple game of catch. The bag in the air, yellow and blue circles on the wrapper floating like birthday party balloons, as it passed through the flickering candlelight.

In the quiet of the room the only sound was the pop of a half-empty loaf of bread, caught and then thrown across an open bed by a sad, aging cop and a young woman, in a frayed black slip, who'd been found and lost again.

21

When the red-eye from JFK landed in Phoenix before dawn on Saturday, the pilot announced the temperature was 103 degrees. Summer in the desert, he added, what else can you expect? Danny Eumont followed his fellow travelers through the wee-hour solitude of Sky Harbor Airport. The terminal was silent except for the hum of vacuum cleaners running over Indian-blanket carpet.

"I can't believe you didn't bring sunglasses," Lainie Mossberg from Tempe, Arizona, said. "You'd better buy a pair."

Lainie Mossberg had boarded the flight in Denver, fresh from a taping session for a rock band she managed. In her late thirties, she was the type of woman who'd come into a bar and take a seat under the TV, so men would look her way.

"I'm not buying sunglasses for one day," Danny said. "Because I'm certainly not wearing them back in New York. Look like some hipster doofus back there. Some West Coast wannabe."

"You're going to regret it," Lainie said.

"I got your regret right here."

"Let's see it," she said.

They were both light travelers. Lainie carried her purse and a small pink duffel. Danny's only luggage was a black canvas briefcase containing an electric razor, toothbrush, tape recorder, two notebooks, a change of socks, underwear, and a tin of Altoid mints. Not even an extra shirt. He'd booked a room in the Phoenix Hilton but figured he might not even stay the night.

"Is that blazer wool?" Lainie said, grabbing the sleeve of Danny's jacket.

"Why, the old cattle rancher mentality? I don't want to start a range war or anything."

"You've got a lot to learn, Eumont."

She said she'd give him his first lesson on the ride home, a ride he hadn't offered or considered. But when she puckered her pouty lips into a promise, he was putty. At that moment Danny thought he understood why young men went west.

At the Avis counter, Lainie held on to Danny's arm while her breasts got acquainted with his elbow. Although he enjoyed the soft pummeling, he wondered why everyone on his flights always chose the same car rental company he did. The young woman behind the counter was far too helpful, patiently describing various auto options to a French couple, who were oblivious of the etiquette of the American queue. The clerk kept squealing, "I love your accent. So cooo-ell."

She apparently didn't dig the inherent hipness of the New York accent because her smile disappeared when she handed Danny his contract and keys. She told him he'd find Soto outside. Soto would point him to the Chrysler LHS he'd just rented.

Danny and Lainie stepped arm in arm through automatic doors and out into the exhaust fan of hell. A pure physical shock. The heat was an actual living, breathing thing. Breathing fire. Danny's shirt immediately attached itself to his ribs.

Lainie told him to quit whining, a little spritz of heat never hurt anybody.

They found Soto of Avis sitting in front of a kiosk in a chaise longue. Soto was a tiny bowlegged man wearing a sweat-stained straw cowboy hat, long-sleeved denim shirt, and Kmart jeans stuffed in dusty cowboy boots. He was listening to *tejano* music and squeezing water from a sponge onto the back of a huge lizard. He introduced the lizard, whose name was Mañana.

"Americans think *mañana* means tomorrow," Soto explained, lubricating his leathery pet. "All it means is not today."

"And maybe not anytime in the near future," Danny said, suddenly impatient.

They followed Soto along a line of rental cars parked under a metal overhang. "Not good to hurry in this heat," Soto said. "One fifteen yesterday. Maybe one seventeen today."

"But a dry one seventeen," Danny said.

Lainie tossed her pink duffel in the backseat and fumbled in her purse. She told him not to take the freeway but stick to Washington Avenue, a dark wide street lined with factories and car repair shops. Fewer eyes this way, she said. She leaned into the dashboard and inhaled the white powder she'd formed into a straight line. Then Lainie Mossberg's entire body flew back from the dash as if she'd been shot out of a cannon. It scared the hell out of Danny. Her head bounced off the roof and slammed back against the headrest, and kept bouncing. "Whew!" she screamed, her head bouncing as though it were on a spring. "Whew, whew, whew."

"I gotta get you home," Danny said.

"Don't be so impatient. Whew!"

"No, seriously," he said. "You need to be home."

"Don't you want to know why they call me twin forty-fours?"

Lainie yanked the sleeveless sweater over her head and proved her breasts were large-caliber. In the flicker of the streetlights they seemed unworldly, too shiny and milk white, the skin stretched dangerously thin. Lainie blinked and rubbed her nose. Then she rolled over onto her left side and threw herself across the center console, her head banging into his sore right shoulder. Danny checked the rearview mirror. Lainie unbuckled his belt.

"Let's wait until we get you home," he said.

"Can't," she said, lowering her head. Her hands felt ice cold sliding down into his shorts.

"I can't drive like this."

"Pull over," she said.

Danny swerved toward the curb, then swerved back. Lainie didn't seem to notice that she'd banged her head against the steering wheel several times. Confusion reigned as cold hands and warm breath descended. Fully facedown, Lainie squirmed to get into position, her legs outstretched, the back of her feet thudding against the underside of the glove compartment.

"Let's wait until we get you home," Danny said. "More room to stretch out."

"My husband hasn't left for work yet," she said.

"Your husband," Danny said. He grabbed a fistful of her hair and bent her head backward. Her eyes opened, and she looked up at him.

"That's my hotel, straight ahead," Danny said. "Right there, next corner. See it? We can go nuts in my room."

Lainie sat up as Danny pulled under the lighted overhang of the Rio Bravo Inn. He waited while Lainie casually put on her sweater. He told her to meet him inside at the bar; he'd park and register. She grabbed her purse and stepped out. When she was safely inside he floored it and drove away. Lainie Mossberg would find a way home. She could take care of herself.

Danny wasn't surprised to see lights on all over the Stone house. No one slept on funeral days. The Stone compound in Scottsdale was a low-slung grouping of stucco buildings set well back off the road behind iron gates, against the foot of a small beige mountain. He stared at the place where Gillian grew up, remembering pictures of her outside in front of the saguaro cactus, wearing prom gowns, graduation gowns, play costumes.

He remembered her pelican story, which he refused to believe. But it's true, she'd always squealed. She'd said that after a big storm blew in from the west, they'd find pelicans on their property. Pelicans were weak fliers, and they'd get caught up in the strong winds over the Pacific and get carried all the way to the desert. Local people crated them up. America West flew them back to California. After every big storm Gillian borrowed her father's Jeep and scoured the desert, searching for lost pelicans.

As the sun rose, in the hours before Gillian's funeral, Danny cruised the geometric streets, talking into his tape recorder. The first thing he noticed was the cleanliness, everything squared off neatly. A strip mall on every block, a gas station and convenience store on every corner. Plants, trees, grass along the highways, somehow growing out of sand. And flat. So flat you could clearly see a traffic light miles ahead.

At Gillian's high school he took the opportunity to get out and brush Lainie's makeup off his pants. He walked around the concrete-block school building that covered enough real estate for two city blocks. Underground sprinklers hissed over an inconceivably green lawn. He made a note that the students' lockers were outside the school, along the outer walls of the building under a small overhang. He could imagine Gillian, a stack of books under her arms, long legs racing to catch her friends, yelling, "But it's true!"

Back in the car, the air conditioner seemed to be losing the battle to the climbing thermometer. Maybe if he kept driving. Everybody seemed to be driving; the freeways were filled with fast-moving cars. Nine out of ten of the cars were white, the drivers hidden behind dark, tinted windows. He whizzed past a road-killed jackrabbit, one long ear stuck upright, waving in the breeze.

The main streets of the Valley of the Sun were endless and arrow straight, flanked by wide, clean, concrete sidewalks. No bums, no vendors, no litter or graffiti. In fact, nothing. No people, no dogs, cats, or signs of life. Just miles and miles of empty sidewalk, houses hidden behind endless block walls. It struck him that except for Lainie Mossberg, the last human being he'd seen was the lizard king, Soto of Avis. Marginally eerie. Where the hell was everybody?

Danny's sources on the *Arizona Republic* had told him that the Stone family had opted for a closed ceremony in a private chapel. It was scheduled for ten A.M., followed by burial in the family plot. He drove straight to the cemetery, thinking he'd get a few minutes of shut-eye before the crowd arrived.

The cemetery was situated between a freeway and a cotton field. All the headstones were flat for easy maintenance. Two rows of chairs were set up under a dark blue canopy. He parked beneath an olive tree, cranked the AC to the max, and waited for Gillian. The last time he'd ever wait for Gillian.

Exhausted, Danny reclined the seat back as far as it would go. He was glad he'd picked a big, comfortable car. A short nap would do the trick. Then he caught a glimpse of something on the floor of the backseat. Something pink. Lainie Mossberg's duffel bag.

Hoping for an address, he unzipped it. The bag contained dirty clothes, makeup, and hairspray. The side pocket had a tube of lipstick called Pagan Pink and a tightly rolled joint. He sniffed the joint; it had the horseshit aroma of quality marijuana. Maybe he'd check the phone book or just mail it to twin forty-fours. He figured the mailmen would know. He tossed it into the backseat.

He'd just started to doze when a long line of cars followed the hearse around a circular driveway. Danny waited until the very last minute, until the pallbearers reached the bier. Then he got out of the chilled Chrysler.

He squinted into the sun as he approached the rear of the crowd. Bits of raw cotton stuck to bushes and gathered against fences and curbs. He wished he'd left his blazer in the car. All the men looked cool in short-sleeved shirts and linen pants; the women looked like money and aerobics. Everybody, including the priest, sported dark sunglasses.

Danny stood at the back of the crowd, rolling a piece of raw cotton between his fingers. He was too far back to enjoy the shade of the canopy, too far back to make out the words of the priest. The priest faced the rows of folding chairs, incanting the rhythms of Scripture. Evan Stone sat in the first row, his arm around Lynnette. Lynnette Stone looked dazed.

Six hours and 117 miles after he arrived, Danny stood in a sparsely treed cemetery somewhere on the outskirts of Phoenix, Arizona, trying to figure out what he'd learned, if anything. He felt far removed from Gillian in this strange place. The girl he knew was a city girl; she loved New York City.

For the first time in his life he felt the sun burning his scalp and wondered how many years he had left on his hairline. He touched it gingerly, wishing his fingertips could spout ice water. Then he tried not to think of ice water, his throat drier than a wine hangover. The priest droned on, and Danny could feel the heat from each individual blade of grass radiating up through the soles of his shoes. The worst was that Lainie Mossberg was right: he was ready to sell his soul for a pair of sunglasses.

He knew the priest's remarks had ended when the crowd started to murmur, then move. The women formed a line behind Lynnette, each holding a single white rose. One by one they placed them on the blond wood coffin. In the crowd movement, Danny lost sight of Evan Stone.

He peeled off to the right and saw Stone alone, walking toward the fence overlooking the freeway. He had his back turned as Danny approached. He turned, looking startled, then took a panicky step back into the fence. Danny extended his hand.

"I'm Danny Eumont, from New York. I'm sorry. . . ."

Stone's overhand right caught Danny in the left temple. He went down hard, stunned more by the act than the blow. He rolled over on his bad right shoulder, and it almost brought tears to his eyes.

"You have the balls to come here, now?" Stone growled. "At a time like this? What kind of scum are you?"

He started kicking Danny, stomping him on his back and shoulders. Danny rolled toward the fence and got to his knees.

"I'm sorry," he said. "I didn't know anything was wrong with her. I should have noticed, I know. But I hadn't seen her in months."

From his knees he tried to look up at Stone, but the sun was right in his eyes. The freeway roared in his ears, little black specks floated across his field of vision.

"Who the hell are you?" Stone said.

"I told you, Danny Eumont."

Men in white shirts and dark glasses sprinted toward them, asking Evan if *he* were okay. Danny felt like an asshole from New York in a woolen blazer with brass buttons hot enough to brand cattle.

"Oh, Danny, I'm sorry, so sorry," Evan Stone said, dropping to his own knees and putting his arms around Danny. "I thought you were someone else."

Danny knew his mouth was open as if words were coming out, but none did. Maybe he'd missed something in the glare of the sun. He wanted to scream something at the righteous bastards surrounding them, in their Ray-Bans and linen, but he was too tired and sore to care. He felt like a pelican, a weak flier caught up in a storm he couldn't handle. All that came to mind was: "Somebody, please . . . turn down the goddamn lights!"

22

The water of Crotona Pool glistened blue green in the morning sun. It lapped at the white-tiled edges rhythmically, peacefully. Victor knew that peace wouldn't last. Soon the wild children of the Bronx would occupy every inch of water. Many would climb over the fence rather than pay, then they'd go running and screaming, kicking and punching like savages. They didn't swim but leaped in recklessly, then bobbed up and down, often fully dressed in pants and shirts, some with sneakers on. The boys would grab the girls by the hair or breasts or brutally lock an arm around their necks and yank them to the edge of the pool. Or a band of them would mob a girl, hold her high in the air, hand to crotch, and throw her toward the water without regard for her safety, without conscience.

He hated these people; they were ignorant, and they'd always be ignorant. Victor knew he didn't belong among them. They had no self-respect. No class. Poverty would be all they would ever know. Welfare their only hope.

He longed for the better life he would soon be living. He remembered his swims as a boy in the Sea of Cortés. For hours he'd swim alongside sea turtles and dolphins. The clear blue water showcased the Technicolor spectacle of the sea, the colors of fish brighter and more iridescent than one could imagine. All he wanted was this life again, but this time a life that reflected his accomplishments. He was once the greatest aerialist in the world. He wanted the admiration he deserved. So many people had more than he, and they were never the greatest anything.

Victor had not been greedy. A quarter of a million dollars was not a lot of money for a man as rich as Winters. He would not miss it any more than the crumbs that blew off his table. Men like Winters had access to incredible wealth, more than these savages around the pool could ever imagine. Most people could not comprehend the true wealth of some people. People who owned five or six mansions around the world. Victor had been in their company. As a young man he'd been introduced to people who had more money than they'd ever need. He'd seen the way they carried themselves, and he wanted that life. It wasn't right that so few had so much. All Victor wanted was enough. Enough to live a simple, elegant life as a man of respect. He deserved it, and no one was going to stop him from getting it.

He'd come to Crotona Pool to work out and stretch his sore muscles in the warm water. He needed the sense of peace that water should impart. The warmth of it, to be enveloped by it. To cut out all distraction, because he needed to think of a plan. A foolproof escape plan. One that was flexible, one that allowed for a variety of contingencies. He wondered how Alain Charnier had eluded the police in *The French Connection*. He'd disappeared on Ward's Island somehow. The movie never explained his escape. Victor knew he could figure it out.

He did a flip turn at the end of the pool and headed back. The sheen of his tanned muscular body glinted as he stroked high in the water. He could hear rap music from the boom boxes. Victor missed the music of Mexico, with its soft trumpets and guitars. Music should be about love, not hate. He could hear it in his head, as he felt the good burn in his shoulders. It was his fiftieth lap.

A commotion by the pool gate drew everyone's attention. A gang of young savages pushed their way through the turnstiles. Victor went underwater to get a last minute of serenity. Swimming underwater was the only peace one could find in this city. That was the last thing he'd told Pinto as he'd dropped his weighted body into the Hudson. Be grateful for the peace, my Russian friend.

When he raised his head his eyes stung from the massive dose of chlorine. He pulled himself up at the end of the pool. Groups of adults and teenagers had staked out portions of space, like refugees, around the fence. His towel was gone. A group of young girls giggled and pointed at him, some making that wet smacking noise they made with their lips that was supposed to be seductive. The air was heavy with marijuana smoke. He walked dripping into the locker room, doing all he could to control his rage. He prayed one of their boyfriends would be in the locker room and would bump him or mouth off. He'd show them what violence truly was. He consoled himself with the thought that he'd completed his last swim among the ignorant rabble of this city.

23

I shoulda knocked that dwarf cop on his ass," Joe Gregory said as they entered Buster Scorza's pink neon world of the Pussycat Palace. "You see the look on that kid's face? Like we're here on some shakedown scam."

They'd parked the Buick in a bus stop on Eighth Avenue directly in front of the three-story sex emporium. Two young uniformed cops from Mid-Town South had pulled up behind them. Using their radio car's bullhorn, they'd ordered the detectives to move the Buick, drive on. Gregory got out and flashed his gold shield and Irish smile. "We're working a case!" he'd yelled, being friendly. He didn't have to tell them anything.

"Bullshit," one cop yelled back.

"They teach them that in the academy," Ryan said. "Cops our age are evil incarnate."

"And that's exactly why they're getting in trouble out there. When we came on the job, we had cops fifty and sixty years old working in uniform, around the clock. Guys with military service and 'boo coo' experience. Taught you how to analyze a situation with common sense. Treat people with respect."

The Pussycat Palace was the McDonald's of porn, all chrome and happy plastic. A mere dollar got the customer in the door, and he got four tokens in the bargain. Gregory flashed his badge, and they strolled past the token seller at the entrance.

The long dark hallway leading to the back was lined with small booths. Above each door was a red light. The red light glowed while money was being fed into the machine, and security came knocking when the light went out. One token worth twenty-five cents bought a minute of filmed sex, the perversion of your choice. Each booth advertised access to 360 flicks on four simultaneous screens. It sounded as if you'd stumbled into a medieval torture chamber. A cacophony of moans, groans, grunts, whimpers, and screams, all coming from behind fifty locked doors.

"We've been announced," Gregory said. "Buster himself is coming to greet us." Ryan figured the token seller at the front desk had buzzed the back room.

Buster Scorza came out from behind a mirrored door in a mirrored wall, protected by a raised desk and manned by an immense black man who hawked tokens and ousted ball breakers. Gregory reached for his ID, but it wasn't necessary. The Mob guy knew.

"Gentlemen," Buster Scorza said.

It had been several years since Ryan and Gregory were last in the Pussycat Palace. A homicide then. A Marielito who'd sliced up his partner in their live sex act. He had a tattoo of a dagger inside his lower lip; she had a daughter in the Bronx named Jennifer. On cue, Ryan and Gregory could recite all the details for every murder they'd handled for three decades.

"Can we talk in private?" Ryan said, raising his voice above the pulsing disco beat.

"Out here is good for me," Scorza said.

He wore shapeless black pants and orthopedic shoes laced

tongue to toe. His white short-sleeved shirt hung outside his pants, the material so thin you could see the straps of his T-shirt. Pleats ran down the front of the shirt, in the casual chic favored by Panamanian dictators.

"You sure about that?" Ryan said. "All these booths, everybody listening to your business."

"Don't worry about them," Buster said. "They all got their hands full."

The Taj Mahal of commercial porn had invested heavily in high-tech gadgetry. But the smell of ammonia was still eye-wateringly strong.

"How about Trey Winters?" Ryan said. "He have his hands full?"

The question caught Scorza by surprise. He'd expected any one of the numerous illegal areas to which he was vulnerable. He decided it might be less noisy to talk in the office. Two steps up, behind the raised counter. Through the looking glass.

"My business with Trey Winters is just that, business," Scorza said, tossing his keys on the desk. The office had been well soundproofed. The carpet was a gaudy red, but the pile was plush. A lime green fake leather sofa served as Buster's casting couch.

"We're not going to play games with you, Buster," Gregory said. "You and Trey Winters don't add up. Something stinks, besides this office. And we're going to come up with it. Now's the time to get on board. First guy on board gets the best deal."

"I have no idea what you're talking about."

"This offer leaves with us," Ryan said. "If Winters spills his guts first, his story is the one we go with. You want your freedom riding on an actor?"

Ryan could understand why Scorza didn't want them in his office. The wall held a bank of TV screens that focused on his little kingdom of lust from every crack and cranny.

"This is bizarre," Scorza said. "What in hell are you talking about?"

"What kind of business do you have with Winters?" Ryan asked.

"Show business," he said, shrugging.

The bulk of the Pussycat's cameras were focused on hallways. Men milled about, peeking into booths, reading descriptions of movies, generally avoiding eye contact with each other.

"So what's your role—producer, director, lead actor?" Gregory said.

"Mr. Winters had some questions regarding the stagehands union. I told him I no longer had any affiliation with the local. That's it."

"Did you laugh when you said that?" Gregory said. "Because it is funny."

"It might be funny to you, but I severed all my union ties five years ago."

"Obeying the court's order," Ryan said. "Like the solid citizen you are."

"The word of the supreme court of this state is good enough for me," Scorza said.

Four cameras covered the basement, where the live nude peep show ran all day and night. On a bare round stage surrounded by booths, an ever-changing parade of beaten women with ghetto faces rubbed themselves against small windows of the tiny cubicles inhabited by a circle of jerks.

"Winters has been in this business a long time," Ryan said. "He knew you were thrown out of the union."

"I might argue with the 'thrown out' part," Scorza said. "But, you're right. I've known Trey Winters for many years, and he did know I left the union. He was asking for advice on what he can expect from the new leaders. Concerning his new show."

"Why didn't he just go to the new union people himself?" Gregory said.

"You'll have to ask him that question."

"How did you meet Trey Winters?" Ryan said.

"Through Paul Klass," Scorza said. "The director. Paul and I had many dealings when I was still with the union. Charming man, fascinating. His death was a blow to the theater."

On the second floor, the seminaked girls in the one-on-one booths lured men into their lairs for a friendly strip and talk. Each side of the glass-separated booths was equipped with phones.

"Nothing is ever easy," Ryan said. "You're forcing us to do this the hard way."

"Do what the hard way?" Scorza said.

Ryan pointed to a camera labeled number three. It was the second-floor one-on-one booths.

"Clear that up for me," he said. "What the hell is going on there?"

"That's one of our touching booths," Scorza said. "Perfectly legal. I have copies of the court decision if you'd like to read it."

"I hope it doesn't say it's legal for her to have her hand down his pants."

Scorza looked at the screen. Then he opened the mirrored door to his office.

"Lonny," he said to the huge man at the raised counter, "go upstairs and tell Gypsy she's fired. Have payroll close her out and tell her I want her ass out of here permanently."

"She with a customer?" Lonny inquired.

"Give the customer his money back and escort him to the street. Tell him he's barred."

Over the loudspeaker came a warning that the lesbian special live show would begin in ten minutes, and don't forget Miss Rhonda Rockies in all her abundance would be on the main stage at noon, three, and six P.M. Seating limited.

"Sorry, Officers," Scorza said, closing the door. "That's why we have these cameras here."

"Now, see," Gregory said, "there's my suspicious mind at work. I would have thought Gypsy would know she's on camera. My thinking was that these cameras were here to make sure nobody holds money out on you."

"Lawyers cost money," Scorza said. "If she brings Public Morals down on us, I'm out real money. Besides, I don't want that shit going on in this place."

"What makes you think we won't lock her up now?" Ryan said.

"Be my guest," Scorza said. "I'll even testify as a witness for you."

"What a great citizen," Gregory said.

"I can certainly promise you, or a judge, she'll never set foot in here again."

"You *are* an actor," Gregory said. "You missed your calling. I was almost convinced by that performance. Weren't you, pally?"

"Almost," Ryan said. "But you have other problems, Buster. Last week a customer had his pocket picked in here. And believe it or not, he reported it."

"Tsk, tsk," Scorza said. "Imagine that, a pickpocket here in our city."

"We're going to help Mid-Town South on this case," Ryan said. "Canvass some of your customers. Maybe locate a potential witness."

"I told you the truth about Trey Winters. You have no cause to harass me."

"Still acting," Gregory said. "The man inhabits his role."

"No one is harassing you," Ryan said. "All we want is the truth about your business with Trey Winters. And while we're waiting for you to remember the truth, we'll try to solve this pickpocket case."

"Suit yourself."

"You're not giving us any choice, Buster."

"You're going to do whatever you want anyway," Scorza said. "No matter what I say."

As Ryan came down the stairs from Scorza's office, big Lonny, fresh from his fake firing assignment, waddled down the hallway of locked booths. Ryan walked to the end of the line and banged on the metal door to the first booth. He yelled, "Police!" loudly enough to alert all three floors. Gregory took the left side, did his own yelling. They walked down the line, banging on doors and yelling. Lonny came hustling to the rescue.

"Here comes your protection," Ryan said, turning back to Scorza.

"The First Amendment is my protection," Scorza answered, and waved the big man away. "Come up here, Lonny."

But Lonny's progress slowed drastically. He had to fight his way back to his perch behind the desk because the crowd came sudden and intense. The halls were filled with men heading for the sunlight, buckling belts, zipping, snapping. It was a pervert's fire drill.

"Nobody seems to want to talk," Ryan said. "We may have to come back later, maybe tomorrow, too."

"Come back every hour if you want," Scorza said. "In the meantime I'll call my lawyer."

Scorza went back inside his office as Lonny shook his head at the mass exodus of men in Armani suits or army fatigues. All manner of clothing in disarray.

At the end of the hallway they split up. Gregory went downstairs, Ryan took the one-on-one booths on the second floor. No one volunteered to speak to them; all were too busy seeking an exit. A sanitation man tripped on his green pants and tumbled down a full flight of stairs. His arm, unfortunately, looked broken. Ryan wondered how that accident report would be written up.

They left through the gift shop, thoughtfully situated on the side street. Convenient enough for the harried and horny commuter to duck in and pick up a movie, a magazine, or a battery-powered love muscle for the little woman waiting in Westchester.

"Got any love potion number nine?" Gregory asked.

Both detectives squinted in the bright sun.

"That went well," Gregory said.

"We didn't hurt him," Ryan said. "He lost a couple of bucks, that's all."

"He knows we can't hurt him, pally. His customers will be back no matter what we do. We need a different angle. All we're doing is trying to get even with him because he's stonewalling us. Sometimes getting even ain't the way to go."

They turned the corner onto Eighth Avenue, and Ryan noticed it first. A parking ticket on the window of the Buick. Under the windshield wiper and directly over their official plate with the seal of the NYPD.

"Remember what I just said about getting even being a bad thing?" Gregory said. "That was all bullshit."

24

On Sunday morning Anthony Ryan sat in the grass of Oakland Cemetery with a penknife, digging deep narrow holes over the grave of his son, pushing little pieces of his life down into the soft turf. First a button off his uniform, then a shamrock tie tack, a tiny NYPD detective's badge, a subway token.

Oakland Cemetery is situated on a hillside in Yonkers, New York, facing the defunct Alexander Smith Carpet Shops, which once wove carpet for the coronation of a Russian czar. Anthony's father, Kieran Ryan, had told him that czar story when he took him through the factory over fifty years ago. He'd wanted him to see it before it was gone. The whir and clatter of the massive looms had frightened the young boy, but he'd never admitted it.

Kieran Ryan, a retired bus driver now eighty-four and residing in Florida, had told his son a million old Yonkers stories. Anthony Ryan couldn't even remember if he'd passed the czar story down to his son, Rip.

Alexander Smith's was built in the mid-1800s and grew into

the largest rug mill in the world. Now "the shop" sat sliced into myriad furniture and appliance warehouses and small woodworking firms. In the beginning Alexander Smith himself drove the daily product into New York City by horse and wagon. Each day's sales gave Smith the money to buy material for the next day. Alexander Smith died on November 5, 1875, on the night he was elected to Congress. He was buried on this same hill, a bit lower than the Ryan clan.

The fact that the Ryan family was above the Smiths pleased Kieran Ryan, who'd purchased twenty plots in the hillside graveyard after he'd hit the number for $600, a small fortune in 1947. Thanks to the reckless lifestyles of Kieran's Irish kin, only five of the twenty plots remained. The deed to the plots was locked in a strongbox in the closet of Kieran Ryan's Florida condo. He'd given Anthony clear instructions that if he should die, neither Uncle Rocco, the brother of Kieran's late wife and Anthony's mother, nor any of the Gagliardi family was to be allowed access to the remaining plots.

Last January, when Rocco's wife, Ryan's aunt Violetta, died, Kieran Ryan disappeared into the Florida Keys with the deed, while his phone rang off the hook. Kieran had vowed that only one Gagliardi would ever be laid to rest in ground that he paid for; and she was already there: his beloved Angela Gagliardi Ryan, Anthony's mother. He'd rather see an Irish setter interred next to him than the likes of Rocco Gagliardi.

Kieran Ryan was the family storyteller, and one of his favorite stories was the day he collected his $600 in the Hollow Athletic Club on Walnut Street, a few blocks away. He took six-year-old Anthony, and they walked down the hill to the neighborhood called the Hollow, because Kieran Ryan never owned a car until he moved to Florida at eighty years of age. Before they entered the Hollow A.C., Kieran bent and told his boy, "Pay attention, son. These men are Polacks." Inside the club, Anthony sat at the bar and drank the best root beer of his life while a man called Singapore Charlie found a quarter behind his ear.

On the way home they stopped in another club. Before entering, Kieran Ryan again told his son to pay attention, "These are your mother's people. These are eye-talians." Inside, he ate his first cannoli and women hugged him and talked about his blue eyes as if he were a movie star. The lesson continued through other neighborhoods as Kieran sipped from a gallon of red wine in an unlabeled jug. On the climb back up the hill Anthony saw a group of people on the steps of a church. Eager to please his father and show his aptitude, he pointed at the group and in a loud voice said, "And they're niggers, right, Dad?"

Anthony Ryan remembered how his father loved to tell that story, always embarrassing his serious, liberal son. But he taught Anthony about a world he came to love: the rich ethnic and racial heritage of the city. Anthony became a regular in the Hollow, a tight community inhabited by proud carpet millworkers, immigrants from Poland, Czechoslovakia, and Romania. Good people, Kieran assured his wife, who'd look out for a small child no matter what neighborhood he'd come from.

The Sunday bells of Holy Trinity echoed throughout the cemetery. He was sure the bells came from Holy Trinity because three churches in the neighborhood, all within blocks of each other, carried that name. The Catholic church, the Episcopalian, and the Russian Orthodox Greek Catholic with its endless name and impressive minarets. As kids they'd called it the "onion" church. Three churches with the same name in the tight neighborhood he once roamed, where nobody had money but everyone had food to share and muscle to loan.

Anthony was always struck by the cleanliness of the Hollow, every front stoop scrubbed daily by the woman of the house, on her hands and knees. He remembered the unintelligible calls of produce vendors pulling their own carts, and the iceman, the rag man, the scissors grinder. Yonkers was a city of neighborhoods, each a world unto itself. He could have passed this on to his own son. It would have been so easy. The stories were in his heart and on the tombstones around him.

In 1954 the sprawling carpet shop abandoned Yonkers for cheap labor in Mississippi, as if they owed nothing to this city of hills. It signaled a death knell. With the loss of the city's largest employer, the Hollow and other neighborhoods began to self-destruct. Now only a few stubborn old women scrubbed the stoops every day. The Hollow A.C. and all the other clubs were gone. The old women stayed indoors at night.

Ryan wondered whether the neighborhoods would have held on if the carpet shop had stayed. Would the children of the millworkers not have fled? He wondered, if he had passed down the old Yonkers stories to his own son, would he have learned to love this funky town between Manhattan and the real suburbs? If Rip Ryan had known that the mile-long factory across the street once wove carpet for the coronation of a Russian czar, maybe he wouldn't have gone west to find his own life and death on the floor of a bleak Utah canyon. But, as the Great Joe Gregory said, reasoning like that was thinking through your ass.

After all these years, Anthony Ryan was again a regular in the Hollow. Around him were other regulars, mostly women carrying watering cans from the spigot, clipping tall grass around a tombstone, lining the stone with flags and small plastic statues of saints and angels. He returned a wave from a woman tending the grave of her husband, Stan, dug twenty years earlier. Ryan considered his wave to be progress.

The grief experts said it took eighteen months to two years. Six months ago he couldn't have lifted his head without tears. Six months ago he was still angry with God. Now he was closer to God than ever and prayed to him to take care of his son. This was progress. He knew that in twenty years he wouldn't be here every day clipping and watering.

The world has become too mobile, Ryan thought. It's too easy to move away to a place where the sun is warm but the history belongs to others. Away from home it becomes too easy to sit by the pool and forget we're responsible for each other. Responsible not only to connect the dots of each other's lives by passing down stories, but to protect the old, the sick, our children, and the children of others who move away to find their own history. Despite our parochial stupidity, we have a contract here.

Ryan's mind was filled with questions about his son's death. The events of that day were still not clear to him, but maybe that was best. He knew if he allowed his natural suspicion to overwhelm him, he'd be on a plane to Utah. He had to trust in his brother officers in Utah, all cops and fathers, mothers, sisters, brothers. They were good and decent people, and he trusted them to act as his surrogate.

Leigh Ryan worried that the circumstances of the Gillian Stone case were too similar to their own nightmare. But this was not about similarities to Anthony; all deaths were different. To him it was about responsibility. It was about looking out for your neighbor's child, no matter how far he or she has come. Trey Winters should have looked out for Gillian Stone. He hadn't. When that happened, cops had to step in and become surrogate fathers.

Although he hadn't held Gillian Stone in his arms at birth, he'd held her at her death. God had delivered this young woman into his arms for a purpose, and that made her his child. Gillian Stone's departing spirit had understood that when she'd made him hear the words "I love you."

He took a small set of NYPD collar numerals from his pocket. The brass forty-eight identified his rookie precinct. During the time he wore those numbers on his collar, his life was full of stories. Stories he should have told before now. He pushed the numbers into the dirt.

25

The ferry rocked gently as Joe Gregory blew a smoke ring that floated in the twilight over the Hudson River. The sounds of a dance band drifted out from the main room. Through grimy windows Danny could see Anthony and Leigh Ryan clinging to each other, moving across the floor in slow motion.

"What were you and Aunt Leigh cooking up before?" Danny said. "Looked like a pretty heavy-duty conversation."

"We're running away to the islands," Gregory said. "She's dying to see me in a Speedo. Now quit changing the subject and finish telling me about Evan Stone."

Danny took a big swig of his gin, though Gregory had warned him that the juniper berry made you crazy. Gregory held a cigar in one hand, a glass in the other. He sipped Irish whiskey and gazed at the city. Sunday quiet, and glittering.

"He was all apologetic," Danny said. "The guy really felt bad about hitting me."

"Okay, let's go over it again: All you said was, 'I'm Danny Eumont from New York,' and he hits you. Did he say why?"

"He said he thought I was someone else."

"Like who, for instance? Who would he punch at a funeral?"

"How should I know? A business associate, some asshole golfing buddy who pissed him off."

"That don't sound kosher," Gregory said. "Not for nothing, but people at funerals are on their best behavior. If everyone always acted like they were at a funeral, this would be a better world, guaranteed."

It's no wonder cops are as paranoid as they are, Danny thought. After a lifetime spent suspecting everyone and everything. Side by side, elbows on the boat's rail, they exchanged opinions on the resurrection of the New York waterfront. The big-shouldered Gregory dwarfed Danny as they passed the new sports piers off Thirty-eighth Street.

"So after all the bullshit," Gregory said, "Stone didn't even give you anything useful."

"All he said was Gillian was doing fine until Faye Boudreau came to New York."

"Well, he certainly wasn't going to say anything negative about his little angel. Parents are always shocked when they find out their kids got bad habits. I hope you didn't tell him you were banging her. He'll wanna blame you. He probably thinks she never had sex in her life."

Manhattan's narrow working waterfront disappeared when containerized shipping chased the industry to New Jersey. Manhattan lacked the space needed to unload the containers and set them onto the backs of eighteen-wheelers. The loss sent the waterfront into a forty-year funk. Now it was coming back, but in a far different form. Gregory said he liked it better when it fed families, not entertained yuppies.

"Let me say one final thing in regards to your Arizona fiasco," Gregory said, getting back to the case. Cops never let the conversation drift away from "the job" for very long. "I'm sure Evan Stone was upset, but guys in our job spend their entire careers in the worst minutes of other people's lives. Day in and day out, we're knocking around in somebody's nightmare. None of those people feel like talking to us. If you don't push them, you're wasting your time."

"Don't get me wrong," Danny said. "The trip wasn't a total waste. I put together some good notes on the landscape, things like that."

"What landscape, coupla cactus? You can copy that stuff out of *National Geographic*. You want the story, you should have been all over Stone."

"Compassion is *not* the worst character trait," Danny said. "Evan Stone was burying his daughter."

"So you're a nice guy. Do I have to tell you the rest of that one?"

"Next time I go on an interview remind me to borrow one of your rubber hoses."

The boat's rail was packed, and almost everybody faced east, watching the skyscraper light show. The bejeweled skyline of Manhattan flashed gold and silver in the setting sun. To New Yorkers, nothing in nature was as interesting as its effect on the city. Gregory said that the few who remained on the opposite side of the boat were conspirators and sleazy opportunists, whispering deals that only New Jersey should witness.

"You think we're all corrupt, brutal bastards, don't you," Gregory said.

"Not all."

"Not your sainted uncle, of course, but the rest of us thieving bullies."

"That's not what I said."

"I'm actually a sensitive guy at home," Gregory said. "An accomplished gardener. Bet you didn't know that. In fact, the only place I use *my* official NYPD rubber hose these days is in my backyard. Watering grass and flowers for the beautification of our planet."

"Is that so."

"I've even managed to grow grass in my backyard, a lovely

shade of blue. Bluer than Kentucky. Want to know how I managed that?"

"Not really," Danny said.

"By accident, my young friend. Like all great discoveries. The blue rises up from all the Maxwell House coffee cans underneath my lawn. That's where I keep my bribe and shakedown money. Buried in my backyard in hundreds of Maxwell House coffee cans. Over the years the blue paint has peeled off the cans and dyed the grass follicles. Royal blue. Quite a sight."

"I'm sure it is," Danny said. "I've got to see it sometime."

Gregory shook his head and flicked his cigar out into the water. "As far as the angel Gillian goes," he said, "a slightly less than perfect picture is starting to emerge. We spent part of yesterday and most of today interviewing chorus girls."

"I don't think they call themselves chorus girls."

"Whatever," Gregory said. "Apparently Winters wasn't the only person who noticed her dark side."

"Who else?"

"I don't do names."

"How about doing a little bit about the Scorza interview?" Danny said.

"I'm not doing anything about *that* at all. But I will tell you something about human behavior. See John Miller over there?"

Gregory gestured over at his date, Cookie Martucci Counihan. Cookie was sitting on the life preserver box, discussing her previous lives with John Miller, the ABC-TV News reporter.

"One time a bunch of us are bullshitting at the bar in Elaine's, and John Miller asks everybody what's the first thing we look for in a woman. Your uncle says, 'Gray hair.' Everybody goes, 'C'mon, stop the bullshit.' They all thought it was a nonanswer, like he was being politically correct. But I knew it was *his* answer."

"The woman would be more his age. I've heard him say that before. He means it."

"Exactly," Gregory said. "I said big tits, and I meant that, too. Although every now and then I go through a great ass phase. But what's important is, John Miller asked a simple question and he wound up getting an answer that spoke volumes about your uncle. It's his character, people act in character. Now apply that to your situation. Evan Stone didn't let all those reporters at JFK rattle him last Wednesday, did he? But yesterday, you walked up to him all alone, and suddenly he gets rattled and knocks you on your ass. It's inconsistent."

"You're telling me there's something suspicious in Evan Stone's reaction."

"You were there. You tell *me.*"

The boat was filled with New York writers, athletes, politicians, and show biz celebrities the cops had pulled out of places like Elaine's, Neary's, and Rao's. Nobody understood the value of contacts and connections better than cops. Someone always knew someone, but even if they didn't, they'd find a way to reach into the most sheltered levels of metropolitan society. Danny was only beginning to understand the immense behind-the-scenes power the NYPD wielded. But they kept it all sotto voce, and that was the main reason the power existed.

Gregory tried to sing the theme from *Gilligan's Island,* but he couldn't get past "a three-hour tour." Anthony Ryan came up behind them.

"You and the skipper keeping out of trouble, Gilligan?" Ryan said, moving into a spot on the rail next to Danny.

"The skipper has taken a vow of silence," Danny said.

"Nothing to say," Gregory said. "We rattled Scorza's cage. The guy held his ground."

As they sailed past Greenwich Village Danny was surprised by the number of water tanks that still remained on the roofs of the older buildings. Cylinders of all colors and sizes. They looked like the homemade rockets of a disorganized militia.

"I'm meeting Wacky tomorrow," Danny said. "I'll ask him about Scorza."

"That string is played out," Gregory said. "So Trey Winters

knows a Mob guy. Big freakin' deal. Everybody on this boat can pick up a phone and call a made man."

At the tip of Manhattan the ferry swung gently west to avoid the path of the Staten Island Ferry. Then it turned toward the East River. The wind changed and carried a brackish odor.

"I'm also having dinner with Abigail Klass tomorrow night," Danny said. "The food editor for our magazine set it up."

"She'll be looking to protect Winters," Ryan said. "But try to get an idea of his mental state that night."

"Winters's mental state was at home, with his bodily state," Gregory said. "At the time Gillian Stone died he was not there. You keep forgetting that, pally."

"You guys really don't agree on this at all," Danny said.

"Was that a light bulb just went on?" Gregory said, waving his hand around in the space above Danny's head. "By jove, I think he's got it."

Near Wall Street they passed some of the newly renovated piers that housed tennis courts covered by block-long bubbled air tents. As night fell, the lights glowing yellow inside made them look like giant radioactive beehives out of a colorized Japanese horror flick.

"You have to admit Winters had motive," Ryan said. "We know he was having an extramarital affair with Gillian. A relationship that was blowing up in his face."

"Right," Gregory said. "We know that from the neighbor Stella Grasso and the sister, Faye. Both interviews you did alone."

"What's that supposed to mean?" Ryan said. "You don't trust me to do interviews on my own?"

"I trust you. But I don't agree with the way you're handling this. This is my freakin' case, pally, and I don't see Winters as a suspect. You got some private hard-on for the guy, that's your business. But I call the shots in this case. And I say we back off of Winters. And, oh yeah, we discuss interviews *before* we do them. No more Lone Ranger shit."

The smell of fish blew from the Fulton markets. Up ahead, the three bridges loomed into view: Brooklyn, Williamsburg, Manhattan; all three huge steel and spidery, like an erector set contest of the gods. Spanning a river that was not a river at all.

"If you guys see a mermaid out here," Gregory said, slapping his big meaty hand on the rail, "ask her what she thinks. Don't bother calling me. I'll be inside dancing with your wife."

"Keep the Holy Ghost between you," Ryan said.

A frowning Ryan stared out over the water, as if he were actually looking for a mermaid. Danny knew that on the way back they'd make one trip around the Statue of Liberty, then linger at Ellis Island. The booze would be flowing by then, the cops full-blown sentimental. Someone would offer a toast to the struggles of their ancestors. McDarby would play the harmonica. Joe Gregory would sing "If Old Ireland Were Over Here," a song he knew in its entirety.

"Should I cancel the interviews?" Danny said.

"No," Ryan said, resuming his thousand-mile stare. "Absolutely not."

Above them, the E train rumbled across the Brooklyn Bridge. Inside, on the main floor, Joe Gregory, with the agile grace of a grizzly bear, danced across the floor with Leigh Ryan.

26

After the boat ride they wound up in Elaine's, their group filling three front tables. The mix of cops and reporters spewed stories faster than you could write them down. Which no one would, because the mere appearance of a notepad indicated a serious death wish. Joe Gregory sang from his one-line repertoire, the doo-wop years, until Elaine threatened to toss his ass out onto the bricks.

In the wee hours the newsmen drifted into their own group, cops into theirs. Anthony and Leigh Ryan were the first to leave, taking Gregory's date, Cookie Martucci Counihan, home to Queens. At last call only the hard core remained. Joe Gregory sat at table three in a hushed conversation with Elaine. Danny moved to the corner of the bar near the window and a zaftig redhead he'd chatted up earlier.

"Where on the West Side?" the redhead said, apparently doubting he was a legitimate Manhattanite.

"On the corner of bedlam and squalor," Danny said, a line he'd borrowed from Tom Waits.

"In a doorman building?" she snapped, and he knew he was outgunned.

He wasn't sure what other idiotic comments he'd made. Thick clouds floated through his consciousness. In his defense he could cite the devastating effects of jet lag, ferry funk, and the juniper berry.

He put his glass down carefully. He didn't want a spill. In the society of late night drinkers the worst thing you could do was spill your drink. Better you should fall off the stool, fracture your skull. Your cranium would heal faster than the scars a spilled drink would inflict on your reputation.

At table three Joe Gregory recited "Dangerous Dan Mc-Grew" while Elaine ignored him, scanning the night's receipts. When the redhead finally went to the ladies' room, Danny leaned over and asked Tommy the bartender if he knew her name.

"Electric Alice they call her," Tommy said.

"What does that mean?"

"I think it's more a warning than a name."

Danny knew that Tommy was right. The prudent thing would be to grab a cab and go home, but prudence jumped ship when man's favorite organ assumed command. Discreetly he checked his pockets to make sure he was armed with latex security.

"Does she live around here?" Danny said, thinking maybe her nickname had something to do with her hair, or she worked for Local 3, maybe Con Ed.

"You think it's wise to find out?" Tommy said, looking directly at him.

Danny paid his tab as Electric Alice came out of the ladies' room, fresh lipstick and all. To the exhausted Danny, with his shoulder aching, she looked as refreshed and rested as Minnesota Fats did to Fast Eddie Felson in that crucial juncture of their nine-ball marathon. He folded.

He caught a ride down Second Avenue with former squad boss Wally Millard, who dropped him off a few blocks before he turned onto the Fifty-ninth Street Bridge to Queens. Danny walked toward Third Avenue, figuring he'd make the left down to Fifty-seventh, where he'd stand a better chance of getting a cab. The air felt cool and clear, benefiting from the breeze and the weekend dip in air pollution. The city was quiet enough to hear the streetlights click through the changes. It was that surreal hour when only cops and psychos were on the stroll.

At the corner of Third Avenue he heard the squeal of brakes, a cab stopping near Caramanica's restaurant. The poorly tuned engine chugged loudly in the hushed city. Danny jogged toward it. The cab's back door opened. The driver wrote on a clipboard. A woman slid money into the safety slot. The cab was a gypsy, "Tremont Taxi" painted on the side. A broken side window covered with plastic taped to the frame. He started to yell to the driver. Then he stopped.

The woman slammed the door. The cab chugged away. The woman paused, a little unsteady on her feet. Danny waited on the corner as a Nineteenth Precinct radio car cruised by. He knew she'd be walking toward him. He knew exactly where she was going.

"Danny?" Faye Boudreau said.

"What the hell happened to your face?"

Her eye was swollen, almost closed, the bruise dark purple and fresh. She put her hand up quickly, but her hand could not hide the welt.

"I fell," she said.

"From where, the roof?" he said, looking closely. "You have to get that taken care of. I'll take you to the hospital."

"I'll be fine."

"Don't be silly, Faye. Get it looked at. You could have eye damage."

"Just walk me home. I'll put something on it."

Faye wore white sandals, a short black rayon skirt, and a black T-shirt from *Cats* with the green eye staring. He could smell the booze, see the shaky gait.

"Who the hell did that?" he said.

The bruise looked worse in the elevator's fluorescent glare. The purple skin around it appeared parchment thin and dead. Outside the apartment door she fumbled for her keys. Danny wanted to persuade her to make the emergency room run, but he kept his mouth shut until she opened the door. He knew how sounds carried in the hall.

Danny knew where to find everything in the apartment. It was exactly as Gillian had left it. Not as neat—Gillian had been obsessively neat. But it still smelled like her, the scented candles and potpourri.

He took a white terry-cloth dish towel from the kitchen drawer and dumped half a dozen ice cubes into it. He held it up to Faye's eye. She winced and stepped back when the towel touched her. Danny put his left hand against her back to hold her still. She took a breath and allowed him to press the ice against her cheek. Danny couldn't help himself, his heart beating faster, being in this apartment again. Nothing had changed. Nothing.

"You really should have this looked at," he said.

"*Mañana.*"

Even Faye's shampoo, her hair so close to his face, was Gillian's apricot.

"She always said you were a nice guy," Faye said.

"I fool a lot of people," Danny said.

"That was a big subject between us. Nice guys."

Faye wore simple gold hoop earrings. Just one hole in each ear, not four like her sister. She wore no other jewelry, no rings, no bracelets.

"I miss her," Faye said. "I never knew I could love somebody like that. Like it hurts. It hurts in my heart. I always heard that in songs. About heartache, you know? I thought it was just something you say."

"Are you going to be all right?" he said.

Faye's profile, in the light of the table lamp, reminded Danny of Gillian. The same bone structure and low thick hairline as their mother, Lynette. She pulled her head away. He was sure the ice was painful, but it would keep the swelling down. She reached up and took hold of the towel and put it on the counter.

"Just hold me," she said, wrapping her arms around his waist. She pressed her body against him, as if trying to go through him. Then she looked up at him and kissed him. Her lips were full and moist, her breath hot.

"Faye," he said in weak protest.

She shoved her hand under his shirt, feeling his skin. Even her hands were hot. She yanked his shirt out of his pants, then stepped back and pulled the *Cats* shirt over her head. She unsnapped her black bra and tossed it. She bunched Danny's shirt up under his chin, then she pressed her chest against him. Skin to skin.

He said her name several times but said neither stop nor go. Just "Faye, Faye, Faye." Her breasts were much fuller than Gillian's, her nipples dark and large. She clawed at Danny's shirt, then his belt, easily frustrated at each small impediment: buttons, buckles, snaps. "Faye, Faye, Faye," he murmured.

In red panties, Faye tossed clothes off the bed, then the red panties. She had a tattoo of something peeking above the vee of her pubic hair. Danny struggled to get his pants off, the condom out. She pulled at him, her legs wrapped around his body as if trying to climb him. He could feel her wetness on his leg.

She fell backward onto the bed, trying to pull him down on top of her. They were too close to the wall, his feet still on the floor, knees barely on the bed. Danny tried to maneuver her longwise, farther up the mattress. But she grabbed his cock and squirmed toward him. Pulling him down.

She came almost instantly . . . violently . . . the second he entered her. Her legs straightened, her heel smashing into the wall. He heard it break the Sheetrock. She moaned and bucked. Then the desperation left her, but she kept riding him. Riding it out. Working on him. Chanting in his ear.

Later he lay there, looking at the wall. His shoulder ached, but he was afraid to wake her.

27

A good tailman gets the glare behind him. Anthony Ryan stood on the east side of Columbus and Sixty-sixth, with his back to the Monday morning sun. The weather had cooled off, the predicted high only eighty-two. Ryan leaned against the front windows of the ABC-TV studio. On the big screen in the lobby Regis and Kathie Lee held up a copy of the *Daily News*. The back page headline was OVERRATED, yesterday's crowd chant at Yankee Stadium for the beleaguered pitcher Irabu.

Ryan pretended to watch, but his attention was focused on the sun-drenched West Side, specifically the front door of the Reebok Sports Club. He was waiting for the wife of Trey Winters to show up for her ten A.M. workout.

Darcy Jacobs Winters met her personal trainer three times a week in the Reebok Sports Club. Ryan knew she'd arrive by nine forty-five in a black Lincoln Towncar. Her driver would be Poochie Englehardt, a former member of the Four Eight Precinct detective squad, who'd rub his face with both hands when he parked. This gesture courtesy of the blue under-ground.

The blue underground consisted of thousands of retired cops and feds working at all levels of big business. With its silver-haired cadre of seasoned detectives, the NYPD provided corporate Manhattan with a ready-made all-star team. A tightly knit network, it knew all the secrets, where all the bodies were buried.

The Lincoln was right on time. Poochie Englehardt picked Ryan out easily, as if he had a badge painted on his forehead. He did the face rub, then threw Ryan one solemn nod, as if to say "This is a gift, don't screw it up." Darcy Winters hit the sidewalk running. She wore a raincoat over black tights and white sneakers. Ryan followed her into the lobby.

Ryan figured Darcy's raincoat indicated her desire not to be caught sporting spandex in public. He made a point not to look at her as they rode the elevator silently to the third floor. Three was as far as the elevator went in the huge building. There had to be another bank of elevators.

The door opened onto a room the size of a cathedral with a thirty-foot ceiling and marble floors. Three steps up to the security desk; the sign read, "Reception Desk." Ryan picked out all the security people in their Gap blue blazers, a pair of them within fifteen feet of the elevator. He had his ID ready.

"I'm looking for Mrs. Trey Winters," he said loudly.

He got the reaction he'd hoped for. They looked right over at Darcy Jacobs Winters, who had stopped at the coat check room.

"Oh," Ryan said, turning slowly. "Are you Mrs. Winters?"

Ryan introduced himself. He extended his hand quickly, knowing that once they'd shaken your hand you'd scaled the biggest barrier.

"If I could have just two minutes," he said, holding on to her hand. "It's about the Gillian Stone case."

"I've already been interviewed."

"This is the follow-up. It's standard."

Ryan transferred his hand to the woman's shoulder and guided her back, out of the way of the people rushing off the elevators. A gentlemanly thing to do, her safety his only concern.

"How did you know I'd be here?"

"I have a friend who works out in this gym," he said.

"Tell Russ I'll be with him in a second," Darcy said to the woman behind the reception desk.

Darcy Jacobs Winters was not a classic beauty. Her face was large and full. Her figure was deceptive, slim up top, pearing out from the hips down. Ryan asked her what she remembered about the night Gillian died.

"The phone ringing in the middle of the night. My husband answering it. He said the police asked him to come down to the precinct on Fifty-fourth Street. Gillian had been seriously injured. We were shocked to find out she was dead."

Ryan remembered his own middle-of-the-night call from the police officer in Utah: Your son has been seriously injured. But Ryan had been a cop a long time. He knew exactly what "seriously injured" meant.

"I'm talking about before you went to bed," he said. "What time did your husband get home that night?"

"A little before twelve-thirty."

"In the previous interview you said twelve forty-five."

"Did I? I forgot what I said. What time does Letterman end? Letterman was still on."

"It ends at twelve-thirty."

"It used to be on until one."

"That was the old Carson show, years ago."

"Then I should have said about twelve-fifteen. I'd fallen asleep on the couch with the TV on. I always wait up for Trey, unless he says he's going to be real late. Letterman was still on when he got home."

Ryan wrote in his notebook. Sometimes it unnerved people if they saw you recording their words in ink. It implied adding teeth to words that might return to bite them. Darcy Winters didn't even blink.

"I know people are going to say my husband was having an affair with Gillian," she added. "But it's not true."

"I believe you," he said, smiling.

"People think because of his looks he's a womanizer. Even my father called him a playboy when we first started dating. Then he got to know him better."

"Your father was a great friend to the cops in this city. The Police Foundation would have gone broke years ago without him. We were all truly sad to hear of his death."

"Thank you," she said. Her eyes filled with tears. "My father was a wonderful man. My whole life, before I met Trey."

They stood on a huge western-style rug near a cactus taller than they. The tinkle of silverware and the screech of chairs on the marble café floor echoed in the cavernous room.

"Did you ever meet Gillian Stone?" Ryan asked.

"At an AIDS fund-raiser in the Sheraton a few months ago. Actually, this may seem cruel, but I wasn't surprised she committed suicide."

"Why?"

"I took a good look at her at the fund-raiser. Real good. After all, my husband gives her this great apartment; I'm curious, right? She was beautiful, truly beautiful, but something was missing or wrong. I don't know what to call it. Something missing in her eyes. My husband says she was doing drugs, but I don't think that's it. Oh shit, I don't know what the hell I'm talking about. Go ahead, ask me something else."

Darcy Jacobs Winters gave her assessment of Gillian with such conviction, Ryan's gut reaction was to walk away. He wondered how a sleazeball like Trey Winters could hook up with a nice person like this. Marty Jacobs was right to object. Any father would do the same.

"Do you know someone named Buster Scorza?" Ryan said.

"I know of him," she said. "My husband has some business dealings with him."

The answer surprised Ryan. He'd had his next question ready, a follow-up on a negative answer. Sometimes you get fooled.

"What kind of business dealings?" Ryan asked.

"Umm, something to do with the theater unions."

"Scorza's been legally barred from involvement with those unions."

"My husband says he still wields influence. Actually he has a meeting with him this week. Wednesday morning, I believe."

A steady stream of tight-bodied women in clingy exercise gear passed by, elevator doors opening every few seconds. Ryan had been prepared to dissect Trey Winters's personal relationship with Gillian, but he decided to switch gears. He knew he couldn't turn this woman against her husband. Better to get on her good side.

"Has Scorza been threatening your husband?"

"Not that I know of," she said, looking alarmed. "Why?"

"I don't mean to worry you. But Scorza has a history of extortion and intimidation."

"It's just a business deal."

"Now *you're* worrying *me.*"

"No, please don't worry," she said, laughing. "It's nothing. Mr. Scorza said he'd intercede with the unions in regard to my husband's new show, and hopefully avoid any problems."

"What's the catch? Scorza always has a catch."

"Everything has a catch, Detective," she said, still smiling. "He asked my husband to speak to my company in his behalf in regards to his Times Square real estate holdings. His buildings are in the renovation zone."

"The renovation zone?"

"One building on Forty-second Street. Three or four more around Eighth Avenue. Mr. Scorza wants to get the fair market price for his buildings, before the city condemns them."

"If your company buys them before the city condemns them, Scorza gets a lot more money."

"It happens all the time. It's just business. Nothing to worry about."

"One hand washes the other."

"That's all it is. But thank you for your concern."

"Just be careful of Scorza," Ryan said.

"Thanks. I'll make sure my husband stays on his toes."

He watched her walk away, a tomboy walk. Heels banging heavily against the floor. Ryan had been wondering where the actual gym was. Then he saw that everyone who walked through the restaurant area wound up at a bank of elevators on the other side. Ryan figured it was those elevators that carried the well-heeled jocks to far-flung corners of the immense gym.

Ryan punched the elevator button, knowing that Trey Winters was smarter than he figured. He didn't have the heart to confront Darcy with the testimony of Stella Grasso, or Gillian's sister, Faye. She'd never believe it. If Trey Winters told Darcy the sky was falling, she'd advance him the money for a billion hard hats.

He'd set her up perfectly. Whatever his deal with Buster Scorza was, he'd sold her on his scenario. In truth, there was no way Buster Scorza, even when he did have influence in the stagehands union, was worth the money he'd make selling his buildings to the Jacobs Organization. It was a deal too sweet. Payment for something else . . . like murdering Gillian Stone.

He took a last look at Darcy Winters waiting at the other bank of elevators, and he wondered what kind of gym this was. There was no clank of iron weights, no squeak of sneakers on a hardwood floor. Only the tinkle of cups and glasses, the whir of a blender. The smell was not sweat or chlorine from a pool, but fresh coffee. And fresher money.

28

It was Victor's first trip to Randall's Island. From the maps it appeared the island's only purpose was to support the pillars of the Triborough Bridge. In the sky above the island, the wide ribbon of concrete and steel connected auto traffic between Manhattan, the Bronx, and Queens. The island itself seemed deserted on a Monday morning. It was certainly a place where no one lived. Even the permanent buildings appeared abandoned. The streets looked like overgrown and unrepaired paths in a forgotten industrial complex.

Victor parked Pinto's car in a lot opposite the main tent of a closed street fair. A line of carny booths stretched along a dirt path. Idle rides, including a small ferris wheel, sat on the opposite side of the tent. The sign read, "Fri, Sat, and Sun Only."

He decided to walk because he couldn't figure out what road to take. It all seemed like one big back alley, and he didn't want to get stopped by the cops for some obscure driving violation. Ward's Island was his destination, and it was close enough.

Ward's Island had been joined by landfill to the south side of Randall's Island. The linked islands sat in the northern part of the East River between Manhattan and Queens and were officially part of Manhattan. The 255-acre Ward's Island was originally purchased from the Indians in 1637 by the Dutch governor. After the American Revolution it was sold to the brothers Jasper and Bartholomew Ward for farmland. The southern tip of the island splits the East River into the Harlem River and the Hell Gate Channel.

From books in the library, Victor learned the island once housed an auxiliary immigration station, an asylum, a hospital for destitute immigrants, and a potter's field. But he was interested in it not as a place for the penniless to die, but as a place to get rich and start a new life. The point was to get the money from Trey Winters and, in case the police were involved, use the island to elude capture. As did Alain Charnier in *The French Connection.*

The trick was to figure out how Charnier did it. The waters surrounding the island were Victor's last resort; he didn't want to go into the water. Swimming would slow his flight, and carrying money and clothes would add to the effort. But if he had to, a strong swimmer like Victor could traverse either the Harlem River or the Hell Gate Channel.

The books said that hundreds of ships had sunk in the Hell Gate's waters, including the British frigate *Hussar* in 1780. The *Hussar* had been carrying gold and silver for military paymasters. Divers still hunted for its treasure. In 1876 the U.S. Army Corps of Engineers blasted out most of the dangerous underwater rocks, but the channel still remained difficult to navigate.

Alain Charnier, in the movie, didn't appear to be a strong swimmer. He was an old man who used guile. Victor couldn't imagine Charnier going into the filthy water. Alain Charnier escaped the clutches of the police in a more elegant manner. Completely dry.

In the movie the police had blocked only the Triborough

Bridge exit, because they knew Charnier had driven onto the island. They assumed he'd leave by car. He didn't. If Charnier did not go in the water, the map showed one other possible avenue of escape: the Ward's Island footbridge to Manhattan.

Victor walked past a golf driving range and New York City's school for firemen. In the pure peace of the summer morning the island seemed an oasis in disrepair. The green grass of picnic areas and ball fields stretched out like shaggy meadows. Off to Victor's right lay a complex of the city buildings: a psychiatric hospital, a men's shelter.

He strolled the peaceful footpath around to the east side of the island. Although it was early in the day he was shocked that no one was using the park. In a city of joggers, it would be so easy to walk across the footbridge from Manhattan and enjoy this bounty. The island was an incredibly quiet haven in the middle of a brutal and noisy city. The breeze blew gently off the water. The sounds of birds came from the heavily wooded area in the center of the island. The smell of trees and plants blooming filled the air. New Yorkers didn't appreciate the gifts nature had bestowed on them.

As he rounded the bottom of the island, Victor saw the Ward's Island footbridge in the distance. It was a thin slice of turquoise metal rising high above the Harlem River. He was now sure the narrow footbridge into Harlem was the route used by Charnier. The police didn't cover this route because they never anticipated a chase on foot. Across the dark river, Manhattan loomed like a fortress of brick and concrete. He began walking up the path to the bridge ramp.

"Hey, buddy," a voice said.

Victor turned to see a man in a dark green khaki uniform leaning out of an official-looking Jeep.

"The bridge is closed," the man said, a glaze of sugar on his upper lip. "You can't get up there."

It was then that Victor noticed an obstruction up ahead, around the next angled turn. A huge barricade of plywood and barbed wire.

"Why?" Victor said.

"They wanted it," he said, pointing across the river. "Those people in the housing project over there. They said the inmates were walking across the bridge. Pissing in their hallways, bumming money, acting weird, shit like that. They had all kinds of stories about rapes and shit. They were picketing, doing everything to get it closed. The city finally said fuck it, closed it down. Over a year ago."

"Too bad," Victor said.

"Hey, makes my job easier. Know what I mean? Less beer cans and rubbers. Only thing, it gets spooky out here sometimes. Nobody but weirdos to talk to. A whole park full of nothing but nut jobs. Tell you the truth, I wouldn't be caught dead out here at night."

"I see," Victor said, wondering how the man knew he wasn't a nut job.

"You're a big guy and all that. But I'd be a little careful anyway. You see somebody, don't make eye contact, whatever you do. Some of these psychos wandering around this park, they're not fucking human. My brother-in-law is a cop, and he says that psychos get this superhuman strength. Can't be stopped. Gotta blow them away. And sometimes that don't even work. They keep coming at you."

The man drove away. Victor looked up at the footbridge. The entrances on both sides were blocked by the barricades. Past the barricades, approaches ran for several hundred feet, gradually sloping upward. Then nothing. The center of the bridge was raised to allow ships to pass underneath. It was raised, not in the center like a drawbridge, but one long section, raised to its highest point, like a pole-vault bar. They'd simply left it in that position. Nothing but air between the two approaches. He couldn't believe his luck.

29

Danny Eumont spent Monday afternoon looking for Wacky Walzak, but he couldn't get Faye Boudreau out of his mind. What happened between them, happened; he wasn't going to analyze it now. The important thing was Faye was in trouble. Maybe he'd missed something with Gillian, but he wasn't going to do it this time. He just needed a few hours to think it through before he called his uncle. To find the right way to say it. After all, he'd been drinking, the juniper berry, and the jet lag. All that. Maybe just be honest: I had sex with her. Maybe not. Either way Joe Gregory was going to be merciless.

He didn't find Wacky until an hour before curtain, coming out of Shubert Alley. The night was warm, and the streets were packed. Office workers, getting out of town, hustling toward the Port Authority and Penn Station, crossed paths with theatergoers traveling in from New Jersey and Connecticut.

"What do you know about Buster Scorza?" Danny said.

"Enough to say cement shoes are not my style," Wacky Walzak said.

Cars idled in front of parking garages, waiting for spots to open, blue exhaust fumes rising. On the sidewalks, early arrivals gathered nonchalantly under marquees, occasionally drifting into the path of a head-down, homebound New Yorker. A full-speed pedestrian shoulder slam was just one more Gotham experience.

"Everybody knows Scorza's a bad guy," Danny said. "All I want to know is, what is Trey Winters's connection to Scorza?"

"Not my area of expertise."

Danny treated Wacky to a hot dog from a street vendor outside Charley O's restaurant. Wacky wore a T-shirt that read, "Send a salami to your boy in the Army."

"This is all I get for my help?" Wacky said. "A dirty-water hot dog. Dinner under the umbrella with Mr. Big Spender. 'Hey, big spender . . . spennnnd . . . a little time with me.' Remember that song from *Sweet Charity*?"

"I still owe you a dinner," Danny said. "Anywhere you want to go."

They were standing near the Booth Theatre on West Forty-fifth Street. The Booth connected with the Shubert Theatre on Forty-fourth. Back to back. They'd been built as one building, but the Booth had half as many seats as the Shubert. Wacky bit into his hot dog with everything, and onion sauce dribbled down his chin.

"My uncle told me you knew more about the theater district than anyone. Yet you can't tell me one simple fact about Buster Scorza."

"Buster Scorza has nothing to do with the theater."

"He used to head the stagehands union."

"He's been beheaded," Wacky said, a dime-size dollop of yellow mustard resting on his purplish lower lip.

"If he's been beheaded, why is he meeting with Trey Winters?" Danny said.

" 'Hey, big spenda . . .' Cy Coleman song. Neil Simon book.

The hookers sang it. Did you know that at that time Neil Simon had four plays on Broadway simultaneously?"

"That's really interesting, Wacky, but I have an important appointment on the East Side in fifteen minutes."

Danny was due to meet Abigail Klass for dinner. He figured he'd get a cab easily; all traffic was coming toward the theaters at this hour, and cabs usually went away empty.

"I've never dined in Twenty-one," Wacky said. "I like those little jockeys going up the stairs."

"Twenty-one's the magic number," Danny said.

The sound of bagpipe music came from the corner of Broadway and Forty-fifth. Danny could see the lone piper in MacGregor kilt and bearskin hat standing behind his open case. In the hour before curtain the streets of the theater district were filled with street performers. Singers, trumpet players, jugglers.

"You must buy these twelve to the pound?" Wacky said to the small Greek behind the hot dog cart. "Thin as a pencil, these hot dogs."

"Shut you crazy mouth," the vendor said. "Nine dogs to a pound, like always. You don't know what you're talking about."

Terra-cotta figures lined the upper portions of both theater buildings. On the capitals of the Shubert were two woolly rams; along the top of the building were heads with bat wings. The capitals of the Booth featured two openmouthed animals; under the cornice at the top of the building were a series of brackets consisting of white glazed human heads, all with their mouths wide open. Danny pulled big-mouthed Wacky away from the Greek bearing a hot fork.

"Am I wasting my time here?" Danny said.

"You know, once I found a Raisinet in a box of Goobers peanuts. Everybody said I was wasting my time. I wrapped it in plastic and sent it back to the company. They sent me a whole case of peanuts."

A woman walking into Charley O's with two little girls

warned them about the long lines to the ladies' room at intermission. Make sure you pee before you leave the restaurant.

"I really don't have the time for this," Danny said, checking his watch. "I'm going to let Joe Gregory talk to you."

"Don't bother the man, he's probably busy beating some hapless miscreant. The truth is I don't know the answer."

"Gregory says you know the answer, because he does. He says Scorza met Winters through Paul Klass."

"He only knows that because he worked in Vice," Wacky said, then mumbled, "Uh-oh. Too much information. Too much information."

Outside the Shubert a guy in a tux and a mask entertained the waiting crowd by singing songs from *Phantom of the Opera*. His top hat sat on the ground in front of him, ready for cash.

"Now tell me what Vice has to do with it?"

"I'm still very hungry, you know," Wacky said, jingling the coin changer on his belt. "Hungry man of La Mancha. Little wieners do nothing for me."

"Don't push me too far, Wacky."

"Paul Klass passed away. I will not tarnish his reputation."

"You're giving me no choice. I'll call Gregory, tell him you sandbagged me."

"It's all ancient history," Wacky said, jingling the coin changer louder and faster. "Only a few alive know the tale."

"Gregory will be here tomorrow night," Danny said.

"So will I," Wacky said. "Haven't missed a performance in five years. Then only because I snapped my ankle in a pothole crossing Forty-third. Streisand hated to miss a performance, too, you know. Once in the Winter Garden Theatre Barbra's understudy in *Funny Girl,* Lainie Kazan, was ready to go on. Babs called in with strep throat. Lainie was so excited; she'd waited fifteen months. She was in costume, curtain ready to go up, when La Streisand drags herself in and insists on going on. She knew Lainie was talented."

"That's it. Adios," Danny said, and turned around.

Wacky grabbed him by his sleeve. He held a roll of bills up to his face. "Subtlety goes right over your head," he said.

Danny finally got the point and handed Wacky two twenties. Wacky placed the bills in a thick roll and snapped a rubber band around it.

"Tell me now, will you, please," Danny said.

"Paul Klass had a nefarious dealing with Buster Scorza. It's no secret. It was well-known on the street. Paul Klass was not ashamed of his lifestyle."

"What nefarious dealings?"

"Did I say nefarious? Was that my line?"

"Don't do this," Danny said, taking a deep breath. "I've had enough."

"Okay, Mr. Impatient. It seems that Paul Klass had certain, shall we say, exotic habits, pleasures, whatever."

"Tell me, you crazy fuck!" Danny yelled.

"Young boys. Paul Klass had a thing for young boys."

"Is Trey Winters going to Scorza for young boys?"

"Absolutely not. The man has been a chippie chaser all his life. It's his reputation, his legacy."

"No boys for Trey."

"Believe me," Wacky said. "That I would know."

On the sidewalk behind them a one-legged pigeon hopped around a discarded lunch bag, pecking at a chicken leg. Danny wondered what kind of bird ate other birds.

"Then why is Winters going to Scorza?"

"You're the detective."

"I'm not a detective, I'm a reporter."

"Whatever," Wacky said. "I know what I know. Scorza supplied young pretty boys to Paul Klass. And others. But I'm talking years ago. Years, years, years. Things were not so wide open in those days. The average person needed somebody like Buster Scorza. To get . . . you know, stuff."

"Like little boys?"

"Little boys, little girls, sex, drugs, rock and roll. Maybe not rock and roll."

The crowd in front of the Shubert burst into applause as the guy in the tux and the mask bowed. The Phantom of the Alley nudged his top hat forward. Danny hoped he had enough money left for cab fare.

"Maybe there was something going on between Paul Klass and Trey Winters," Danny said. "Could he have been one of Klass's young boys?"

"You're not listening to the lines. I said Paul liked young boys. Young, very young. I'm talking twelve, thirteen years old. Pretty-boy Winters was already too old when he arrived in New York."

"And you know that for a fact."

"I delivered enough Cokes and cheeseburgers to apartment eighteen-K in those days."

"That's it? That's your forty-dollar guess?" Danny said.

"That's a century-note gem, not a guess, sonny boy. I gave you a discount because I like your uncle."

Danny turned and ran for a cab dropping passengers off on Broadway. He thought about Faye getting out of the gypsy cab from Tremont Taxi, her face swollen. He wondered how she was. The rolling lights on the ITT news billboard read, "First rule of success: Subscribe to *The Wall Street Journal.* . . . Yanks lose to Brewers 6–2."

"We still on for Twenty-one?" Wacky yelled.

30

A "forthwith" in the NYPD is an order to get your butt to a specified location. It means now. *Right now!* "Immediately" is not a strong enough word. Death is not an excuse. At 1845 hours on Monday evening, forty-five minutes after their tour ended, Ryan and Gregory received a telephone message from the night desk man in the Chief's office. He'd guessed correctly that they'd be in Brady's Bar, behind headquarters. The message he relayed was a direct order from the chief of detectives to meet him at the Downtown Athletic Club. Forthwith! Both cops knew that good news never followed that word.

The Downtown Athletic Club is a thirty-five-story brick structure that faces the Statue of Liberty, at the southernmost tip of Manhattan Island. The Retired Detectives Association of the City of New York held its monthly meetings in the club's Heisman Trophy Room. Guest speakers were culled from the current power structure in law enforcement. That night's honored guest was Chief of Detectives Patrick Ferguson.

"This isn't a social thing," Gregory said as he pushed the

elevator button marked *H.* "No, no, no, no, we're not talking sentimental old times tonight."

"Paddy's not a sentimental guy anyway," Ryan said. "Remember when the PC wanted the bosses to come up with their own Christmas anticorruption program? Paddy had a huge poster put on the wall showing Santa Claus in a coffin."

The walls of the Heisman Trophy Room were covered with portraits of every winner since the first award in 1935. The trophy, named after the club's first athletic director, John W. Heisman, was presented in the first week of December to the athlete voted the outstanding college football player for that year. Visitors to the club often wanted their pictures taken next to the portrait of their hometown or alma mater hero. Visiting cops posed next to the portrait of O. J. Simpson, their handcuffs dangling.

Dinner had not yet started when Ryan and Gregory arrived. The cocktail hour was more popular than the chicken breast. Most of the big, happy crowd lingered at the bar, telling war stories and plunking down plastic chips for drinks. The Chief sat at the dais, laughing with a handful of old-timers. He wasn't worried about his speech; he had only one basic speech, but it was a work of art.

Although many of the people around the Chief knew him from the bad old days, none would call him "Paddy Roses" tonight. Tonight he was "the Chief," with all due honors and respect. Some were there to seek his blessing, hoping to engineer a "contract." Hoping the Chief might, in his infinite wisdom, make the phone call that would transfer them or a loved one into a prestigious assignment on a high floor in headquarters. Most came, "hat in hand," as Gregory always said, because memories and past loyalties were the only collateral they could bring to the table.

As soon as the Chief spotted Gregory he waved everybody off and pointed toward the far window. The window overlooked the Hudson. Ferries and cargo ships floated gracefully around the river like sailboats in a park pond.

"What the hell is going on with the Stone case?" the Chief said.

As soon as he said that, they both knew the case was over. The chief of detectives didn't issue a "forthwith" just to inquire about status.

"We got one or two questions, Chief," Joe Gregory said. "It'll be closed tomorrow."

"It's closed now," the Chief said. "It's done, stick a fork in it. I spent half the afternoon on the phone with the mayor's office. They think you're trying to set the records for lawsuits in a single case."

"Scorza, right?" Gregory said.

Ryan looked out the window at the stunning view. The city's new Holocaust museum was in the last stages of construction. Along the river's edge the line of new high-rises stretched north as far as the eye could see. Everything built on landfill. Twenty years ago only water bordered the West Side Highway.

"I can understand you hassling Buster Scorza," the Chief said. "I might even enjoy telling his lawyer to go fuck himself. But tell me why you're still breaking Trey Winters's balls. Following his wife into her health club."

Ryan could feel Joe Gregory glaring at him. He hadn't mentioned his interview of Darcy Winters.

"Whatever you say, Chief," Gregory said. "We'll go back to the office now, drop off the paperwork."

"Give us until the end of the week," Ryan said.

"Why?" the Chief said. "Everything points to suicide. Even the lab report shows she was taking depressants."

"The lab report isn't back yet," Ryan said.

"Go get Coletti," the Chief told his night driver. "Look for the guy in the loudest suit."

The tech man strutted over, wearing a red satin bow tie that appeared to be made of curtains from a Sicilian whorehouse. He was preceded by cologne and trailed by the fumes of his faux Cuban cigar.

"Get that cigar out of my face," the Chief said, "then fill these guys in on the lab report for the Stone case."

"I didn't know the report was in," Ryan said.

"Check your box once in a while," Coletti said. "I put a copy in there myself."

"I checked it," Ryan said. "Right before I left at six."

"Your age, you probably just think you did."

Ryan grabbed Coletti by the bow tie. Gregory inserted an arm between them and said, "Not again, pally, please. Let's not come to blows in here."

"That's not a fucking clip-on," Coletti gasped.

Ryan released his grip and stepped away from Coletti.

Coletti said, "I called in a favor for you, Ryan. Got preliminary results back in less than a week. Then you act like this in front of the Chief."

"I didn't see a thing," the Chief said. "Give him the results, quit jerking around."

"Besides alcohol," Coletti said, "she had only one drug in her system, but she had enough to knock a linebacker on his ass. It's a drug called Lorazepam, also known as Ativan. It's a strong muscle relaxant, like a tranquilizer for the nervous system."

"I never heard of it," Ryan said.

"Then I'll enlighten you," Coletti said. "It's four times the strength of Valium. It's potent shit."

"Mark it closed pending further information," the Chief said, and walked back to the dais.

An old-time detective who'd been watching walked up and jabbed his finger at Ryan's face. "Next time you got a beef in here, you take it outside like a man," he snarled.

The old-timer had to be pushing ninety. He was a regular, part of several tables of classy old detectives. Out for the night with their best suits on, like old times. Sipping a few martinis, sniffing a little perfume.

"How come you didn't find any Lorazepam when we searched?" Ryan said.

"My guess is she swallowed her whole stash before she jumped. She was stoked."

"Is this a prescription drug, Armand?" Ryan asked.

"Yeah, but she didn't have one. We checked her pharmacy, and her doctor."

"She bought it on the street?"

"You can get anything on the street. But I'd bet she has some jet-set supplier."

"I never heard of it before, either," Gregory said.

"Out west, down south, places like that, you hear of it more."

"Could it have been given to her without her knowledge?" Ryan asked.

"Stop it right now," Gregory said. "I see where you're going. Enough is enough."

"Wouldn't be the first time," Coletti said.

Ryan shook hands with Coletti and apologized. Coletti waddled back to the bar. Ryan wrote on an index card.

"Now Coletti's your buddy," Gregory said. "You think he gave you fresh ammunition."

"I love that guy," Ryan said.

"The Chief says it's closed, pally. It's closed. Finished. You go anywhere else with this case, you go without me. I ain't bullshitting here. You work one more minute on this case, you do it without me. You listening? That's the last thing I got to say on it."

"Drive me to the office," Ryan said. "Then you can go wherever the hell you want. I won't have to worry about dragging you down with me."

"You want to fuck up your life," Gregory said, punching the elevator button, "that's your business. But I'm not the one you should be worrying about."

31

Danny Eumont thanked the gods of etiquette that only two forks appeared to his left. He'd feared a murderous row of silverware, a lineup formidable enough to fluster someone who gave a rat's ass about proper forkage.

"So you spend your life just going around eating shrimp?" Danny said.

"Pretty much."

Abigail Klass was younger than he expected. The picture on her column showed only the back of a woman's head, a woman holding a knife and fork in the air. This was too bad, because the other side of that image deserved presentation.

"I'm glad you're not allergic," she said. "You'd be surprised how many people are allergic to shellfish."

"My teeth get a little sore crunching the shells. Otherwise, no problem." Slow down the wiseass act, he thought. Let her discover the shallow man at her own pace.

Pier Seattle was an in joint and had a great crowd for a Monday night. It was a takeoff on the seafood restaurants of

the Pacific Northwest. "Sophisticated seafood," the menu announced. Charlie the Tuna need not apply.

Despite linen tablecloths, the decor was spare: hardwood
floors, fish memorabilia, and racehorses on the walls. Work in
the stainless-steel kitchen was observable through a huge picture window. The walls, according to the menu, were painted
kayak yellow and Laramie blue.

"How about this," she said. "We'll order three appetizers,
and two entrées, then do a couple of desserts."

According to the menu, the fish were line caught and hand
harvested. The meat and vegetables were organic, the game
farm raised. Every entrée came with a story. If Joe Gregory
were here, Danny thought, he'd ask the waiter, "How much
would it cost without the story?"

"Why don't you order for both of us," he said.

"I'll pick something, but you order it. I don't want to give
them any clue as to who I am."

Danny never realized that food writers worked this covertly.
She had made the reservations in his name and waited outside
until he arrived. She insisted on a corner table, then picked the
seat against the wall so she could see the entire restaurant.
She'd been schooled in the art of undercover.

"Are we allowed drinks?" he said.

"Just don't be a lush. They go over my expense account
with a jeweler's loupe."

Abigail Klass had short dark hair that curled up slightly
under her left ear. She had dark brown eyes and a blockbuster
smile set in a face that reminded you of the all-consuming
radiance of your first high school crush.

"When you called," she said, "I figured you wanted to discuss leaving your Johnny-come-lately outfit and moving over
to a real magazine."

"Why would I do that? *Manhattan* is the weekly of the future in this town."

"A future of maybe a year," she said.

Abigail's columns appeared regularly in *New York* magazine.

Her yearly "Best of the West Side, Best of the East Side" ratings were its biggest-selling issues. Restaurants framed favorable reviews and displayed them in the window. Each review was a little plotted story, with characters and overheard dialogue. Her readers came away with more than a vague idea about certain meals; they felt as if they'd been there with her.

Their waiter was an aspiring actor with Pierce Brosnan looks but a flat midwest accent. Abigail had picked out a variety of menu items, trying to cover as many specialties as possible. Then Danny played his part suavely, acting as if he really knew what the hell fois gras was. Sophisticated fish demanded the sophisticated diner. He could play that part.

"I see your columns all over the place," Danny said. "And I never realized you were Paul Klass's sister."

"I was wondering how long it would be before that came up. Most men just want the free meal; now I get one who's looking for information."

"Oh no, I want the free meal, too," Danny said.

Abigail smiled and said, "The truth is I never met Gillian Stone."

"Actually, I was more curious about Trey Winters."

"I was afraid of that, too. I already told the police everything I know about that night. Not much, really. He never mentioned her during dinner. And to tell you the truth, I wouldn't say a bad word about Trey Winters if I knew one."

Pierce Brosnan brought the wine and an assortment of oysters on the half shell: Hood, Pearl Bay, and Kumamoto. Danny wondered about sucking them down, but the vinegar dip had bite to spare. He decided to change the subject away from Trey Winters; he'd learned from his uncle to circle around to a different angle.

"I bet you're quite the cook," he said.

"You've got to be kidding. My last boyfriend used to run from the house screaming whenever I touched a pan."

"How did you learn about food?"

"From books. Reading. Actually, I'm getting a little sick of it. After a while there's only so many things you can say about risotto."

He sampled the roasted mussels from the wood oven. Much of the food came from a wood oven. She told him that wood ovens were the latest fad.

"Let me ask you something," Danny said. "I noticed that you always review high-ticket places like this. Why don't you do some places where real people eat."

"You mean like Burger King?"

"That Johnny-come-lately outfit? No. I'm talking about the fast-food pioneer who changed the way America eats. Since 1921, the one and only White Castle."

"I might have to pass on that one. I worry about food sold by the sack and referred to as belly bombs."

"That's a shame, because you're missing out on the best cheeseburger in town. It's the steam grilling. Part grilling, part steaming."

"Sounds damp."

"A little mushy. But that's part of the whole experience. Like little meat loaves. These little squares of beef, one point five ounces, perforated with five holes. Steam grilled to perfection. Covered with onions. That pungent aroma of onions."

"Why five holes?"

"Actually, that's a good question," he said. "I'll look into it. But the Castle cheeseburger is the pinnacle of the cheeseburger mountain. See, in most places they never get the cheese right. You know how it's always hard, undermelted? But at the Castle it's all steam grilled, and this tangy cheese flows down and inhabits the very soul of the burger."

"I feel like I should make the sign of the cross."

"I always do," Danny said.

The last appetizer was smoked salmon, with Russian osetra caviar. Abigail put a portion of everything on her plate. She stopped every few bites and made notes on a pad she had hidden on her lap.

"What do you think of the decor?" Abigail said.

"I wondered why they had pictures of racehorses on the wall of a seafood restaurant."

She looked around and made a note on her pad.

"Last week," she said, "I ate at a place where they sat me next to the Heimlich chart."

"Was that the night you ate with Trey Winters?"

"You're not going to give up," she said. "Okay, let's get it over with. I've known Trey for more than ten years. Both he and Darcy have been wonderful to me and my brother. Especially Trey, he's been amazingly supportive."

"What was his mood that night?"

"Sounds more like a cop question," she said.

Danny poured himself a second glass of wine. He couldn't even remember drinking the first.

"Trey was relaxed and charming, as always," she said.

"Your brother got Trey his start in show business, didn't he?"

"Paul thought the world of Trey. He always said that once Trey got the Shakespeare bug out of his system, he'd become one of the finest light comedy actors in the business. Paul said that Trey had a Cary Grant appeal."

Danny wondered if Abigail knew the appeal that little boys had for her brother. He doubted it; Paul was much older than she was. Probably already dying when she was in her early teens.

"Trey and your brother must have been very close," Danny said.

"I hope that question doesn't have some hidden agenda. For some reason people refuse to believe a normal friendship is possible between a gay man and a heterosexual one."

"No agenda, I promise," he said. "All I'm trying to do is get a feel for Trey as a person. To be honest, he comes off a little cold."

"He's not. I'll tell you exactly what kind of person he is, Danny. Trey Winters supported my brother through the last five years of his life, and it wasn't a cheap proposition. He paid for all his medical expenses and living expenses. When my brother was near losing his apartment in the Broadway Arms, Trey had his theater company buy it, at a healthy profit to Paul. Then he let him live in it until he died. Over three years, rent free."

The waiter delivered Danny's entrée, wood fire–roasted Maine sea scallops. Abigail reached over, took his plate, and spooned a trio of scallops onto her own. She chewed slowly, then wrote on her hidden pad.

"Actually, my brother introduced Trey to Darcy Jacobs," she said. "Darcy's father, Marty Jacobs, backed several of Paul's shows."

"Lucky break for Trey."

"Marty Jacobs wasn't happy about it. Not at all. In fact, he never spoke to my brother again after that. He didn't want his baby to marry an actor. There's a pretty detailed prenup involved in that marriage."

"I forgot that was your brother's apartment," Danny said.

"Gillian was the first person to live in it since he died. I think Trey was trying to be a mentor to her, the way Paul had been to him."

"Did he mention bringing a costume over to her, or offering a role as understudy?"

"I told you, he never mentioned her at all."

Abigail held up her plate and slid a stack of her prawns onto his plate. She asked him if he could taste rosemary. Groucho had a line here, but Danny held it back. He liked this woman too much.

"Her drug problem must have devastated Trey," Danny said. "She was so young, such a talent."

"I'm sure it did."

"That's why I was surprised he was so relaxed when he had dinner with you. It was just a few hours after telling her he wanted her to be tested for drugs."

"I'm not saying he was giddy or anything," she said. "But he certainly wasn't nervous, or anxious. Concerned, maybe.

The man is weeks away from a major Broadway opening. He has a million details on his mind at all times. In fact, when I was waiting for him outside the restaurant, I saw this guy hand him an envelope. Trey said it was business. And it obviously concerned him."

Danny wondered if Winters had ever mentioned this envelope to the police. Who gave it to him? He'd check with his uncle; he knew Joe Gregory wouldn't tell him.

"Some people were saying Gillian Stone was more depressed than anyone realized," he said.

"I wouldn't know about that. But I have no idea why anyone would want a terrace in this city. For the last few months of my brother's life, when he was in such pain, I worried about him doing something like that. I've stood on that balcony and looked down. It always sent shivers through me."

She sat back and wrote something on her pad. Danny knocked off the wine, thinking he could handle this again.

"You've got me thinking," she said. "The food of the people. Not a bad idea at all. Where do I find a White Castle in the city?"

"Sunnyside, Queens. But you'll need a guide, and I'm the best. We'll get a sack of everything."

32

Anthony Ryan sat at the computer in his upstairs den, scouring the Internet for drug information. He was searching for Lorazepam, the drug Armand Coletti had told him about a few hours earlier. Also known as Ativan, it was an effective muscle relaxant, depressant, or tranquilizer to the nervous system. Imprinted with the company's logo, it usually appeared as a small, round, oblong, or football-shaped tablet. Legitimate doses ranged from two to six milligrams a day.

He could hear Leigh hammering away downstairs. She'd begun the process of cleaning out Rip's bedroom, converting it into a pink palace for their granddaughter, Katie. She wanted it ready when Katie and Margaret returned from Ireland next year. And as with everything Leigh did, she jumped in with both feet. The smell of paint, the rustle of wallpaper, furniture trucks in the driveway: every day something new for Katie's room.

The Ryans' Cape Cod had four bedrooms. The two downstairs had belonged to Margaret and Rip. Margaret's room, still intact, always awaited her return from an adventure abroad or a bad marriage. Upstairs were two bedrooms and a small bathroom, all with sharply slanted ceilings. Anthony and Leigh used one bedroom. The other, across the hall, was a guest room/den combination. The past few years it had become more of a computer room. He heard Leigh coming up the stairs.

"You're not in some porno chat room, are you," Leigh said. "Hot, lonely cops, something like that."

"Hot cops are never lonely," he said.

She wore one of Rip's old Baltimore Orioles T-shirts and paint-stained khaki shorts. She told him she was going to shower, get the paint off, but he couldn't see any paint on her. He couldn't understand how she could paint without getting any on her. Leigh walked to the wall and began adjusting pictures. That was how she was: whatever caught her eye that minute, that was what she did.

Family pictures filled the walls of the den, hung frame to frame, running up the slanted ceiling. His favorites were the black-and-whites taken in their backyard when neither the trees nor the kids were tall.

"What are you doing?" she said.

"Researching that drug from Gillian's blood test."

"Oh," she said. He could hear the disappointment in her voice. She wanted this case over.

"I've been meaning to ask you," she said. "What is the Duck's real name?"

"Why would you want to know that?"

"Just curious. I've heard you and Joe talk about him for years. Joe introduced me to him on the boat ride Sunday, but I didn't catch his name."

"He probably said the Duck," Ryan said. "Now that you ask, I can't remember myself. Donald something."

"Is that a joke?"

"No, it's Donald, really. I can't even remember why they call him the Duck. If I ever knew. He's Gregory's buddy. All I ever knew was the Duck."

"Men have strange ways," she said.

"I'll find out for you."

"Don't bother. I was just curious."

Leigh dropped her clothes in the hamper and went into the bathroom. Men have strange ways, he thought. Leigh washes off mystery paint and wonders about people's real names. Faye Boudreau, by herself, has more strange ways than an entire village of men.

Ryan scrolled the Web page of a Nevada investigative agency until he found something that made him sit straight up. It was a mention of Lorazepam in a report on a drug called scopolamine hydrobromide. The agency reported that both drugs were being used by hookers as knockout drops. The hookers picked up businessmen in hotel bars in Vegas and Reno, as well as five other states. Lorazepam was water soluble, so the hookers kept it in small plastic containers, such as those that originally contained over-the-counter eyedrops. Odorless and colorless, it was so powerful that just a few drops in a drink could render the victim unconscious within twenty minutes. He printed it out.

33

Tuesday morning Danny Eumont awoke to a banging on his door. Who the hell banged on an apartment door at seven o'clock in the morning? Totally beyond the rules of common courtesy.

"Take it easy!" he yelled as he stumbled toward the noise.

He had no idea who it could be this time of the morning. His uncle wouldn't bang this hard, and it wasn't Gregory's shave-and-a-haircut. This knocker lacked form as well as courtesy.

"Keep your pants on," Danny said as he peered through the fish-eye lens of the peephole. His eyes were as blurry as the optics, but he could make out a color: blond. Big blonde, big blond hair, big blond chest. *Speaking of knockers,* his Groucho persona whispered.

"You in there sniffing my dirty underwear?" Big Blonde yelled.

"I think you have the wrong apartment," Danny said.

"Are you Danny Eumont from *Manhattan* magazine? The pervert who stole my luggage?"

"What the hell are you talking about?" Danny said, recognizing Lainie Mossberg from Tempe, Arizona.

"Is that your gig? I hope your neighbors keep an eye on their laundry with you in the building."

"Lower your voice," Danny said, quickly unsnapping the dead bolt. He slid back the chain lock and opened the door. "I've got a lease to protect. If not a reputation."

Lainie wheeled her Pullman into the room. She looked as if she'd been up all night. He closed the door behind her. He could smell cigarette smoke in her clothes and big hair.

"You thought you were funny dropping me off at that hotel, a regular comedian."

"I had an errand to run. I intended to come back, but I had car trouble."

"Lying bastard. You weren't even registered."

"I panicked when you mentioned your husband. I draw the line at the H word."

"We're separated, idiot. He lets me crash in his place. But, don't worry. While I was waiting for you I met this guy in the lounge who works for the Arizona Diamondbacks, the new baseball team. I got seats whenever I want them. In the frrront rooow. Losing you was the best thing that happened to me that night."

Lainie wore a sunshine yellow business suit and white high heels with alligator tips. Very businesslike. She pointed to her carry-on bag, which held the logo of the new baseball team: a turquoise *A* with the hint of a snake.

"How did you get here?" he said.

"By plane, asshole. The big bird in the sky."

"No, I mean from the airport."

Danny looked out the window, expecting to see a cab or a broom idling at the curb. He caught his half-naked reflection in the window but figured Lainie Mossberg was not offended by men in boxer shorts.

"I got a ride from a *nice* guy," she said.

Danny remembered he had once been a *nice* guy who

chauffeured her from an airport. He brushed his hair back with his fingers and ran his tongue over his teeth. He tried to remember where he'd put her pink bag.

"How did you find out where I lived?" he said.

"From your own big mouth," she said. "You bragged to me on the plane. Big-time magazine writer. How they sent you to Phoenix to write an article on Gillian Stone."

"Someone at the magazine gave you my address?"

"Do the math," she said.

Danny put on his pants and found her duffel bag at the back of his closet. It was on top of the strongbox that safeguarded his cop novel. The hot pink plastic bag looked as though it should have had a picture of Strung-Out Barbie on the side.

"You did steal it. You are a weird shit."

"Not steal. I was going to return it."

Lainie rifled through the bag. She pulled out everything and tossed it on the kitchen counter. Clothes, hairspray, a pair of baby blue panties she dropped onto a stove burner. He made a mental note to check his renter's policy.

"I see something is missing," she said. "Apparently Mister High and Moral has no reservations about stealing the personal drugs of another."

"I threw that away," he said. "I didn't want some pot-sniffing beagle hassling me at the airport."

"Oh yeah, right. But you did go through my stuff."

"Only in self-protection," Danny said.

Lainie turned the bag upside down and shook it. Bits of cracker and tissue fell onto his counter and floor as she peered inside. Danny wondered if she was scheming to discover the loss of her life savings. Finally she found a tube of hand cream, unscrewed the cap, and squeezed some onto her hands.

"Why didn't you just call me at the magazine?" he said. "I would have gladly mailed the bag back to you. You could have saved the price of airfare and still insulted me."

"I'm here about something else," she said, rubbing the excess cream up her arms. "I have a proposition for you. A quid pro quo."

"I should have told you earlier, Lainie, but next month is ring time for me. The lovely Margaret Mary Houlihan, her father is a big Irish cop."

"This is business, faggot. I have a business proposition for you. I have information that you can use in your story on Gillian, but you also have to help me out."

She brushed past him, going into the kitchen. "You at least have coffee?" she said, opening cabinets. "I'm having coffee."

"I recommend the decaf."

Lainie found the coffee can and washed out the pot. She kept looking around the apartment as the coffee dripped.

"This apartment is all wrong," she said. "You have no flow. You got all your shit stacked up by the window. You need proper flow. Read a book on feng shui, why don't you."

Danny's Groucho persona whispered a crack about Chinese food, but he filed it away. Maybe he was maturing.

"Good coffee," Danny said as he followed Lainie back into the living room, where she plopped down on the couch.

"Coffee always tastes better when someone else makes it."

Danny sat across from her on the brown corduroy lounger that had once sat in his uncle's computer room. Lainie removed her relatively conservative yellow jacket and folded it carefully. Under it she wore a white tube top, a testimony to the miracle of man-made fabrics.

"I'm going to give you a taste of what I know," she said. "Just a taste. Then I want a commitment from you."

"I can listen."

"I have this girlfriend, very close. We did a lot of shit together in our lives. You don't even want to know about it. In and out of drug programs, some voluntary, some not. The thing is, this friend of mine is now in Silverado, which is the Betty Ford of Scottsdale. For the past two years she's been in the same therapy group with Lynnette Stone. Is that interesting to you?"

"Depends on what she said."

"My information is money. You'll be all over it."

Danny put his coffee on the floor. He decided he needed to buy a coffee table and brush his teeth.

"What do you want from me?" he said.

"An easy one. I have a group coming through New York next month. The same group I was with in Denver, Lunatic Nation. The next Nirvana. They have three upcoming dates in New York. Their biggest gigs so far. I want an article on them in your magazine, plus a review by your music critic."

"Maybe I can manage one or the other. Maybe."

"I need both."

"What if the critic pans them?"

"Won't happen. If your critic happens to lack vision, then so what. The main point is I got them coverage. Besides, no such thing as bad ink."

"I'll do the best I can."

"I need a firm commitment. You're going to love my information."

"Like what am I supposed to love?"

"I know why Evan Stone acted crazy to you at the cemetery that day."

"You know about that?" Danny said. He had no idea if he could arrange coverage of the new Nirvana, but he couldn't pass this up. "Okay, you got a deal. Now show me what I bought."

"I get both? Article and review."

"Twin forty-fours."

Lainie removed her alligator-tipped pumps and sat up on the couch cross-legged. Her legs were tan and smooth, but an angry array of tiny Band-Aids clung to her toes, like a swarm of flesh-toned worms.

"Lynette Stone has been in therapy half her life," Lainie said, massaging her feet. "She's a talker, too; Evan mustn't let her say shit at home. Lynnette's story is that she found out she was manic-depressive in her late thirties, ten years after the problem raised its ugly head. Ten miserable years thinking she was nuts, according to her. Well, now she thinks that maybe that's what happened to Gillian. She was the exact same age as Lynnette when the strangeness hit her."

"So she believes Gillian committed suicide."

"Of course, what else? Lynnette blames it on a bipolar disorder."

"What does Evan say?"

"I don't think he knows shit. He blames the sister. But Lynnette says she noticed that Gillian was starting to have problems long before the sister got there. She says she begged Gillian to get some help, but she was too worried about her career. Lynnette says when she was Gillian's age she did street drugs to cope. Now she feels guilty because she thinks Gillian was doing the same thing, and she wasn't strong enough to help her."

"Evan Stone never knew?"

"Men are dense when it comes to noticing things. In case you haven't noticed."

"Okay, why did he punch me when I spoke to him at the cemetery?"

"I wish I'd've been there to see that. I would've kicked you right square in the balls."

"I fully believe that."

Lainie pulled herself upright and leaned forward. Unlike most women who wore clothes too tight, she seemed unbothered by material constricting her flesh. Most women unconsciously adjusted and yanked at such attire. Not twin forty-fours.

"Evan Stone thought you were the sister's boyfriend," she said.

"Faye Boudreau's boyfriend?"

"That's the name, Faye. I couldn't remember. Lynnette hardly ever says her name, calls her 'my other daughter.' She says that Faye wanted a ton of money from them. Money to go away forever. A quarter of a mil. Evan said no way. He offered a small trust fund. Said he'd put some money in it every year."

"They go through with it?"

"Faye wanted no part of that deal. One big cash payment and good-bye was what she wanted. Evan said he didn't have that kind of cash, so they made some other deal, I'm not sure of the exact amount. Faye said she'd send her boyfriend out to collect the money. Evan said he'd call when he had the cash together, but he never got the chance. This was right before Gillian died."

"He thought I was there to collect the money."

"He heard that New York accent and freaked out. Then he decided, Screw her, meaning Faye, I ain't giving her shit. After the funeral he called and told her. They haven't heard from Faye since."

Danny thought of Faye's bruised face. The last thing she'd told him was not to come to see her again. She was moving away.

"What's the boyfriend's name?"

"Not a clue," Lainie said, yawning. "I don't think the Stones even know it. He's from Florida, but he's living in New York, too."

"The Bronx?"

"I have to do everything? New York is all I know."

Danny knew he had to call his uncle. He'd put off telling him about Faye. Her late-night excursion in a Bronx gypsy cab, her battered face. He hoped it wasn't too late.

Lainie stood up and stretched. "Coffee makes me sleepy," she said, and began to unzip her skirt. "I'm going to crash right here for an hour, if it's okay. You have an extra pair of pajamas so I don't wrinkle this suit?"

"There are some T-shirts in the top drawer."

"You don't mind, right. I don't want a problem if your new

fiancée, Mary Beth McGillycuddy, drops by. Is that her name?"

"Something like that."

"I knew that was bullshit."

34

In the early morning hours of Tuesday, Anthony Ryan strolled past the Times Building and turned west on Forty-fourth. He wore a telephone installer's nylon windbreaker, light blue with a swath of yellow and white down the front. The jacket had been acquired by the Organized Crime Intelligence Unit through a connection in the phone company. The NYPD's bug and wiretap teams lived in Ma Bell apparel. But the disguises of legitimacy worn by undercover cops were an unspoken matter, since no group was flattered when imitated by the law.

On Eighth Avenue he stopped outside a botanica and checked his notes in front of a window full of saints and angels. He'd pulled old bookmaking files, looking for locations of past wiretaps. He wanted to know the basements where the telephone boxes were located.

Besides the windbreaker, Ryan wore work boots and an old pair of chinos, and he carried a nylon gym bag with a few tools. He'd spent the entire morning looking for a telephone box that held a specific set of screws and wires: the bridging points to the phone in Trey Winters's office. He wanted to hear any conversation between Winters and Buster Scorza. At least get the specifics on their meeting. He knew it was to-morrow morning; he didn't know the exact time or location.

Ryan's search began on the outskirts of the area, picking buildings a safe distance away from Winters's office. He knew that the hardware that connected a particular telephone to the main system appeared in more than one location. But trying to find it without the assistance of the phone company was like trying to find two needles in the crumbling haystack that was the infrastructure of this aging city. Calling the phone company was out of the question. He closed his notebook and walked away from the botanica and the eyes of a 3-D plastic Jesus.

Each telephone box he looked at contained its own history: ancient wiring weaved among space age filament, advanced technology layered over spit-and-a-prayer ingenuity. On Eighth just north of Forty-sixth, Ryan found an unlocked box in a dirt-floored basement trimmed in rat poison. He'd flashed phony ID to a Pakistani T-shirt dealer, announced himself as a troubleshooter, and descended a set of concrete steps no wider than a hand span.

Sitting on a wire milk crate, he faced the wall, opened the box, and again began the laborious process. The huge metal box was jammed with the usual spaghetti-pot labyrinth of col-ored wiring. He took a telephone handset with alligator clips from his gym bag. He began working down the rows of screws, looking for the line to Trey Winters's office.

What he was doing made him sick to his stomach. His en-tire career had been built on doing the right thing. Now here he was, setting up an illegal wiretap. If they caught him, he could always retire. He'd waive his vacation and terminal leave and he'd be out tomorrow, before anyone could figure out ex-actly what he'd done. Saving his pension mattered most, an in-come for Leigh; he'd worry about jail time later.

Ryan's back was getting stiff. He'd spent most of the morning poking through rusty telephone boxes in ancient basements. This one was the worst. He was almost finished when he hit the jackpot.

Either the excitement or the smell of mothballs made his eyes water. He needed to double-check. He pulled a second headset from his gym bag and borrowed a dial tone. He waited for someone to answer; then the unmistakable voice of Trey Winters's secretary, a rasping voice Joe Gregory said was better suited to the reception desk of *Ring* magazine. Ryan didn't say a word; he hung up.

He built a nest in the corner by stacking T-shirt boxes in an el shape, forming a cardboard cave against the wall. He spread a large mover's quilt over the floor and used smaller boxes to sit on. He squeezed in and made himself comfortable in the tight space, his feet resting on a box with the official logo of the NFL. He turned off the headset. He knew he'd be able to feel the vibrations of the next ring. The last thing he did was remove the voice-piece from the headset, so they couldn't hear him breathing.

Anthony Ryan's instincts assured him that the deal between Scorza and Winters was wrong. It had nothing to do with Scorza's union connections, but everything to do with Gillian Stone. Ryan didn't know exactly how or when the knockout drops were administered to Gillian. But someone knew. If not Winters, surely Buster Scorza knew exactly what Lorazepam was.

It occurred to Ryan that the basement nook he'd built was like a kid's rainy-day fort. The kind Rip and Danny used to construct of blankets and sofa cushions. The happiest days of his life were those days of bad snowstorms, when he'd take the day off work, the schools closed, kids all over the house, building forts and playhouses. The fireplace would be blazing, Leigh in the kitchen, the smell of vegetable soup and freshly baked bread. Mostly it was the comfort of knowing that everyone you loved was perfectly safe. Right under your wing.

The next phone call came ten minutes later. Winters's secretary put Syd from the William Morris Agency straight through. Something about percentages. Ryan yanked the alligator clips, and the voices went silent. He couldn't do it. He thought about Leigh, and Margaret, and Katie. His dad. He had other forts to build, a woman to get old with. A woman that he would hurt so badly.

It would be more work, but he could do it the right way. After all, he knew Scorza wouldn't let Winters talk business on the telephone. Darcy Winters said the meeting was tomorrow morning. All Ryan had to do was sit on Winters for the morning. He could do a morning. He could do two days . . . standing on his head. But he'd watch him today, just in case of a change in plans. He knew Winters was in the office at this moment. He scrambled to his feet.

For the rest of the day Ryan stood vigil outside Trey Winters's office in the Theater Guild Building. At lunchtime he followed him to Barrymore's, waiting until Winters stepped down into the restaurant. Ryan checked for Buster Scorza, but Winters dined alone. So did Ryan. He ate a slice of pizza in the outer lobby of the Plymouth Theatre, watching Barrymore's front door. Behind him stood a constant line of people at the box office, all buying tickets for *Jekyll & Hyde*.

Winters ate quickly, then returned to his office, where he stayed until after five.

At rush hour a lone pigeon squatted on the bronze head of George M. Cohan as Winters walked north on Broadway, a street that was once an Iroquois war path. Ryan stalked him from the other side of the street, slightly behind. Like most New Yorkers, Winters walked extremely fast. His lanky stride chewed up the blocks.

Winters was an easy tail. Tailored clothes hanging on a six-foot-five frame, chiseled features, and a hundred-dollar haircut. Ryan could tell he liked the minor buzz he left in his wake; he'd even turn a little to give his deluded fans a generous glance at his fast-moving profile. Tourists stared at him, confident it must be "somebody."

A red double-decker bus passed between them, the open upper deck packed with tourists. It obscured Ryan's sightline, but Winters could have been wearing feathers, he was that easy to spot. Winters passed the Broadway Theatre, *Miss Saigon* in its sixth year. The line at the Ed Sullivan Theater stretched around the corner, everyone vying for the standby tickets for the taping of that evening's *Late Night with David Letterman*. Letterman groupies congregated underneath the yellow-and-blue marquee, looking up continually to check the street cams.

Ryan followed him past the theme restaurants on Fifty-seventh Street, all the way to Park Avenue, then ten blocks north. Winters was too self-involved to notice a guy in a Ma Bell windbreaker strolling behind him for twenty-five blocks. When pedestrian traffic dwindled Ryan broke off the tail and walked over to Lexington Avenue. He knew Winters was going home. No sense pushing his luck, getting made by an actor. He'd never live that down. Besides, he had more questions for Faye Boudreau.

Ryan walked down the subway steps, searching his pockets for a token. He never used his shield in situations like this. On the platform, a slender black man wearing dreadlocks stood against a pillar, playing "Manhattan Nocturne" on a dented silver trumpet.

35

Danny Eumont knew that every Tuesday night Joe Gregory had dinner in Jimmy Neary's on East Fifty-seventh Street. The restaurant was crowded when he walked in, not an empty seat anywhere. He spotted Gregory in a corner booth in the dining room.

"Where the hell's your uncle?" Gregory said.

"That was my question."

"I covered for him all day," Gregory whispered. "He calls me this morning, tells me some bullshit story about having errands to run. Last I heard."

"Did you call Aunt Leigh?"

"Are you freakin' nuts?" Gregory said.

Danny shut his mouth when the waitress approached. He'd learned the rhythm of cop-speak. Certain subjects for certain ears, and when any possibility existed that your voice could be overheard . . . shut up. His uncle said that Joe Gregory hadn't spoken in an elevator in twenty years.

Danny ordered a Tullamore Dew and water. He reminded

himself to drink slowly because the bartenders in Neary's rationed the H$_2$O as if it had dripped from the sacred shrine at Knock in County Mayo.

"Then where is he?" Danny said when the waitress left.

"Either working Trey Winters, or he's with the sister. She's putting an evil spell on him."

"I tried to call her all day, no answer."

"You have her number? Give me her number."

Gregory wrote in his notebook while Danny laid out the story. How he'd spotted a battered Faye Boudreau at three-thirty in the morning getting out of a gypsy cab. Danny stopped talking briefly when his drink arrived. Then he filled Gregory in on Lainie Mossberg's tales from the desert about Gillian's possible manic depression, Faye's quarter-million-dollar shakedown, and the boyfriend up from Florida.

"That's why Evan Stone took a swing at me," Danny said. "He thought I was the boyfriend out there to collect."

Joe Gregory sat in a booth with one leg outside, as if ready to pounce at the flash of a muzzle. The handle of a delicate teacup was pinched between his ironworker's fingers. He asked Danny to tell him everything he knew about Faye. Danny complied but never mentioned anything about the sex.

"I'm going to Florida first thing in the morning," Danny said. "I made an appointment with the private detective the Stones hired to find Faye. Maybe I can find something on the boyfriend."

"Last week Arizona, this week Florida, *Manhattan* magazine must be duking out some major expense money."

"This trip comes out of my pocket," Danny said.

"Call me if you get something hot."

"I can use something hot right now," Danny said. "Those lamb chops look good."

"They are. But you don't have time."

Neary's clientele was older and polished. The silver-haired class of Wall Street, City Hall, and the archdiocese were there for the nourishment and the nexus. And as always, where power congregated in the city of New York, the welcome mat rolled out for a few good cops.

"You don't think he's with Faye, do you?" Danny said.

"Naw, he thinks she's a victim. My money says he's on Winters; he's been dying to make a case against him."

"Then where's Faye?"

"Howling at the moon, who knows? She gives me the screaming meemies, that broad."

A few detectives were at the bar, conversing with the lawyers and the trust funders. Gregory called them "old school cops," a reference to how they carried themselves and their worldly secrets. Old school cops considered themselves gentlemen, and in places like Neary's they acted as kindly consiglieres to the citizenry. In here they would never show the drink or mention the ugliness.

"You got a medallion number on the cab?" Gregory said.

"It was a gypsy. Tremont Taxi, on the door."

Gregory grabbed his notebook and stood. "What time does your flight leave?"

"Six oh-five A.M. But I'll be back tomorrow night."

"Finish your drink," he said. "I'm going to make a few phone calls. Then we're going for a ride."

36

Victor's thighs pressed against the towel he'd draped over the sink. The tiny bathroom was poorly lit and not half the size of his own in the Bronx. He preferred a lighted mirror, preferably one with 5X magnification. This one was cheap, like everything else in the apartment. The mercury that silvered the back was peeling badly. Black images dulled and deadened his reflection.

His face needed care. He'd spent too much time on the city streets, his skin absorbing soot and car exhaust. He searched the medicine cabinet for a little oil or cream. One tube was all he found. The label listed aloe as the first ingredient, but the smell was lilac. Too feminine for him, but better than nothing. With a circular motion he massaged cream into his cheeks and the tiny lines around his eyes.

Soon there would be time to relax and stroll on the sunny beaches. In Mexico he could buy pure aloe from street vendors for a fraction of the price of this designer cream. His face would be tan and healthy as he walked among the blond *turistas* from Seattle and Minneapolis who came into his restaurant.

He planned to invest in a nice restaurant. Not too high end, but classy. One that didn't serve the Sonoran food of northern Mexico, with its heavy sauces, all tortillas, tacos, and lard, the kind of cooking most Americans think is the sum of Mexican food. Cheap and heavy. He'd specialize in the fresh vegetables and seafood. Take advantage of the fishing boats that returned daily with the day's catch. Octopus would be the house specialty.

He was only days away from his dream. Today had gone beautifully, his plan delivered. At nine-thirty A.M. Victor had handed an envelope containing instructions to Trey Winters. He'd met Winters just as he was entering his office in the Theater Guild Building. His hat pulled low over his face, Victor had shoved the envelope into Winters's hands and walked quickly away. It was even easier than the first envelope, in front of the El Bravado restaurant. This time Winters had clutched the note to his chest, as if expecting it.

Victor heard a key in the lock and instinctively grabbed the straight razor. He flattened himself against the wall.

"You shouldn't be here, Victor," Faye said, quickly locking the door behind her. She was dressed in black jeans and a blue blouse that he knew Gillian had bought for her. French blue, she'd called it. She wore dark glasses, but they didn't hide the bruise. The eye was less swollen, less purple, than yesterday.

"You expecting your policeman?" he said.

"My face like this? I hope nobody ever sees me."

"It was your own fault."

She took a six-pack of Coronas from a paper bag and put them in the refrigerator.

"I came to get you," he said.

"I already told you I'm not going. What is that cooking?"

Red sauce was cooking on the stove. A bag of corn tortillas sat between the burners, steam fogging the inside of the bag.

"I know it won't be as good as Mama's," he said. "But I try."

"I'm not hungry."

"The way you eat. It's a wonder you're not sick."

"I am sick," she said. "Sick in the head."

"Mama's cooking will fix you."

"Mama's food won't help what's wrong with me, Victor."

Faye saw her suitcase opened on the bed. Victor had found it in the closet, and he'd packed some of her clothes and others he'd left folded next to it.

"Remember how she fixes the house with flowers, Faye? Bouquets in every room. Her eyesight is going bad, now. She has to feel her way along the street to get to mass. Along the walls and the parked cars. But every morning she goes."

"I miss her, too, Victor," she said.

"Come with me. We'll stay in the Bronx. One night. To-morrow we'll drive to see Mama."

"I'm not going to Mexico with you."

"Stop being stubborn. You have no life here. You belong with us, your family."

"Gillian was my family."

She opened a beer and put on the television. An old movie with Bogart and Bacall. She pushed the suitcase aside and sat on the open sofa bed. Victor picked up the clicker and changed it to the all-Spanish station.

"We better get used to the language," he said.

"How many times do I have to say it, Victor?"

"Faye, I'm sorry for what happened to Gillian. Sorry with all my heart. But it didn't have to happen. All she had to do was tell him she didn't know how it was missing. Someone could have stolen it. A burglar. Thieves steal every day in this city."

"But you stole it, and I have to live with that."

The phone rang, and Faye ignored it. It kept ringing, and Victor looked at the phone, then back at her.

"Answer your telephone," he said.

"I don't answer the telephone anymore."

"Answer it!" he yelled. "Or they will come over here to find out why."

Faye picked up the phone with a soft "Hello." She listened, then said no several times before hanging up. She told Victor it was a detective wanting to know if Detective Ryan had stopped by.

Victor knew where Ryan was.

After delivering the message to Winters, Victor had stayed around and watched the Theater Guild Building for signs of police activity. But all he saw was Detective Ryan following Trey Winters to lunch. He suspected only Trey Winters, saw nothing else. Ryan would be Victor's Popeye Doyle.

"You should go now," she said.

"We haven't eaten."

"I'm not hungry, I told you."

He snatched the beer out of her hands and poured it down the sink. She went to the refrigerator for another, and he grabbed her and held her by the wrists.

"It was fine when I fixed your police friend in Miami," he said.

"I never asked you to kill him."

"He was beating you, Faye."

"So you beat me now, instead."

"You make me do that, *querida*. With your disrespectful mouth. These people did nothing for you. Your own birth mother did nothing. That's not family. Your own sister didn't help you."

"Gillian loved me."

"You were a novelty to her; she would have forgotten."

Faye slapped him in the face.

Victor hit her back, quick and hard with his open hand. Faye fell backward and slammed into the stove. She slid to the kitchen floor, and red sauce spilled down the white porcelain stove and onto her French blue blouse. Victor knelt down. He touched her cheek with his fingers.

37

Gregory came off the Cross Bronx and made the left on Webster Avenue. Skeletons of Chevys and Fords sat helter-skelter along the sides of the sad streets, as if abandoned in haste by the conscripts of a retreating army.

"We should have stopped at Faye's apartment," Danny said.

"I called her from Neary's."

"She was home?"

"Yeah, and she said Ryan wasn't there."

"And you believed her."

"If your uncle was there, he wouldn't let her tell me he wasn't. Besides, he'd never miss a trip to the Bronx. My guess is he's going to put Trey Winters to bed, then we'll hear from him."

Anthony Ryan loved the Bronx. He loved talking about how much the South Bronx had improved in the past few years. A new dawn was rising over Fort Apache, he said. Every other block showed evidence of new construction. But to Danny the predominant look was still the bombed-out landscape of a battle lost. Rubble-strewn lots seeded with shards of shattered brick; abandoned five-story walk-ups shuttered blind with tin; the twin war orphans of poverty and apathy playing on cracked sidewalks.

"Tremont Taxi, right?" Gregory said.

"That's what it said on the side of the cab."

"There used to be an eye and ear clinic over here on Tremont Avenue, right off Webster. I used to drive a cop there once a week for treatment. This was in the late sixties, maybe early seventies. Treatments lasted three hours sometimes. Some psycho woman tossed lye in his face, partially blinded him. Lye used to be a big thing. Big danger to cops. This woman nailed five or six cops at once. Coming up the stairs, some Harlem tenement. He was one of them. You don't hear so much about lye anymore."

When the Bronx was all one big farm, they named this section Tremont for its three hills: Mount Hope, Mount Eden, and Fairmont. The gypsy cabs congregated atop Mount Hope, outside a storefront on Tremont Avenue near the Grand Concourse.

"He'll call you, right?" Danny said. "If he needs you."

"He knows my beeper number by heart."

Joe Gregory said the reason the city allowed the gypsy cabs to operate was that they'd go into areas like this. Gregory parked in front of Tremont Taxi, behind a primered Plymouth Aries with a plastic taxi sign on the side door.

The front window of the taxi office had once been the showcase of a bakery or butcher shop, some place with wares to display. Inside, a bitter smell, coming from the dark green leaves steaming on the hot plate. A two-way radio crackled.

The dispatcher was a heavyset black man in a wheelchair with "Property of Bronx-Lebanon Hospital" stenciled on the back. He sat beside a rickety card table, the shiny pages of a skin magazine open before him, all flesh and hair.

Gregory identified himself and told him that he needed to speak to someone who worked late last Sunday night. Someone with knowledge of a fare dropped off at Third Avenue and Sixty-fourth in Manhattan. The dispatcher gave him the obligatory sneer, then spoke into the radio.

"That's two one one five Bathgate," the dispatcher said, his mouth against the mike. "Two one one five."

A smattering of porn mags spilled over a greasy vinyl sofa against the wall. Coke cans jammed with cigarette butts. A poster of Pam Grier as Foxy Brown was taped to the wall above the sofa. The radio crackled again, the voice unintelligible.

"Return to base," the dispatcher said.

Then he said to Gregory, "Sorry, I can't help you."

Gregory walked behind the desk and put both hands on the back of the man's wheelchair. He yanked it quickly and powerfully, as if he were going to dump the dispatcher onto the floor. He leaned down and whispered something to him.

"Miguel is the dude you want," the dispatcher said. "He probably took that run. Probably coming in at midnight."

"Two probablys," Gregory said.

"Sometimes he shows, sometimes he don't."

"What's his phone number?" Gregory said.

"You gotta be joking."

"Maybe it's in these files," Gregory said. He opened the single file cabinet against the wall and took out a bottle of Gilbey's gin. He opened the second drawer and threw movie cassette tapes onto the vinyl couch.

"You don't need to screw up my files," the dispatcher said. "I can't speak for last Sunday, but Sixty-fourth and Third is a regular. . . . We pick her up around the corner, Two Ten Echo Place. Three, four in the morning, maybe once a week. Maybe less, I don't keep no statistics."

"What apartment at Two Ten Echo?" Gregory said.

"She calls, we pick her up out front of the building."

"Our little talk won't get back to her," Gregory said, picking up a stack of mail on the counter.

"I'm not exactly planning to sweet-talk the bitch, myself."

Gregory gave him the zipped-lip sign. "How did that happen?" he asked, pointing in the general direction of the dispatcher's lower body.

" 'Nam," he said.

"Sorry, man," Gregory said quietly. "Sorry I hassled you."

He took a business card from his pocket and told the dispatcher to call him if he needed anything. He apologized twice more before they got out the door.

They had no trouble finding 210 Echo Place, a large private house carved into several apartments. Three metal garbage cans sat out front, with the number *210* painted vertically in black. A thick chain looped through the lids. Seven steps led up to a stone stoop. Gregory kept driving past the building.

"We passed it," Danny said. "Two Ten is back there."

"I know. That was just a look."

He went around the block and came through more slowly the next time.

"What are we doing now?" Danny said.

"Looking for your uncle."

"Why would he be here?"

"Because he's capable of getting Faye to admit she had a boyfriend up here. And he's crazy enough to look for the guy himself. That's why I went through the block. To check for his car."

"I thought you said he wasn't at Faye's?"

"Never assume, Daniel."

Gregory parked at a hydrant three houses away. He turned off the lights, let the car idle.

"What we got here is tricky," Gregory said. "The trick is to find out exactly who lives here without raising anybody up."

"How do you do that?"

"Several ways. Con Ed billing tells us who's paying the electric, but maybe this place isn't broken down to individual meters. The phone company is a source, but maybe our subject doesn't have a phone. My personal favorite is the mailman. The mailman knows it all."

"It's almost midnight," Danny said. "Good chance the mailman's been here already."

"That's the conundrum."

A radio car from the precinct cruised by slowly. The heavily muscled cop driving had his bicep propped up on the door ledge. He threw a glare to let them know they were trespassing on his turf. And he knew who they were. Danny wondered why it was so important for some cops to establish fear. The weight lifter's glare suggested he was one small provocation away from steroid rage.

"They think we're Internal Affairs," Gregory said.

Danny knew that two white guys from different generations wearing suits would be perceived as being from Internal Affairs. Cop reasoning went as follows: This neighborhood, this hour, who else could they be?

"Years ago," Gregory said. "Everybody in the Detective Bureau used to wear fedoras. The same fedora. Cops would know we were from the bureau because of the hat."

"I left mine home," Danny said.

"When you first got made detective they sent you down to Izzy's on Delancey Street. You walked in, told Izzy you just got made, he sold you the right hat. We all had the exact same hat. Ribbon band. Izzy always threw in the pearl pin. I still got mine home."

"Leave it to me in your will," Danny said.

Gregory made a note on a Neary's cocktail napkin with an old golf pencil he found on the dash.

"I wish your uncle was here," Gregory said. "He knows the Bronx a lot better than I do."

"What's going on with him, Joe?"

Gregory looked up at the windows of 210 Echo Place. For a guy who'd been a cop over thirty years, he seemed unsure of what to say next. He was not comfortable as the final word.

"Your uncle is a guy who dwells on his regrets, Danny. He

thinks he's responsible for everything and everybody, including Gillian Stone. When something goes wrong he blames himself. Always did. Since Rip died he's been eating himself alive with regrets. I told him, as my old man always said, it's a late day for regrets."

"I think Eugene O'Neill said that."

"He probably heard it from my old man."

The same radio car passed them again. This time the recorder, a young black woman, checked out their license plate number. Danny thought about how his own regrets had been eating at him this past week. He knew he hadn't listened closely to Gillian. He thought about his uncle, and how his granddaughter, Katie, would sit on his lap, look up at him. He remembered watching his uncle's face, the absolute concentration on every word she said; bombs could go off and he wouldn't know anything but her. He decided he'd give Abigail Klass another call. He'd learn to listen. Really pay attention.

"How about you?" Danny said. "You have any regrets?"

"Regrets?" Gregory said. "I've got a few. But then again too few to mention."

"That's the first Sinatra you've done tonight."

"I must be slipping," he said.

A male voice came over the Buick's police radio. Gregory had switched bands to pick up local precinct calls. "Rat Squad on Echo Place," the voice said. "Rats on Echo."

"Where?" said another voice.

"Two Ten," the first voice answered.

Gregory ignored the veiled threats on the radio, as if accepting the paranoia of late-shift ghetto cops. Danny preferred not to be the target of mistaken identity.

"Take a walk up and check the names on the mailbox," Gregory said. "At least we'll get something out of the trip."

"Maybe there are no names on the mailbox."

"Maybe if the queen had balls, she'd be the king," Gregory said. "Go up and check the names. It's worth a shot. Take two minutes."

"What do I do with them when I get them?"

"You write them down, take them to Florida, and ask the people down there if any of them ring a bell."

He handed him the golf pencil and another Neary's napkin.

"What do I say if I get caught?" Danny said.

"Say you're looking for Nilda Rosario. About five two, dark hair. A little mole on her neck, just below her left ear. Big ass."

"You just make that up?"

"Naw, she's a broad I used to know. She lived in that apartment building on the corner. I used to visit her for those three hours while the lye cop was getting treatment."

"Thirty years ago and you think she still might be around?"

"It's worth a shot," he said.

Danny walked up the stairs and opened the vestibule door. The smell of disinfectant was strong enough to bring tears to his eyes. In the ground-floor window a TV flashed blue behind the curtains. The light was dim, but he could see names written on the mailbox. Above each mailbox, on a strip of fresh adhesive tape, appeared a name. Five names: four Spanish, one Russian.

38

After he stopped following Trey Winters, Ryan caught the number six train downtown. He switched to the westbound E at Fifty-first. At the Mid-Town North Precinct, he picked up his Olds, stuffed his bright windbreaker into his gym bag, and put it all back in the trunk. He donned a black sweatshirt from his emergency clothes bag, then drove back to Faye Boudreau's and knocked on the door.

He could hear Faye's TV from outside her apartment door. The sound of rapid-fire Spanish and a loud laugh track like Telemundo. He knocked again, harder this time, and the sound of the TV stopped.

"Just a minute," Faye said.

Ryan was ready to knock again when he heard footsteps coming toward the door. Locks unsnapped.

"I didn't expect you," Faye said.

"I just have a few questions."

"You can't stay long; I'm leaving in a few minutes."

Faye's face was badly bruised, her body language too tight,

her voice too shrill. Something was very wrong with Faye Boudreau. He felt the prickly hairs on the back of his neck. Ryan decided he'd ask her what happened but wouldn't push it. He knew she'd lie, and he didn't want her to go off on a tangent.

"What happened to your face?" he said.

"Fell down the stairs. Going to the laundry room."

She wore black jeans that looked new, and sandals with leather thongs braiding up her leg. The fact that Faye had been barefoot every other time he'd seen her made Ryan think she truly was leaving. But over the black jeans was an old, ripped Florida Marlins T-shirt.

"I heard the TV from out in the hall," he said. "I didn't know you could speak Spanish."

"You grow up where I grew up, you learn to speak Spanish damn quick."

"*Pronto.*"

"*Sí,*" she said.

The bed was made. On it, a half-packed suitcase. It struck Ryan that he never considered she had a life outside this apartment. A life outside her grief. The curtain blew away from the partly open window. First time he'd seen that.

"Where are you going?" he said.

"Florida. Taking the bus."

"When?"

"Right now."

"Just like that?"

"Just like that," she said.

He followed her into the kitchen. He felt the stove burners and found one still warm.

"Did you ever know Gillian to take a drug called Lorazepam?"

"I told you she didn't take drugs."

"Blood tests proved she had Lorazepam in her system, Faye. A lot of it."

"I don't know what that is."

In the sink, a single pot soaked in red water. Except for slicing limes for beer, that was the first domestic act he knew her to perform.

"Let's talk about your last conversation with Gillian," he said. "I want you to think about each word."

"You always this thickheaded?"

"Gillian told you she was wearing the white costume, didn't she?"

"She said she tried it on."

"Do you know what she had around her neck that night?"

Faye fiddled with silverware and dishes, drying things that already appeared to be dry. Taking them from the dish rack and putting them into various cabinets. The stove and counters were clean, wet swipe marks on both.

"Gillian came to me today," she said.

"Faye, don't."

"Please, don't think I'm crazy. Please, please, please. Just listen to me."

She went into her suitcase and took out a plain white envelope. She took out a feather and held it between her fingers. A small white feather.

"Outside on the street," she said. "I was going to the store, and a dove came above my head. I heard it and looked up. It just stayed there, above my head. Fluttering its wings. Making sounds. Coo, coo. Right above my head. Just staying there. Then this feather fell."

Ryan could hear street sounds from the street, high heels clicking on concrete. A gust of wind sent the venetian blinds swaying, clacking against the window frame.

"I thought you would understand," she said. "If anybody, I thought you would."

Faye searched the kitchen for something else to do. She hadn't made eye contact again. She was beginning to cry.

"I do understand," he said, wrapping his arms around her.

Ryan told her about a phone call just days after his son died. It was a very young boy. He couldn't understand what the child was saying. He kept asking the boy to repeat the words. The boy made the same sounds over and over. Maybe infant gibberish, maybe a foreign language. Over and over. Ryan became frantic, begging the boy to try again. Make me understand, he'd said. He'd begged. It went on and on, until he couldn't handle it any longer. He believed the voice was Rip telling him that he was fine.

"I believe it was Gillian above you," he said. "Telling you not to worry about her."

Faye tried to push him away, but he held her tightly. Then she relaxed in his arms, breathing deeply and exhaling, as if letting all the air out of her.

"I did a bad thing," Faye said.

"Probably not as bad as you think."

"I knew Gillian was going to die."

"Did she tell you that?"

"No. But I knew. I know what she had around her neck. White rosary beads."

Ryan had never said anything about rosary beads. Gillian had to have told her.

"I gave them to her as a gift," she said. "She told me she planned to wear my rosary beads when she played Maria. Then she jumped off the terrace."

"She didn't jump," Ryan said. "She was thrown off the terrace. Whoever gave her that drug threw her off."

Faye looked up at him, startled. At first Ryan thought another gust of wind had caught the venetian blind behind him. He heard the clatter, then it slammed back against the window frame as Victor bounded across the bed, two quick steps, and grabbed Ryan from behind.

"No, Victor!" Faye screamed.

Victor's arm wrapped around Ryan's neck. They banged against the wall, against the refrigerator, glass falling inside. The man was powerful; Ryan couldn't budge his arm. He reached back for his gun, but it was trapped against the big man's body. Victor squeezed tighter. Ryan stretched his head forward, his chin digging into the huge forearm, then he snapped his head back as hard as he could. He heard the crunch of nose cartilage. At the same time he raised his leg and slammed his heel into the top of Victor's foot. He pivoted hard against the open hand.

The big man staggered back against the wall, holding Ryan's gun. He licked at the blood that ran down from his shattered nose. The cop's eyes recorded the pedigree: Hispanic, about thirty years, six feet, one eighty, thick black hair. He had an athlete's build, and his black eyes were fixed on Ryan.

"Don't do this," Ryan said. "I'm a police officer."

"Please, Victor," Faye said.

"Put the gun down, Victor," Ryan said, hearing the name. He inched forward, watching his eyes. Beads of sweat like drops of fine oil ran down from Victor's hairline. "We can work this out."

"Do as he says," Faye said. "We'll run, Victor. Don't hurt him. We'll go together. Fuck the money."

Victor waved the gun at him, pointing him back. Trying to lick the blood off his mouth.

"Trust me, Victor," Ryan said. "Let's stop this. Before something bad happens."

"Something bad has already happened," Victor said, then he blinked, the sweat in his eyes, and Ryan reacted.

He slapped the gun hand away and drove his elbow into Victor's throat. The gun fell to the floor as Victor let out a gurgling cry and surged forward, digging in with his powerful legs. Ryan fell backward. His head cracked off the corner of the metal bed frame.

Ryan could hear Faye yelling in Spanish as he groped for the gun. He was dazed and nauseated, and he could feel the swelling above his temple where he'd hit the bed frame. The swelling came quickly, like inflating a balloon. Swelling, until the skin could stretch no more and began to split. He saw the gun against the wall and struggled to his knees, reaching; but the big man got there first. Ryan got to his feet and lunged;

he wasn't going to die on the floor. He clutched a fistful of black hair and twisted, trying to lock Victor's gun arm against the wall.

Ryan saw Faye pick up the bat. The first blow hit both of them. She came down hard, with a big high swing. The full weight of the Bobby Bonilla model struck Ryan's hand and crushed it against Victor's head. The second blow caught only Victor. The gun fell to the floor. Ryan dropped and cradled it into his stomach. He heard the door slam.

39

Danny Eumont arrived in Tampa on Wednesday morning on the tail end of a tropical storm. He made two phone calls before he left the airport. The first to Joe Gregory, who reported that his uncle was still in the wind. Even Gregory sounded worried, not a good sign. The second call was to *Manhattan* magazine to commence begging the music editor to cover Lainie Mossberg's rock band.

Danny's head still buzzed from an excess of bon voyage drinks in Kennedy's on West Fifty-seventh. Gregory had bought the first drink, then called Ryan's beeper. Three calls and three drinks later, Ryan still hadn't answered the beep. One last time, Gregory promised. One and done. Anthony Ryan never called. One and done was bullshit.

With a dry mouth and the sun overhead, Danny drove the rented Toyota across Old Tampa Bay, the tempting blue water flat as glass. The rain stopped, and a hazy steam hovered over the roadway. Evan Stone had told him where he'd find Valentine Carlson, the private detective he'd hired to locate Faye

Boudreau. Danny called ahead, and the PI agreed to meet him.

Valentine Carlson, once a promising infielder in the Milwaukee Braves organization, retired from the Tampa PD into his own investigative firm. His "offices" were located in a rusting travel trailer on a forgotten corner off Route 175 outside Gulfport. The blue sign above the trailer read, "Honest Val's: Used Cars and Discreet Investigations." A dozen old cars sat in the sandy lot in front of the trailer. Not one of the grimy vehicles had rolled off its respective assembly line subsequent to the presidency of Jimmy Carter.

When Danny drove up, Carlson was stretched out in a hammock on his porch, reading the sports page. He wore a green Hawaiian shirt covered with toucans. The porch was a flatbed truck backed up to the trailer door.

"Welcome to Honest Val's," he said, extending his hand, as Danny came up the makeshift stairs to the wooden truck bed. "Finest auto showroom in the subtropics."

As if he'd sensed Danny's need, Honest Val Carlson moved to his ice chest with the grace of a shortstop going into the hole. He had a deepwater tan and a big smile and looked too young to be retired. Only the gray on top hinted that the engine might have a few more miles than it appeared from the body.

Danny accepted a seven-ounce Coronita and brushed ice chips onto the truck-bed floor. He sat across from his host on the backseat of a late fifties Chevy. Like his yard adornments, Honest Val's porch furniture had its origins in Detroit.

"How's the car business?" Danny said.

"See something you like? I can put you in the car of your dreams. Low credit, no credit, don't matter to me. Get you out of that rice burner, into a real machine."

"These cars drivable?"

"Probably not even pushable," Honest Val said. "About six months ago a guy stopped, looking to buy. He wanted to cannibalize that Fairlane for parts. I chased him."

"Business is so good you're chasing customers away."

"The last car sold here was in 1988, the year my dad died."

Carlson said his father was the original Honest Val. He'd inherited the nickname, the auto business, a huge Hawaiian shirt collection, and a love for life. The original Honest Val had taught him everything about life except how to hit a curveball.

"I worked here as a spinner when I was a kid, turning back odometers," Val said. "By the time I was fifteen I had standing arrangements with every major car dealer in the country. Made more money rolling back miles than I did in triple-A ball."

The beer tasted good, as a cold Mexican brew always did on a hot, hungover morning. The seven ounces went quickly, and Danny was tempted to reach for another. But he thought better of it.

"I came down here after the funeral," Val said, gesturing at the trailer behind him. "You could still smell his cigar. This place was a clubhouse more than anything else. Him and his buddies. They'd play cards, have a few beers, work on tout sheets. Laugh . . . Jesus, those guys would laugh. They'd all pile in that big red Caddy and head for the dog track. I couldn't let it go. So I retired and opened this dynamic PI business."

Danny made a call to Joe Gregory to see if Ryan had surfaced. He hadn't. They left in Honest Val's old pickup; he refused to ride in the rice burner. They drove south toward Sarasota on the Sunshine Skyway, the Gulf of Mexico vast on the right. Below Bradenton they picked up Route 70 and headed inland toward Lake Okeechobee and the Everglades. Honest Val began the story.

"Lynette gave birth to Faye in a Chevy Impala in the parking lot of the Pier House Hotel in Key West," Honest Val said. "The Impala had the keys in it, so she turned on the AC and gave birth. Security called the cops. Lynette and the baby went to the hospital for a couple of hours. Then she split with the baby. She walked back to the hotel parking lot. See, they never took the car keys from her. While the town was toasting the sunset, fifteen-year-old Lynette stole the same Impala and drove straight here with the baby."

"Why here?"

"Lynnette grew up in St. Pete. She knew the convent was back here."

"What convent?" Danny said. " 'Sisters of the Swamp'?"

Danny didn't see any signs of a convent as Honest Val made the left down a gravel road cut in the cattails and marsh grass. They drove about a mile past an "Alligator Crossing" sign. The Convent of the Blessed Sacrament was hidden in a grove of dormant orange trees, marked only by a rusting mailbox atop a wooden post.

"The only thing Lynnette Stone told me when she first called," Honest Val said, "was that she placed the baby on this doorstep. She rang the doorbell and ran. She waited in the stolen Impala until a nun came to the door. Then she floored it and never looked back."

The doorstep was a red brick patio under the shade of a *ramada,* the slats heavily braided with shiny green vines. Danny got out and took half a dozen pictures. Except for a wooden cross on the wall, the building was not overtly parochial. Just a simple Sun Belt stucco with a red tile roof.

Inside, it was cool and dark as a cathedral. They followed Sister Mary Celeste down a long hallway as she proudly filled them in on the order. Once strictly a cloister, Blessed Sacrament now served as a retirement home for the exploding population of aging nuns. Mostly they sewed altar cloths and vestments and baked for the archdiocese. Honest Val's sneakers squeaked on the hardwood floor.

They entered a round room with a high arching ceiling and three metal filing cabinets. It smelled of candle wax and abstinence. A long oak table sat in the center. On the ceiling was a mural depicting thirteen nuns of the order beheaded during the French Revolution. Sister Mary Celeste opened a folder and spread it out on the table.

"This was the information we showed Mr. Carlson when he was last here," she said softly. "It's all we have. Faith only stayed with us for a few hours. We had to call the police. We had no facilities to care for such a small child. The county took her. Social Services."

"I thought her name was Faye," Danny said.

The nun put her finger to her lips, the universal Catholic school warning to lower your voice. The first warning.

"I've heard she calls herself Faye now," the nun said, almost whispering. "But Faith is her birth name. The county asked Sister Mary Elizabeth to name her, and she picked Faith. It's the name on her birth and baptismal certificates. Sister Mary Elizabeth has gone on to her reward, but she kept in contact with Faith for many, many years. She thought a lot of the child."

"What about the name Boudreau?" Danny said.

"As you see in this entry," the nun said, "Faith was adopted by the Boudreaus at the age of three months. The Boudreaus were a circus family from Canada. Dancing bears. Sister Mary Elizabeth was worried about the baby, with the bears and all. We prayed for her, and hoped all would be well."

"It wasn't."

"Not because of the bears. Mrs. Boudreau died of breast cancer when Faith was five, just starting school. Her husband disappeared soon after. He left Faith with the neighbors and just vanished. They found zoos for the bears."

Danny was startled when he heard noise directly behind him. What he thought was a wall was really a black screen. He could make out the dark habits of the sisters as they rose from their knees, rosary beads clattering. They came around the screen and walked through the room, smiling and nodding politely. Nine ancient Marys with ebony crosses on their chests. *Give me nine Hail Marys,* Groucho whispered.

"Where did Faith wind up?" he said.

"In foster care, with the Nuñez family. A trapeze act. Lovely people."

Danny's head was foggy, but he remembered the list he'd copied off the mailbox at 210 Echo Place in the Bronx. He took out the Neary's cocktail napkin. Nuñez was not on the list. He used the convent phone to make one more call to Gregory's office. Gregory was out in the field, and he couldn't get a straight answer from anyone else. On the way out, past the kitchen, he could smell communion wafers baking.

40

Wednesday morning a tropical storm moving up the coast brought wind and rain to New York City. Anthony Ryan in his Ma Bell windbreaker and bloody chinos stood at the corner of Broadway and Forty-seventh under the overhang of the Morgan Stanley Building. Times Square was a sea of black umbrellas. Taxis pulled their foul-weather fade. Street people wore paper-bag hats, neatly cuffed. Some chose plastic as their headgear and tied the bag handles around their ears. Ryan's head was covered by his Yankee hat, which also hid a gash that should have been stitched. His hair, gelled and sticky with dried blood, curled around the bottom edge of the sweatband. His right hand was broken.

Across the street, Trey Winters remained in his office in the dingy Theater Guild Building. Ryan waited. He figured they'd meet in Scorza's office above the Orpheus Lounge or a neutral location like a restaurant. The odds were that he'd be walking west toward Eighth Avenue. He had set himself up so he'd be behind Winters. A tailman anticipated, bet with the odds. Fifty stories above Ryan's head the electronic ticker of stock market prices raced in three huge, Vegas-like bands of yellow lights.

Ryan leaned against the skyscraper's green metal squares and realized he was hungry. That had to be a good sign. He'd called Leigh, told her he was fine but tied up on a case. She hadn't even pretended to believe him. They'd lived together more than half their lives, and Leigh saw through his most artful stories. He wasn't sure how much she'd intuited, but he didn't tell her he'd been hurt. And he certainly didn't mention he'd spent the night in Faye Boudreau's bed.

He remembered Faye pulling him onto the bed. He remembered being sick, and Faye cleaning his face and bloody scalp with a damp cloth. In the morning she and her suitcase were gone, and he had more questions than ever.

Who was Victor? What money were they talking about? Was it possible they were working with Winters or Scorza? His head itched and ached. He reached his hand up to touch it as Trey Winters came out of the office door.

Quickly Ryan came off the green metal and began backing up. Winters fooled him, turning east, walking directly toward him. Ryan ducked around the corner into the driving rain. He looked for an alley or nook, but before he could find one Winters entered the huge office building Ryan had been leaning against.

Ryan needed to take only a few steps to the glass doors to watch Winters traverse the block-long lobby. The center of the lobby's marble floor was empty, roped off to limit damage from wet feet and dripping umbrellas. A path of carpet steered all traffic around to the left. Ryan lost sight of Winters. He wondered if he was heading for the elevators, but then he came around, back into view. He'd made a half circle. He was cutting through the building in the rain. When Winters got to the revolving doors on the other side, he stopped and looked behind him. Then he exited onto Forty-eighth Street.

Ryan ran directly across the center of the lobby as a security guard yelled, "Hey, yo! Hey, yo!" He reached the north door in time to see Winters cross the street and pull the same stunt again. This time he used the covered driveway entrance of the Crowne Plaza Hotel as his personal umbrella. The hotel underpass led all the way through the block. Ryan waited, listening to the *whoomf, whoomf* of the revolving door. Winters was using all the shortcuts to avoid rain on his expensive haircut, and he was looking back continuously.

Winters turned left on Forty-ninth. In the rain and against moving traffic, Ryan dashed across to the hotel underpass. He could smell the chlorine from the waterfall on the west wall, the water echoing as if in a cave. Slamming taxi doors reverberated like bombs going off in his head. He got to Forty-ninth in time to see Winters duck into St. Malachy's Church. The Actor's Chapel.

Ryan was breathing hard when he got to the church and looked through the glass doors. Reflected in the glass was the hot pink exterior of the Eugene O'Neill Theatre, across the street, behind him. He could read the graffiti painted on the building for the run of *Grease*. Rama lama dingitty ding da dong, wah, wah, wah. Backward it looked like Latin.

He slid into a pew, behind a pillar, opposite the ninth station of the cross. Jesus falls the third time. He removed his hat and a little skin with it. With his fingers he wiped a trickle of blood near his hairline. A few worshipers were scattered in the angled pews. One was a cop in uniform, kneeling in a front pew. An old woman just looking into space. And on the altar, a priest in a baby blue cardigan sweater puttered near the tabernacle, softly whistling "Stardust."

Opposite the pews a few dozen folding chairs had been set up for sold-out performances. Stars floated on a blue ceiling, angels flew in the curves of the arches, spotlights angled down from the pillars. On the seat next to him was a brochure, the history of the Actor's Chapel. He picked it up as the uniformed cop blessed himself and came down the center aisle.

The cop looked hard at Ryan, probably sizing him up as a

local drunk grabbing a few minutes' peace. Ryan kept reading: a list of former altar boys, including Jimmy Durante and Don Ameche; the funeral of Valentino; the wedding of Joan Crawford and Douglas Fairbanks Jr. Ms. Crawford signing her name Lucille Le Sueur. The cop walked around a white marble baptismal font the size of a hot tub and out the door.

Ryan stood up and started looking for other exits. He wondered if Winters had merely cut through again. If so, he'd won; he'd beaten the tailman. Ryan walked around to see if he could pick up a trace of fresh raindrops or wet shoes on the hardwood parquet. Then he saw the elevator.

The elevator went up only one flight to the choir loft. Ryan pressed the button and nothing happened. He could hear the murmur of voices echoing in the shaft. Someone was holding the door. He pressed the button again, more insistently. After a few minutes the door closed and a motor whirred. Cables and pulleys rattled and squealed. The cab stopped. It bounced once, then balanced itself. The door opened onto the stunned face of Trey Winters.

Ryan shoved Winters back into the elevator and let the door close. Winters had gone stone white. He was breathing hard and clutching a brown attaché case to his chest. He began sliding down the wall. Ryan pushed the button and the elevator rose.

"Stand up straight," he said. "Let's meet the rest of the choir."

Trey Winters closed his eyes and slid all the way to the floor. Ryan wanted to lean down and hit him, but he'd never had a decent left. So he kicked him. Once, in the side. Hard. Winters gasped as the elevator door opened.

"Gimme that old-time religion," Buster Scorza said.

Ryan pulled Scorza into the elevator. When the door closed he pressed the red stop button.

"You need a doctor, not a priest," Scorza said, staring at Ryan's head.

"We're all going to feel better when we leave here," Ryan said.

"Hope nobody's fucking claustrophobic," Scorza said.

Ryan raised his leg and kicked Scorza, planting his heel above the porn king's knee. Scorza yelped and grabbed his leg, kneading the muscle.

"What is this, kung fu night?" he said.

The priest stopped whistling. Scorza's cologne threatened to devour the oxygen. Ryan knew he couldn't be too loud. He waited, still unable to breathe comfortably. Winters rolled over in a fetal position.

"We're in church," Ryan said softly. "Watch your language, and I won't kick you again. Now open the case."

"It's not in my nature to handle the property of others," Scorza said, brushing Ryan's heel print off his Burberry.

"Mr. Winters has no objection. Do you, Mr. Winters? . . . I thought not."

"It's not my nature to jam up a cop, either," Scorza said. "But I'm making an exception here."

Scorza took a cell phone from his pocket. Ryan grabbed it out of his hand and stuck it in his own pocket.

"So much for the U.S. Constitution," Scorza said.

Ryan picked up the case and jammed it into Scorza's chest. He told him to turn it around and just hold it. He wondered why the priest wasn't whistling. Maybe he was poking around, looking for the source of the noise.

"What happened to your head?" Scorza said.

"I got mugged."

"Where's Joe Gregory?"

"Getting married."

With his left hand Ryan unsnapped the locks of the attaché case. It was full of money, no surprise. Stacks of fifties tied in thick green rubber bands.

"Who the hell would marry Joe Gregory?"

"Lucille Le Sueur," Ryan said as he rifled through the attaché case, looking for anything other than money. Scorza, holding the attaché case across his forearms like a Bensonhurst butler, stared at him.

"You're cowboying this case," Scorza said. "You got no backup, no partner. Dressed like that. Looking like a truck ran over you. You're playing commando out here."

"Shut up, and close the case."

"I'm betting this is something we can work out right here and now, my friend."

"I'm not your friend."

"I might be the best friend ever," Scorza said. "See, the truth is that me and Winters found this money up here during our morning vespers. So I'm thinking we split it, coupla nice Catholic boys like us. Do whatever you want with your share. Buy a nice wedding present for Gregory."

"Look at me," Ryan said. "Do I look ready to play your goddamn games?"

"Hey, we're in church," Scorza said.

"And this is where we're going to stay. Until someone tells me what this is for."

"It's a simple American business deal," Scorza said. "I'm the lendor, he's the lendee. My friend just has a little cash flow problem right now. I'm helping out."

"A member of one of the richest families in the city has a cash flow problem, so he comes to the local porn guy. I really believe that, Buster."

"Don't kid yourself, cash is cash."

"I'm being blackmailed," Trey Winters said from the floor.

"Jesus Christ," Scorza said.

The priest resumed whistling. God and Hoagy Carmichael would be proud.

"I want this to end," Winters said. "I'm sick of it all."

Ryan reached around for his gun. The attaché case fell, and money spilled over the floor and Trey Winters's body. Although they practiced at the range, the gun felt awkward in his left hand. He planted the barrel in Scorza's forehead.

"Artillery is not a good idea in cramped quarters," Scorza said.

"Is this guy blackmailing you, Winters?"

"No, no. I don't know who it is. All I know is I have to have the money ready by tonight. Be in my office, by the phone, at one A.M."

"You see the flaw in your logic?" Scorza said. "If I were involved in this scheme, would I act as the lendor? Steal my own money?"

"Have you seen the blackmailer?" Ryan said.

"A man hands me envelopes on the street. Dark skin, hat pulled down. I think his hair is black, he's not as tall as I am. Maybe six one or two."

"Spanish accent?" Ryan asked.

"He hasn't spoken," Winters said.

"I have no idea what you two are talking about," Scorza said, a little red loop of a gun barrel on his forehead.

Ryan put his gun away and took out Scorza's cell phone. He handed it to him and told him to dial Joe Gregory's beeper number.

"Keep the phone," Scorza said after he dialed. "It's prepaid to a hundred bucks. I'll just take my money and get out of here. Never say a word. My lips are sealed."

He bent down and scooped stacks of bills into the case. Ryan waited until he'd finished and then put his foot on it.

"Why didn't you go to your wife for the money?" Ryan said to Winters.

"I didn't want her to know."

"Too late now," Scorza said.

"You didn't want her to know about you and Gillian Stone," Ryan said.

"Yes," Winters said slowly. "That's it."

Scorza's phone rang.

41

Danny Eumont, his arm out the window of Honest Val's pickup, ventured farther into the swampy center of Florida than he ever wanted to. They'd driven an hour since they'd left the convent. The sun beat down on slash pines and bald cypress. A sour odor hung in the air over the saw grass. On the radio Billie Holiday sang "Strange Fruit," a song once banned in the South.

"Ringling Brothers used to winter in Sarasota," Val said. "A lot of performers live out here in the off season."

"Way out here in the boondocks."

"That's the way they like it. Away from the stares."

"I think I hear dueling banjos."

The roadway was stained with thousands of road-kill remains, fur and blood everywhere. Occasionally a few curled strips of blown truck tire retread. Rickety wooden stands advertised muskrat, melon, and croc. Water stood on both sides of the road.

"Ringling doesn't winter here anymore?" Danny said.

"They moved the operation down the coast to Venice. At the same time they cut down on their side show operation. Some of these people tried to hook up with other circuses, state fairs and such. No welfare for them. No way. These people I'm taking you to now . . . are only strange to look at. Their hearts are all in the right place."

"Tell me about the Nuñez family."

"Faye stayed with them until she was a teenager. Premier trapeze act. Then the father got hurt, or sick, I forget which. After that he started drinking. Died of cirrhosis in record time. My source tells me the rest of the family moved back to Mexico. He can tell you more."

They turned off the highway onto a path of crushed clamshells, bleached white from the sun. Shells crunched under the pickup's tires for a quarter of a mile, then Honest Val threaded through a narrow opening in overgrown hedges. They came out into a collection of trailers and shacks that seemed to be set down helter-skelter, dropped carelessly like Gypsy luggage.

"The Nuñez family lived in that white prefab. Some Romanian tumblers have it now. My source lives in that place over there, the double wide."

"Wouldn't it be better if they lined up these places in rows?" Danny said. "Then the plumbing and the electrical work would be uniform."

"Yeah," Honest Val said, shrugging. "Probably."

They snaked between trailers. In the yards kids ran and played games. Normal-looking kids. He'd expected lobster boys, bearded ladies, lizard-skinned fire eaters, and eight-foot-tall tattooed Chinese hermaphrodites.

"Most of the performers are on the road," Val said. "This is show season for the ones with contracts. You come here in January. You'll see something then."

They stopped in front of the double wide. Tied to a large doghouse in front was an odd-looking animal with long white hair and one horn in the center of its head. A sign read, "Beware dangerous unicorn."

"Puff is a special breed of goat," Honest Val said. "At birth they pull their horns together and try to braid them into one big horn in the center. It was the big attraction a couple of years ago, until animal rights people got into the act. He belongs to Jake Bugel, he owns this park."

Honest Val knocked on the screen door, and the unmistakable squeak of a geriatric Munchkin warned him not to do that again if he valued his kneecaps. Val pushed open the screen door.

"You bring a sprocket wrench?" Jake Bugel said.

"What's a sprocket?" Honest Val said.

Bugel sat on a milk crate in the middle of the living room floor. He was staring at a motorcycle in the center of a bedsheet that protected the rug. It was the tiniest motorcycle Danny had ever seen. Assorted engine parts were scattered around the bedsheet.

"What's the mileage?" Honest Val said. "I'm your odometer man."

"Nine thousand original. All under a tent."

"Call a real mechanic."

"It's Russian made," Bugel said. "Nobody around here will touch it."

"Call the junk truck," Val said. "You're too old for that thing anyway."

"It's not for me. It's for Sasha's kid. The bareback rider. You met her. Nice heinie, lives with the asshole who thinks he's the next Houdini."

"He'll make his escape soon," Honest Val said.

The furniture was a mixture of low and high, but the low was made specifically to be low, not furniture with the legs cut down. Or sawed off. A picture of a dining set with the legs sawed off jumped into Danny's mind. His Groucho persona was tapping his cigar, ready to jump in anytime armed with his repertoire of jokes. The short program.

While coffee brewed, Jake Bugel brought out a stack of old circus programs. The Nuñez family was a featured act for several years. They were a handsome group, two men and two women, all dark skinned and raven haired. Danny looked closely at the women, bookends, but neither woman was Faye Boudreau. Bugel walked in a rocking motion back and forth from the kitchen, the coffee sloshing back and forth in the pot.

"Sugar or Sweet'n Low?" he asked.

"Sweet'n Low," Danny said. *Like your last wife,* Groucho whispered.

"That's Francisco, the father, in front," Bugel said, pointing to the thinner man in white tights. "We called him Frankie. The muscular guy is his son, Victor. The girls were twins, Ava and Ana. This Frankie Nuñez was the greatest trapeze performer I ever saw, and I seen them all. Believe me. The good Lord played a cruel joke on Frankie Nuñez. He gave him all the talent in the world and then made it impossible for him to use it. Arthritis so bad he couldn't make a fist."

"You know what they say," Danny said. "God laughs when we make plans."

"Amen, brother," Val said.

"I'm glad to hear that Faye is doing okay," Bugel said, still walking back and forth in the painful-looking style. "She had a rough road, that kid. Boudreau beat the shit out of her, and did who knows what else."

The host came in with a plate of cookies. Groucho wondered if they were shortbread. Why not? Bugel had a sense of humor. On the living room wall was a print of da Vinci's *Last Supper.* Jesus and the Apostles were little people. And who was around to say that was wrong?

"Frankie died about eight years ago," Bugel said. "The mother and two sisters live in Mexico."

"What about Victor?" Danny said.

"Another talented son of a bitch," Bugel said. "He stops by every winter. Summers he does some kind of street performing in New York. Juggling, I think. Could be fire eating. These kids learn it all growing up here. Works with a partner, a Russian clown named Pinto."

"Would this Victor visit Faye if he knew she was in New York?" Danny said.

"They were always tight, those two."

"Would you consider him her boyfriend?"

"Off and on they had a thing going for a while, then she moved to Miami. Victor has that whole macho thing going for him. He's got a few skeletons, real ones, if you know what I mean. He likes to whack women around. He roughed Faye up a coupla times, and she split. But don't get me wrong about Victor. He can be a sweetheart."

"Sounds like it," Danny said.

"Some people say he has a mean streak. But they were a tight family. Faye was a lot better off with them than those Canuck bear humpers. I tell you something: When Frankie Nuñez couldn't perform anymore, they disbanded the act. They wouldn't even go on performing without Frankie."

"Tell him that cop story," Val said.

"Oh, right," Jake said. "About three years ago the word comes back here that Faye took a bad beating from some psycho cop she was living with down in Miami. He got locked up, but Victor comes back from New York and hears about it. He drove down to Miami to see what was going on. After that the cop disappears off the face of the earth. Never showed for trial. Everybody around here figures Victor turned him into alligator lunch."

"Did you say Victor has a Russian partner?"

"Yeah, Pinto. His last name is Timoshenko. Drives an old beat-to-shit Chevy Nova, the vinyl top peeling off. They have an apartment in the Bronx."

"Two Ten Echo Place," Danny said, recognizing the name Timoshenko from the mailbox list.

"That's it," Jake said. "I grew up in the Bronx, Walton Avenue near East Burnside. Sometimes they stay with my cousin, who, believe it or not, still lives in that fucking hell-hole."

Danny thanked Jake Bugel and asked to borrow a copy of the circus program with the picture of Victor Nuñez. Val checked his watch and looked at Danny.

"We've got time to make a couple of matinee races before your plane," he said. "Don't worry, I'll get you to the airport on time."

"I'll get my lucky hat," Jake Bugel said.

"Let me make a call to New York," Danny said.

"Make it quick," Honest Val said. "I've got a new system. Can't lose."

"Hey, Carlson," Jake Bugel yelled from the bedroom. "You might have to lend me a couple of quid. I'm a little short."

42

Jesus, you scared the shit out of me," Danny Eumont said. He kicked his apartment door closed, then dropped his flight bag on the floor.

"Is that any way to greet your favorite detective?" Joe Gregory said. "No 'Hi, honey, I'm home'? No cute souvenirs from your trip?"

"Who let you in, the super?"

"I don't need no stinkin' super."

Gregory filled Danny's La-Z-Boy. He was stretched out watching a Bogart movie, drinking a cup of tea, the string and tag hanging over the side.

"You picked the lock."

"That's against the law," Gregory said.

Danny knew he'd never get a straight answer. He hung his blazer over a chair and emptied his pockets on the telephone table. The apartment was frigid, the AC blowing on max. A blue nylon jacket and a pair of dirty chinos lay in a heap on the floor. Other clothes he recognized as his own were strewn across the couch. Pants, shirts, and jackets.

"Don't blame me for this mess," Gregory said. "Your beloved uncle needed to borrow some clothes. Where do you shop, anyway, Preppy City? Nothing but Dockers and blazers. Your poor uncle's gonna look like Biff the Yuppie Cop."

"Where is he?"

Gregory pointed to the bedroom. "In there, asleep. Don't wake him up, he's had a rough day."

"What happened to him?"

"It's a long, sad story, but it has a happy ending. He'll tell you himself when he wakes up. Right now, you'd better call your magazine—your machine is full of messages."

"Is it okay if I use my own bathroom? Or is the chief of detectives in the shower?"

"The chief is a bubble-bath man," Gregory said, waving his hand toward the bathroom.

On the way in Danny saw his uncle, the covers pulled up to his neck, his head wrapped in bandages. Danny turned around quickly.

"Tell me what the hell happened to him. Right now."

"Use the bathroom, kid. Before you start dancing around. Then I'll tell you."

"Tell me now, goddamn it."

"Relax, for chrissakes, will ya? You'll wake him up, screaming like a banshee. Just be quiet. Your uncle will be all right. He was involved in a minor tussle, that's all."

"I'd hate to see a major tussle."

"He has eight stitches in his scalp, and his right hand is in a cast. Some little bone is fractured. But you should see the other guy."

"Who is the other guy?"

"You'll find out soon enough. We're gonna snap him up tonight."

"Does Aunt Leigh know about this?"

"She knows we're here, and he's okay. But don't you dare call her. I'll personally kick your ass if you talk to her."

Danny hated the way cops like Gregory thought they had to spoon-feed bad news. As if their knowledge required a warning label: Weaker doses recommended for civilians. In the bathroom he found a blood-streaked towel tossed across the shower rod. The sink looked like a butcher's tub. A black sweatshirt balled up in the trash can. When Danny came out of the bathroom Gregory was looking through the items he'd dropped on the telephone table.

"You went to the track today," Gregory said.

"How do you know that?"

"Two-dollar bills," he said. "Anyone with a roll of two-dollar bills is coming from the track."

"Must be great to know everything."

"It's a heavy burden, my boy. Now sit down and we'll talk."

"I'll stand."

"Fine," Gregory said, and he handed Danny a glass of chillable red he'd poured from the box in the refrigerator. "Your uncle got jumped in Faye Boudreau's place, by some guy whose name I can't tell you right now."

"Because you don't know."

"Oh, we know," Gregory said. "Guy named Victor. Complete ID is forthcoming. We'll know it all by sunup, podner."

"Muscular guy, dark hair," Danny said. "Born in Mexico. Lives in Florida, but currently residing in the Bronx. Spends summers here working as a street performer in midtown, most likely a juggler."

Gregory looked at him, appraising, then said, "It appears that Victor is involved with Faye Boudreau in a scheme to extort money from Trey Winters."

"Her name is Faith," Danny said. "Her real name is Faith."

Danny knew Joe Gregory wouldn't tell him anything he could avoid saying. To Joe Gregory information was a one-way street. It went against his nature to tell a civilian anything at all.

"We have a team watching Two Ten Echo Place," Gregory said. "If we had the right information, we could execute a search warrant within the hour. You got something specific you want to tell me?"

"You don't need me. You'll know it all by sunup, podner."

"I hope you're not holding back information."

"That's against the law," Danny said.

Gregory smiled. "I can only tell you so much," he said.

According to Gregory, Winters told them that last Tuesday night he was going to meet Abigail Klass when this dark, bodybuilder-type man handed him an envelope. Inside the envelope was a note outlining money demands and threatening exposure of a sexual relationship between Winters and Gillian Stone. Pictures were involved. Yesterday the same man delivered a second envelope with instructions on how the money was to be delivered.

"Who took the pictures?"

"Winters doesn't know," Gregory said. "He denies he slept with her. He claims he's being set up all around."

"If there wasn't some basis in truth, he would have called the cops last week. Why is he even paying if it's not true?"

"Because he's full of shit all around," Gregory said.

"This muscular guy is Victor," Danny said. "The same guy who jumped my uncle."

"That's the story as we see it."

"His name is Victor Nuñez. A few years ago he was considered one of the world's best trapeze artists. He lives at Two Ten Echo with a guy named Pinto Timoshenko. The lease is probably in Timoshenko's name."

Gregory wrote on the back of a magazine, around the edges of a Gap ad. "Whatever you got, kid, you better give it all up. We haven't got time to play games. This exchange is going down in a couple of hours."

"Then talk faster," Danny said. "Was Gillian involved?"

"Not directly," Gregory said. "At first Winters thought she was involved, trying to get even with him somehow. That's why he brought the costume that night. Figured he could change her mind. But he realized she didn't know shit, the way she was acting. And she wasn't a good enough actress to fool him."

"What a bastard," Danny said.

"We figure Gillian told Faye about the affair. And Faye and this guy Victor set up the scheme. We don't know how they're connected yet."

"They grew up together," Danny said. "In a circus family outside Sarasota." He handed Gregory a circus program and pointed out the picture of Victor Nuñez.

"I'm going to wake your uncle up, see if he can identify this mutt. Then I'm going to Mid-Town North and get this picture out. Get a warrant going. They're probably long gone from Echo, but we'll give it a shot."

"What was Scorza's role?"

"The bank. Winters says he couldn't ask his wife for the quarter of a mil. He was protecting her."

"What happens now?"

"At one A.M. Winters is supposed to get a phone call telling him where to meet. The exchange is the money for the pictures. We're going to grab him then."

"Where did you get so much money on such short notice? Are you risking Scorza's money?"

"What money?" Gregory said. "No reason to risk real money. It's not like someone's life is hanging in the balance. We got about five hundred bucks on the outside of the stacks, the rest is fake. Just cut-up paper."

"So who killed Gillian?"

Gregory shrugged. "Right now we don't know any different than we did last week, and we may never know."

"That's bullshit," Danny said. "That's not right."

"I hate to be the bearer of all this bad news. But you can't write about this affair, either. Your uncle says he doesn't want to hurt Darcy Winters any more than he has to."

"That's the meat of the story. That's everything."

"I know," Gregory said, smiling. "Sometimes your uncle is a little too much of a bleeding heart, isn't he. And don't bother asking . . . you can't go with us tonight."

"You fucking bastard."

"Hey, it wasn't my decision," Gregory said. "Call the chief of detectives, you want to bitch at somebody. You got anything further you want to tell me? How does this Victor get around? He own a car, or anything?"

"No," Danny said. "Victor Nuñez does not own a car."

Gregory went into the bedroom. Danny rubbed his arms in the icy cold room. He walked over to the telephone table and put on his seersucker jacket. He picked up his wallet, the roll of two-dollar bills, and his car keys. He yelled that he was going out to grab something to eat. Gregory said something from the bedroom, but Danny was already out the door.

43

Hats and bats, they call it when the NYPD goes all out. The phrase had its origin in the riotous sixties, when cops were hurriedly summoned from precincts all over the city and ordered to bring helmets and nightsticks. In the last hour of Wednesday twenty cops jammed into two chaotic rooms at the Hotel Edison. Another three dozen waited in cars spread out around the Times Square area. The chief of detectives spared no expense, determined that the life of a high-profile citizen like Trey Winters would not end on his watch. Hats and bats was the order.

"Know what, pally?" Joe Gregory said from the queen-size hotel bed. "From the back you look like the Invisible Man."

"Then pretend you can't see me," Ryan said.

Ryan wore his Yankee hat over the white hospital turban. His borrowed wardrobe consisted of Danny's blue woolen blazer, tan chinos, and a blue oxford button-down. His head was mummy wrapped, his arm in a sling, and his gun hand encased in blue molded plastic. He looked more as though he should be marching with a fife than working a case. But he was thinking about Trey Winters. Wondering if he was getting away with murder.

"Or that old Bogart movie," Gregory said. "The one where he gets all the plastic surgery. What the hell was that movie? Lauren Bacall. Bogie's whole head is wrapped in bandages, and he's walking around in a suit."

Gregory reclined like a man of leisure, tie loosened, pillows stacked behind him, a copy of the *Post* in his hands. He kept glancing at Ryan, talking him up. Mother hen watching. On TV Letterman waved the top ten list.

"Dark Passage," Ryan said.

"What's that?"

"The movie where Bogie wears the bandages."

Both Ryan and Trey Winters recognized Victor Nuñez from the picture in the circus program. In his last message Nuñez had instructed Winters to be in his office at one A.M. with all the money in one soft bag. He was told to have a cell phone and a car ready nearby.

"Couple more cops in here and we could open a gin mill," Gregory said. "All we needed were two experienced detectives. Me and you, pally. We coulda pulled off this caper with half a load on."

The Major Case Squad was running the show. With their youthful crew running around the overcrowded hotel room, they made Ryan and Gregory look like chaperons on a high school field trip.

More than fifty cops were linked into the hotel room base by radio. The husky voice of Sergeant Rosalie Minardi, born in New Jersey, directed all movements from the adjacent room, via the airwaves. They called her "Totowa Rose."

Ryan asked, "They execute the warrant in the Bronx?"

"Place was cleaned out," Gregory said. "Except for some weight equipment and three banged-up bowling balls. Perfect tenants, the landlady said. Quiet, paid their bills. She ID'd

Nuñez from the circus picture. Ringling Brothers is supposed to be faxing up a picture of the Russian."

"The landlady say if they had a car?" Ryan said.

"The Russian had a beat-up old Chevy, but she hadn't seen the car or them in a coupla days. And Faye is still among the missing."

With slightly more than an hour to go, Trey Winters was in his office, learning his lines with remarkable composure. The star awaited his cue with wires running across his upper body and a battery pack taped to the small of his back.

Winters had been briefed on exactly what was expected of him when Nuñez called: Make sure you make a strong plea for the pictures. If you cooperate too easily without doing the natural thing, the extortionist will suspect a setup. But say the minimum, then drive normally to wherever directed, drop the money, and leave. That's it. Don't improvise. Don't linger.

"We'll only be in here for one phone call," Ryan said. "This is going to be a road rally."

Tech Services equipped Winters's car with a new tracking device based on the technology used in the map locator systems in expensive cars. The car had also been chemically marked on top, so it could be seen from the NYPD helicopter. But the helicopter was grounded because of the weather. Letterman ran a canned ham out into the audience.

"No way this amateur gets away," Gregory said. "We'll be in Brady's by last call, guaranteed. I definitely want to be there when you walk in. We should get some more bandages, cover your whole face like Bogie. For laughs."

Funny money had been provided to Winters. A backpack containing stacks of paper had been topped with a veneer of U.S. currency. It was wrapped to mimic the exact specs of a quarter of a million dollars in old fifties. The weight was the trick. The fake boodle was broken down into five bundles, each six and a half inches tall. Weight had to be added because plain paper, like new money, was feather light. Grit, grime, and body oils added surprising heft to greenbacks. The total actual weight of a quarter mil in old fifties was twelve and a half pounds.

The call came at two minutes after one. Winters picked up on the first ring.

"You have the money?"

"Yes," was all Winters said.

The male caller asked for Winters's cell phone number, then said, "Drive to the corner of Central Park West and Ninety-fifth Street and wait for my next call." He asked Winters to repeat the location, told him to leave immediately, then hung up.

"Winters is being too brave," Ryan said, fishing his nephew's blazer out of the closet. "He should be more nervous. Worried that we might lose him in traffic. Worried about something."

Gregory helped Ryan on with his jacket. Ryan slipped his left arm into the sleeve. His right arm stayed inside the jacket, which Gregory laid over the sling.

"It's too easy," Ryan said. "It's a bad omen."

Gregory began to sneeze. Hotel doors opened and closed, and the sound of heavy footsteps hurried down the hallway. The weighty bump of cop gear *thunk*ed against walls, the squeak of leather shifting on a moving hip.

"You shouldn't think so much, pally," Gregory said. "It takes all the fun out of being a cop."

44

Danny Eumont walked out on Joe Gregory and drove straight to the Bronx. For two hours, he scoured the area around Walton Avenue and East Burnside until he found a battered Chevy Nova with Florida plates. It was a piece of the puzzle he hadn't surrendered to Gregory. Jake Bugel had told him that Victor Nuñez and Pinto Timoshenko sometimes stayed with his cousin, who still lived in this "hellhole." Danny knew they hadn't returned to the Echo Place apartment. He figured Jake's cousin was worth a shot. He parked his Volvo on the next block and waited.

The Chinese-Spanish takeout on the corner handled a steady stream of customers. Danny locked his car doors. A man sold compact music disks out of the trunk of a Lexus. Danny rolled up the windows, despite the heat. Luckily, he didn't sweat for long. At nine-thirty P.M. Victor Nuñez and Faye Boudreau came around the corner, Nuñez pushing an old bicycle, a blue duffel bag slung across his shoulder. Faye slid behind the wheel of the Chevy. Nuñez tried to wedge the bike into the trunk, but the lid wouldn't close on the handlebars, so he tied it down with rope. Danny wondered where the Russian was.

As soon as Nuñez got in, Faye pulled away from the curb. She made the left on Jerome Avenue. Danny followed them down the Major Deegan Expressway onto the Triborough Bridge. At the bridge toll, Danny was two cars behind the Nova. He prayed the drivers in front of him had the correct change and no stupid questions. Faye handed her money to the toll collector. Danny leaned out his window, trying to see if they'd take the Manhattan exit or go on to Queens. But the Nova cut immediately to the left, its trunk lid bouncing. Fifty yards past the toll, it disappeared down the ramp to Randall's Island.

Danny knew there was only one way to drive off the island: they had to come back his way. He cruised down the ramp onto the broken and unmarked pavement. Very slowly, very carefully. The island was a spooky place, abandoned by cars and people. A lost world between Manhattan and Queens, junky and overgrown. All roads seemed to lead to traffic circles that spun you around to where you began. He spotted the Nova pulled up onto the grass near the high chain-link fence that surrounded the NYC Fire Department's Training Academy. Danny parked and snapped off his lights.

Victor Nuñez took the bike and the duffel bag out of the trunk. He slung the bag over his shoulder, said something to Faye, then pedaled away. Danny scrunched down in the seat as Faye drove straight toward him. After she passed he sat up and followed her off the island, to Queens. First to a liquor store on Ditmars Boulevard, then to this spot on Shore Boulevard. Directly across the Hell Gate from Ward's Island.

Danny wished he'd brought a cell phone. He should call his uncle, let him know that Nuñez was on the island. But he was already committed. In for a penny, in for a pound, as Joe Gregory always said. Danny had already lied about Timoshenko's Chevy Nova and the fact that Victor Nuñez might be at Jake

Bugel's cousin's apartment. But if he'd told Gregory everything, he still would have been cut out. Police business, Gregory would have said. Danny couldn't let that happen.

This wasn't about closing a case to him, and it wasn't even about writing a story. It was about a phrase his uncle always used: "Do the right thing." He made it sound so simple. The "right thing" in this case was to find justice for Gillian. If the police weren't going to do it, he was.

The rain had stopped as Danny got out of the olive and walked along Shore Boulevard. Just a light drizzle fell through the lights of the Triborough Bridge far above him. He walked under the massive stone highway, traffic a low, steady roar.

He came up behind the Nova, on the passenger side. Faye was behind the wheel. She had her head back, eyes closed as if sleeping. He knocked on the glass. Her reaction showed no hint of surprise. No fear. Between her legs was a pint of dark rum. And something shiny, which she held in her hand. He was already in the car, sitting next to her, before he realized it was a gun.

45

Perched fifty-five feet above the Harlem River, on the Manhattan side of the Ward's Island footbridge, Victor Nuñez wrote Trey Winters's cell phone number on the palm of his hand. His first call had sent Winters to Central Park. It was a move designed to confuse the police . . . if Winters had actually called them. It also gave him a few minutes to rest and think. Carbon monoxide from traffic on the Harlem River Drive hung in the air like a grainy black cloud.

For almost two hours he'd worked on the bridge as rain fell. The rain had stopped, but the weather was still humid. His hands had tightened up, but everything was in place, all checked and rechecked, just as his father had taught him. Victor had well absorbed the Nuñez family's methodical approach to safety.

The closing of the Ward's Island footbridge had been a blessing for him. Not only did it create the element of surprise, one that would confound any pursuer, but he was able to work without interruption. He'd attached a measured length of rope to the raised portion of the bridge. His plan was to get the money from Winters at the barricade near the Manhattan entrance, run up to the top, then swing underneath the raised portion, across to the other side.

In seconds he'd be on Ward's Island, where he'd stashed a bike in the bushes. No one would see him swing across the open space. Even if they did, he could ride around to the Hell Gate Channel in a matter of three minutes. If the cops were involved, they'd certainly close the exit on the Triborough Bridge, which they'd assume was the only exit. Then they'd search the island for him. But he'd be gone. He planned a swim, a short swim across Hell Gate Channel to Shore Boulevard in Queens.

Victor had dressed in loose black clothing, under which he'd worn a wet suit. He didn't want to go into the water, because he was having trouble breathing, his nose still swollen from Anthony Ryan's hard head. His right shoulder ached from the blow delivered by Faye. But he had no choice. He couldn't take the chance on the police blocking the one exit. They'd never think he'd swim the treacherous Hell Gate.

These cops with their flabby bellies would never believe a man could cover so much ground so quickly. In less than twelve minutes he'd be across an island and two rivers, in another borough entirely. So much movement, so quickly, would create a communications and logistical nightmare for the pursuing police. If Winters had notified them.

Alain Charnier would be proud. Victor's plan was far more brilliant than *The French Connection.* In twelve minutes, while the cops were scratching their flaky bald heads, he'd be a rich man, driving south in a car no one would be looking for.

He sat back against the barricade. And a formidable barrier it was. Like the one on the Ward's Island side, it was built by the city, designed to keep people away from the center of the bridge. Eight feet tall, it was constructed of heavy plywood covered with thick sheet metal and ringed on the top and sides with looping barbed wire. It was an imposing challenge for any street athlete who thought he could scale it or swing around it. The flabby police could never get around it; they'd have to tear it down. Even if they did that, they couldn't get across the open span over the river. They'd have to drive around, which would eat up their precious time.

Victor took the portable drill from his duffel bag. He made a peephole in the plywood, so he could see whoever was coming up the ramp but they couldn't see him. He'd make his escape with only one cop, Anthony Ryan, ever getting a good look at him. He began to stretch and go through the yoga exercises his father had taught him.

In five minutes he'd pick up the cell phone and make a second call to Winters. Ten minutes after that he'd make the last phone call, until Winters appeared at his feet.

46

"Winters is driving too fast," Ryan said. "What the hell's his hurry?"

"Nerves," Gregory said.

They rode up Central Park West in light rain, both partners keeping the sneeze count. They were the third backup tail team, with two main functions: try to spot Nuñez and stay out of the way.

"Nuñez is going to take Winters into the park," Gregory said, tallying sneeze number seven. "Not a bad strategy. Give him an opportunity to scope out a tail. Probably figures he can lose us on foot in the woods. Eight hundred and forty acres to get lost in, foliage is dense and heavy. Unlimited points of escape. The guy's a trapeze artist, maybe he'll swing through the vines like Tarzan."

"I thought you said we'd be drinking in Brady's before the night's over."

"It ain't over till last call, pally."

As Ryan studied a city map with a flashlight, Gregory

wondered aloud as to why they called them trapeze "artists." Then he sneezed for the eighth time.

"I think I'm allergic to your jacket," he said.

Ryan sniffed at his nephew's jacket. It smelled like wet wool and perfume. He felt through the pockets and came up with a rolled piece of raw cotton and a phone number written on an America West napkin. Lainie Mossberg. It was sealed with a red lipstick kiss.

They parked in the east crosswalk at Ninety-second Street, three full blocks below the action. Lights out, engine off. Totowa Rose came on the air, her voice purring with late night implication. She calmly warned Winters not to walk as fast as he'd driven, he'd lose his backup if he did. She announced that a second phone call had ordered Winters to take the money and stand by the park wall. Rose gave the order to deploy pedestrian undercover into the park.

Major Case leaked people into the park, one by one. A jogger in a bright orange sweatsuit. A young couple holding hands. A man in a beret walking a doddery old cocker spaniel. A few others they didn't know, but who qualified as cop possibilities only because it was one-thirty A.M. and this was Central Park.

"That guy in the beret always brings his dog on these things," Gregory said. "Think he adds doggie treats to his expense sheet?"

Ryan picked up the binoculars and looked at Trey Winters, wondering what was taking Nuñez so long. Was he out there watching, checking for police manpower?

"You figure Faye is out there with him?" Gregory said.

"If not here, somewhere waiting for him."

"I don't know whether I told you this before, but you've acted like an asshole on this case."

"Now you know how I always feel," Ryan said.

People spend most of their time and energy promoting and reinforcing their self-image. The self-image of Anthony Ryan, star detective and family man, took a heavy hit. So who was he now? Was he playing a part in an old gangster movie, a guy in a suit trying to change his identity? Or was he really the Invisible Man, and nothing was beneath the gauze?

"What did Leigh say when you talked to her?" Ryan asked.

"What they always say: 'He could have called.' "

"She's right."

"No shit," Gregory said. "Women are always right, I live by that motto. But she sounded relieved. And goddamn happy she gets to spend one more night of wild passion with somebody named Bruno, the Italian stallion."

Gregory checked his watch. He was enjoying himself, a big Irish smile on his face. Ryan wondered how long it would be before he started singing.

"Ten minutes now," Gregory said. "He's biding his time."

"Not anymore. Winters just answered the phone. Now he's walking toward the car."

Totowa Rose said that Winters was told to drive east through the park across the Ninety-seventh Street transverse road. She ordered everyone to hold fast for a few minutes. The subject might be watching for a tail on the narrow park road. Maintain your present position. Winters started his car quickly and made the turn into the park.

"There he goes again," Ryan said. "Taking off fast. He did everything but leave rubber."

Gregory started the Buick, made a squealing U-turn, and headed south, in the opposite direction.

"Must be that New Jersey accent," Ryan said. "I thought Rose said hold your position."

"I take no orders from Jerseyites," Gregory said. "Besides, you're right, pally. He took off too fast. Like he's trying to lose us. We'll run parallel to him."

Gregory made a hard left into the park at the Eighty-sixth Street transverse road. Ryan figured Winters's car was even with theirs, but on the other side of the reservoir. They might even be a little ahead with the speed Gregory was driving. In less than a minute they were through the park, blinking in the glitter of Fifth Avenue.

Joe Gregory was the most instinctive tailman Ryan knew. He was vamping. Winging it. Flying through the red at Madison. Dodging pedestrians, dodging raindrops. Ryan sat up straight. They'd become boy cops again, buzzed by the adrenaline of the chase and the juice of defiance. Chug-a-lugging from the fountain of youth.

They were halfway to Park Avenue when the excited voice of Totowa Rose ordered all personnel to resume the tail forthwith. Winters was on his way to First Avenue.

"Good gamble, right, pally?" Gregory said.

"You're a gambling fool."

"Stands to reason. This time of night he's going to move across town. They told him to drive naturally, that's what he's doing."

"It's not natural, he's flying."

"We'll fly faster."

They caught Winters's car going north on First Avenue. Then Winters made a hard right. Ryan had to twist around to pick up the street sign: E. 102nd Street. Winters stopped at the end of the block, just before the entrance to the Harlem River Drive.

Gregory pulled to the hydrant and cut the Buick lights, half a block back. He sneezed for the ninth time. Winters got out of the car quickly.

"The Ward's Island footbridge is closed, isn't it?" Gregory said.

"The center section is."

Winters walked toward the turquoise metal ramp that zigzagged upward to a pedestrian walkway across the highway and farther up to the closed Ward's Island footbridge.

"He could still walk over the highway," Gregory said. "Maybe he's got somebody waiting in the Harlem River."

"Call Totowa Rose," Ryan said. "Tell her to notify Aviation.

Ask her if it's clear enough for that helicopter. We're going to need somebody up there."

"We should have brought a wheelchair," Gregory said. "Pushing a bandaged guy in a wheelchair is the perfect cover."

"Let's go," Ryan said. "I'll let you hold my arm."

47

Victor Nuñez watched Trey Winters get out of his car, and his heart began to pound. The police weren't following him; at least he couldn't see them. Maybe this would be easier than he thought. He dialed the phone one last time. Winters answered, looking all around.

"On the bridge," Victor said. "Walk up the bridge."

Winters kept looking back up the street, as if expecting someone to be following. Victor couldn't see very far down the block because of the red brick housing project. He could see only a few car lengths beyond the corner.

"Faster!" Victor yelled.

But he didn't have to yell; Winters was walking fast. If Winters had contacted the police, they would be closer, Victor thought. Perhaps the Central Park ruse had worked. It was meant to stall them, throw them off their rhythm. He knew from his act the importance of timing and rhythm. The slightest hitch could be devastating.

"Quickly!" Victor yelled in the phone again.

Winters started jogging up the first ramp. He was carrying the bag in one hand. It didn't appear to be heavy. Victor had no idea how heavy that much money would be. He threw his cell phone in the duffel bag and took out the waterproof backpack. Winters was close enough to hear him without it. He moved into position behind the barricade, at the hole he'd drilled in the plywood.

Winters came around the corner and stopped. The actor stood on the platform, confused. The platform ran straight across the Harlem River Drive, then down to a narrow park that ran along the Manhattan side of the river. The only other way was halfway up the next ramp. To the barricade.

"Up here!" Victor yelled. "Come to this wall."

The barricade, built by the city, was clean on Victor's side, but he knew that on Winters's side the sheet metal was marked with graffiti. Street names and gang logos, painted by the local thugs the barrier was meant to stop. Victor could hear Winters breathing hard. He was inches away now, only plywood separating them.

"Throw the money over," Victor said forcefully.

Winters took a few tentative steps, then threw the bag with one hand. It caught in the loops of barbed wire atop the wall and fell back at his feet. Victor could hear him repeating the simple instructions over and over. He was rushing and talking to himself.

"Throw it harder!" Victor yelled.

The second time the bag cleared the barrier, and Victor caught it one-handed. He dropped to his knees and opened it. Then Winters started saying something that Victor couldn't make out at first. He was begging for him to throw the letters over.

"Hurry, please," Winters said, sounding dry throated from the other side of the barrier.

Victor took an envelope from his duffel bag. He threw it long and far, way over the head of Winters, so he had to run to retrieve it.

Victor's hands shook as he shoved stacks into plastic bags. *Madre de Dios,* he'd never seen so much money. The plastic bags went into his own backpack, into the sealed rubberized compartment. He slipped his arms through the straps of the backpack and tightened it.

Then he heard the voice of Anthony Ryan. He turned the corner to the next ramp and sprinted for the rope.

48

Ryan and Gregory reached the platform just as Trey Winters was coming down. He looked pale and shaken. He tried to walk past them. Gregory grabbed him by the arm.

"Where did he go?" Ryan said.

"I gave him the money," Winters said.

"No kidding. But where did he go?"

"He was behind the wall. I threw the money over."

"You're not finished here," Gregory said. "Show us."

Winters trembled as Gregory walked him up the ramp to the barricade. He told them how he threw the bag over the barricade. He never saw Nuñez or where he disappeared to. Then Winters begged to leave, saying he wasn't feeling well.

"He give you the pictures?" Gregory said.

"He didn't give me anything."

Ryan looked up toward the crest of the bridge as he struggled to put his gun away with his left hand.

"This is no time to be shy," Gregory said, patting Winters's chest. "What's this bulge in your jacket?"

"It's just some personal papers," Winters said.

"You brought office work with you? Do a little paperwork while you're racing around the city, right?"

Winters pulled away as Gregory reached inside his suit jacket.

"You can't do this," Winters said. "That's illegal search and seizure."

"I'll let the Supreme Court worry about that later," Gregory said. "But right now you can either give me what you have, or I can rip that jacket off you."

Car doors slammed on E. 102nd Street. The hollow beat of footsteps shook the ramp as boy cops made the climb in leaps and bounds. They didn't have to ask where the action was. Totowa Rose had followed the path. Winters handed the brown manila envelope to Gregory. Inside was a stack of paper that looked like handwritten notes.

"Where are the pictures?" Gregory said. He held Winters at arm's length while he shoved the envelope into his own jacket pocket.

"There are no pictures," Winters said, snatching vainly at the envelope. "Just give those back to me. I can make it worth your while."

Gregory spun Winters around, shoved him against the side of the bridge, and patted him down. Ryan looked across the river, wishing he'd brought the binoculars from the car.

"You'll get it all back as soon as we voucher it," Gregory said.

Winters stormed away, looking for the Major Case commander. Ryan studied the structure of the bridge, trying to figure out how Victor Nuñez had disappeared. He thought the Mexican trapeze artist should have asked for more money, all the trouble he went through. But the NYPD would have stiffed him with an even weightier hoax.

"He's in the freakin' river, isn't he," Joe Gregory said, looking out on the water of the Harlem.

"No, he's not in the river," Ryan said. "If he planned to escape by water, he wouldn't have set this meet on a bridge, then jumped from . . . what does that say, fifty-five feet. That's crazy."

"He didn't just vanish," Gregory said. "He's in the *agua*, guaranteed."

"What did you take from Winters?" Ryan said.

"Looked like letters. Maybe he wasn't lying."

"He's lying. Whatever they are, he didn't bring them with him."

Major Case arrived in full force. Up above, the helicopter, no longer held back by weather, circled over Winters's car like a bird dog standing its prey.

"We got Aviation working now, pally," Joe Gregory said, taking the portable out of his pocket. "I'm gonna tell Totowa Rose to send that helicopter to check the water for speed-boats."

"Speedboats?" Ryan said. "What is this, *Miami Vice*?"

"I'm calling Harbor anyway."

"Call Jacques Cousteau if you want. But he's not in the water. I think Nuñez either climbed up to that raised bar in the center and crawled across, or he swung over somehow. He's on Ward's Island, and I bet he has a car parked over there."

"This guy might be Superman, pally. But he can't outrun the radio. I'll call Rose, tell her to block the Triborough Bridge. That's the only exit from Randall's, isn't it? We'll drive over like the gentlemen and detectives we are. Then we'll hunt him down like a dog."

Gregory talked tactics and trash with Totowa Rose as they walked quickly down the ramp. Both of them ignored the Major Case boss calling them back. They made a U-turn against traffic on E. 102nd Street. As they drove up First Avenue to the Triborough Bridge, Gregory sneezed for the tenth and eleventh times.

49

All was quiet at the top of the bridge. Victor threw the duffel bag into the Harlem River, then wedged himself behind a steel beam. He took his time, tightening the straps of his waterproof backpack. Over water now, he heard only the sound of his own breathing, coming hard and fast after the run. The steamy hissing of tires on the wet pavement barely a whisper. The voice of Anthony Ryan could not be heard.

Victor had attached the rope to the north side of the bridge to lessen the chances of being seen. Then he knotted it at the handhold and tied a scarf at the knot. It had worked perfectly on his first try, the trip from Ward's Island.

Behind him, cops were milling around the barricade, but no one was chasing him. They had no idea where he was. He'd be visible for only three seconds, in the night, over the black water.

He took the bag of resin from his pocket and sprinkled it on his gloved hands. He wrapped his hands above the scarf and pulled the rope. Taut, perfect. As a boy the ropes felt like an extension of his hands, his arms, his shoulders. He could do it all then, with his eyes closed, swinging high above the dirt floors of countless arenas.

He took a deep breath and let go.

Victor had forgotten the exhilaration. The pure freedom of flying through soothing darkness. For those brief seconds all was silent except for the hum of his body through God's black sky. Whether above a dirt floor in Mexico City or a polluted river in New York, to fly was to experience a miracle. The swing, the grab. He made it easily.

Victor first saw the helicopter as he ran down the ramp on the Ward's Island side. He'd never thought they could get one up this quickly. But they were guessing; they didn't know where he was. Or where he'd go. The edge was still his.

The helicopter spotlight swept over the river as he found his bike in the bushes. From the footbridge to the Hell Gate was almost a mile. A trip that would have taken only three minutes by bike, but he'd ridden less than a hundred yards when the helicopter spotlight swept the exposed path. He scrambled into the woods, pulling the bike with him.

Victor knelt on the wet grass behind a dripping spruce as the helicopter moved away, north along the footpath, the light glinting off specks in the macadam. He could see only the one chopper, but he knew more would be coming. Cops would soon flood the island. Anthony Ryan would be coming. He left the bike and began to run diagonally, through the thickest part of the foliage.

The denseness of the woods was a fortunate covering, but a branch slashed his cheek, and blood ran into his open mouth. In the leafy darkness, he could see the intense white beam of the helicopter searchlight. He thought about his first time in the tunnel in Madison Square Garden. He'd stood behind his father, peeking out into the arena, marveling at the vastness of it. The pure brightness of the spotlight was the thing that most impressed him. The smell of the animals, the bustle of the acts changing, performers speaking strange languages . . .

he was used to all that. But the enormity of the crowd noise. Tens of thousands, his father said. The light show, the music, the sound of the organ reverberating in his chest. Most of all the powerful and seductive glare of the spotlight.

Victor leaped over fallen trees, crashed recklessly through heavy bushes. His slashed cheek stung from sweat, and he'd begun to feel heavy legged, his face burning up. The heat was unbearable in the rubberized suit, but he was getting close. He could hear the halyard slapping against the flagpole of the psychiatric center. Then he saw a car, moving slowly on the path below. He waited for it to pass.

He was exhausted when he reached the pillars under the roadway of the Triborough Bridge. Hidden from the helicopter's view, he bent over and gasped for air. He was glad he'd chosen a spot under the roadway. Minutes had been added to his trip, perhaps ten. But he was less than twenty yards from the spot where he would enter the water. Victor Nuñez's quad muscles burned, and his skin itched from the sweltering rubberized suit. He sucked air into his lungs as he removed his sweatshirt and pants. A mist of steam rose from his body. He walked to the edge of the water and pulled off his sneakers. His feet were burning. The water would feel good.

50

Gregory guided the Buick down the dark back paths of the island. They drove past the ball fields and the hospitals down to the footbridge. Ryan got out and jogged up the ramp, the run causing his head to ache even more. Halfway up the footbridge he saw the rope, the scarf blowing in the slight breeze. Gregory notified Totowa Rose that the subject was on Ward's Island.

"Try some of these other paths," Ryan said.

"We might have to wait for daylight to find this guy out here."

"Unless he goes in the water," Ryan said. "Take the paths along the water's edge. Along the Hell Gate."

"I thought you said he wasn't going in the water."

"I meant the Harlem, not the Hell Gate."

They cruised slowly along the path, Ryan scanning the bushes with the flashlight, Gregory trying to pick up silhouettes in the high beams. Ryan saw something near the edge of the Hell Gate Channel, under the Triborough. It was a mound of clothing. Black clothing. One shirt, one pair of pants, and a pair of sneakers. One left, one right.

"He went in here," Ryan said. "Go cover the other side. I'll stay here."

"I'll leave the radio with you," Gregory said.

"No, just go. Get going. It won't take this guy that long to swim this. And tell Aviation to concentrate on this spot."

Gregory sneezed for the twelfth and final time, then left. Ryan waited, scanning the surface of the water. The helicopter appeared in seconds, scanning the water with the intensely hot white light. On two occasions Ryan thought he saw ripples in the water, but he couldn't be sure. The helicopter kept tightening the circle, getting lower and lower.

Behind Ryan, cars were starting to filter onto the island. The heavy-duty search beams of Emergency Services cut through the depth of the foliage. He kept staring across the water, looking for the outline of Gregory's Buick. He should have kept the radio; he could have contacted Rose, gotten backup for Gregory.

Then the pilot scoured the rocky edge of the bulkhead, and the wide beam of light strafed onto the roadway of Shore Boulevard. Ryan saw a car, but not the Buick. The old style, 1970s, was unmistakable, the boxiness pure Volvo. In the extreme brightness of the searchlight he even saw the color was green, olive green. He kicked off his shoes.

51

So Jake Bugel told you my whole life story," Faye said.

"Not everything," Danny said.

"Ain't much more to know. Tended bar in Florida. Let my sister die in New York. That about covers it."

The upholstery in the front seat of the Chevy Nova was badly worn; little pieces of foam stuck to Faye's black skirt. The car smelled of brake fluid, onions, and BO. Faye held a small silver automatic in both hands. Her arms were extended around and past the pint bottle clutched between her thighs. Danny asked her to put the gun away. She said Victor had told her not to let it go.

"Jake told me all about Victor," Danny said.

"Don't let Victor hear that. Victor hears it, Jake Bugel winds up in some swamp."

She made a knife-slitting motion across her throat. Danny could hear the sound of a helicopter off in the distance.

"Like the cop from Miami," Danny said.

"Like him. Like Pinto. Like you, when he finds you here.

Like all the fucking cops in New York. Victor wants something, nobody can stop him."

"I'm not afraid of Victor."

Her laugh rumbled with late night hoarseness and too many cigarettes. "He'll chew you up like Puppy Chow."

"You said Victor killed Pinto?"

"Strangled him. Then he made me help him dump his body in the river."

She took a left-handed swig of the rum. She'd killed two-thirds of it already. Her right hand, and the gun, were partially hidden in the folds of her skirt. Danny turned slightly on his hip, toward Faye. Watching the gun.

"It was Victor's idea to blackmail Trey Winters, wasn't it," Danny said.

"Yeah, but it was all my fault. *I'm* the one who told him about the safe in the first place. He took *my* key for the apartment, went over to the building, sneaked in the back way, and stole the shit out of the safe."

Off to Danny's right, the helicopter searchlight scanned the Hell Gate. He tried to look out at the water. A thick, greasy film coated the inside windows.

"Were the pictures in the safe?" Danny said.

"What pictures?"

"The pictures, I assume, that showed Gillian and Winters having sex."

"Who told you that? There were no pictures, just letters. Letters that had nothing to do with Gillian. I wouldn't let Victor do that to Gillian."

"Letters?"

"Yeah. Paul Klass wrote these letters addressed to people who he was forgiving for shit, before he died. A couple were to Mr. Winters, forgiving him for screwing over his wife's father."

"Darcy's father . . . Marty Jacobs?"

"Marty Jacobs, that's the guy. I never heard of him before, but Gillian knew who he was. She knew the whole story. In one letter Paul Klass talks about these videos of him and Marty Jacobs blowing these young boys. Having sex and shit, with these little kids. And Mr. Winters knew about the videos and used it to get something over on Marty Jacobs. So Marty Jacobs got mad at Paul Klass for telling. Then before he died Paul Klass wrote all these letters forgiving Mr. Winters and all these other people who fucked him over in his life. I thought it was a nice thing to do, forgive everybody. People should do that."

"Victor was using the letters to blackmail Winters."

"It worked," Faye said.

"Not for Gillian."

"Victor said Gillian wouldn't get in any trouble, because she didn't do anything. So when Winters asked her about the letters that night, she called me, and I said . . . Yeah, Victor has them. Then she told Winters she could get them back. Victor went over there that night to give them back. But Gillian was acting crazy. She said she was calling the cops on Victor, no matter what."

"So he killed her?" Danny said.

"Gillian never liked Victor. She tried to get me to stay away from him. But he was my brother. What could I do? He was more than my brother."

"What does that mean?" Danny said.

Faye looked straight ahead. She took a deep drink of the bottle. It was almost gone.

"Victor murdered Gillian," Danny said. "He threw her off the terrace."

Faye waved her hand as if to dismiss him. Danny heard the butt of the gun hit against the bottle.

"He didn't have to kill her, Faye. He killed her because he wanted the money. Like you said, nothing stops him."

Danny tried to look out across the water. The windows were now foggier with the breath of two. He rubbed a clear circle with the side of his hand. Ward's Island was all lit up like Christmas with red turret lights and searchlights.

"He's my family," Faye said.

"Bullshit. He knew you loved Gillian, and he killed her anyway. For himself. For money for himself."

Danny caught a glimpse of something in the side-view mirror. A figure in the darkness behind them. Crouching. Moving toward them. He hit the button on his door, locking it.

"Somebody's behind us, Faye," he said. "Let's get out of here. You didn't do anything wrong, and I can help you. Just let me help you."

"You can't help me, Puppy Chow."

"We'll find my uncle. He can help you, before you get in too far over your head."

"Your uncle the judge and jury?"

"No, he's Anthony Ryan, the detective you've been talking to."

"Oh, Jesus," Faye said. She banged her head against the side window, two, three, four times. Danny couldn't see the gun; he thought maybe it had fallen to the floor. "I am no goddamn good. Never was, never will be. Your uncle. Jesus. I wanted to fuck him, too. And he's your uncle. Jesus. Nice guys. All my life I've been looking for some nice guy."

"Start the car, Faye. Just drive the car, please."

"To where, Puppy Chow? Where can you go?"

Danny saw the man's shadow outside his fogged-up side window. Faye screamed. The hulking figure grabbed the door handle and tried to open it, yanking the locked door with such force the entire car rocked. The bottle of rum clanked off the steering wheel and fell to the floor. Mouth open, Faye brought the gun up. The barrel clicked against her teeth. Danny lunged, wrapping his hands around hers. The force of his weight slammed them against the window. The gun went off, shattering glass, reverberating, as if an explosion had occurred inside the tiny car.

Danny's ears rang in the silence, as Joe Gregory reached in and took the gun from him.

"It's okay," Gregory said, his voice soft, soothing. He opened the car door. "Everything's going to be fine."

Faye Boudreau stretched her arms up toward him, as if he were the father she never knew.

52

Victor Nuñez dove deep and fast to avoid the spotlight. He didn't know how far the bright light of the helicopter could penetrate into the water. He dug for the bottom, then turned smoothly underwater and swam toward the rocky shoreline. He needed to find a spot, an air pocket under an outcropping, a place he could breathe and rest.

The helicopter had destroyed his timing. Having to run across the island, instead of biking, cost him time and energy. Now the copter had zeroed in on the area under the bridge. They must have found his clothes and shoes on the other side. If so, they'd found Faye by now.

It was a good thing he had an alternate plan. Always have a backup plan, his father had taught him. This one he'd devised because he didn't trust Faye. Strange Faye, always so unpredictable. He didn't know if she'd be there when he came out of the water. So he'd stashed a stolen car, a few blocks south, near a small Queens park filled with dozens of indecipherable hunks of metal they called sculpture. He'd attached a second rope to a metal pole at that spot to pull himself up. Maybe two hundred yards away. But he had to get there underwater, and the crossing currents of the Hell Gate were stronger and trickier than he'd expected.

Victor broke the surface quietly, for a quick breath. The helicopter was at its farthest point, an opportunity to surface swim. He drove his powerful legs, pushing toward the shore. He needed a fuller, stronger stroke, but between the backpack and the pain he could not rotate his shoulder all the way back. The shoulder was worse than he'd thought.

He didn't have far to go, only thirty yards, but he lost track of the helicopter, and then it was behind him, its brilliant spotlight fixed on the water. He dove again, turning over as he did. The bright light penetrated like a match through fog. He reached out, hoping to touch rock. Pain shot through his right shoulder.

He stayed under for as long as he could, then popped up. The light was even brighter, the sound greater. The helicopter seemed to be hovering out in the middle of the water, the surface churning from the wind of the blades. The outside edge of the spotlight was only a few feet away from him. He dove again and noticed the backpack seemed to be getting heavier. He kicked desperately, then his knuckles grazed rock. If he could only find a pocket in the jagged shoreline, a haven in the shards of rock formed from the explosives of the engineers over a century ago. A spot where he could breathe, away from the lights.

His lungs burned as he felt his way up the shore wall. Then his head struck an outcropping. Don't panic, he told himself. With his back to the floor of Hell Gate Channel, he grabbed slimy rock, trying to find his way up around the cruel ceiling. The gods were with him as he felt the curve of rock and the clear water above. He pushed and kicked. But he couldn't rise. Something was holding him down. He twisted and turned until he realized the backpack had snagged on something.

His lungs felt about to burst. He slid his arms from the bag and tried to wrench it free, digging with bare hands into the rock. But he was too weak. He placed his feet against the rock and tried to use his body weight. But as he turned, he retched, the sick air bursting from him. He gulped, his throat and chest in spasm. He gulped, taking in the filthy water. It soothed him. Cooled him. Like the waters of the Sea of Cortés. A dolphin swam near, touching his face, wanting to play.

Anthony Ryan had kicked off his shoes the second he saw the green Volvo. He struggled with his socks, pants, and jacket. He managed the tie over his head, then ripped off the shirt with his one good hand. He was already in the water when he heard a single gunshot. Breaking glass. The sounds went through him like an electric shock. Always a good swimmer, Ryan jolted ahead, and he drove for the spot where he'd seen a head come out of the water.

It won't happen again, he told himself. Not this time, not while I have a chance. It won't happen. It won't. He sliced through the water, hardly taking a breath. The cold water felt good on his itchy head, and the blue hospital cast on his right hand acted as a paddle.

Ryan concentrated on the spot on the bulkhead where he'd seen the head surface. But he had to squint in the bright light of the helicopter hovering right above him. Someone was yelling something over a loudspeaker. He swam harder as the helicopter came closer, the downdraft rippling the water. They'd mistaken him for Nuñez. No way he could correct that now. He hoped for the best. Hoped some cowboy cop didn't take it upon himself to pick up a high-powered rifle. He saw a knotted rope hanging, probably attached to a roadway guard-rail. When he reached the rope the figure had disappeared. Ryan dove. He wasn't sure why. His arm scraped along the slimy wall, jagged rocks, and pieces of metal. His foot touched something different. He felt around, trying to make contact. Then he surfaced, took two deep breaths, and dove again. He scraped his hand along the rough walls. Nothing. He pushed, telling himself to dig deeper. He tried. He tried with all his being. Then there was no more in him. He floated to the surface.

Exhausted and starting to shiver, Anthony Ryan dog-paddled in the circus atmosphere. All around him were lights and movement; bullhorns and sirens; cars, trucks, and boats. Cops yelled at him to stay right where he was. They called him by name now, their voices reassuring, as if he were an old man lost in a park. Divers jumped from a Harbor Unit launch. The new NYPD, all technology, equipment, and youth. Isn't youth grand, Leigh had said.

On Shore Boulevard the lights were even brighter. He saw his partner in the luminous haze, standing next to his nephew, both of them looking down into the water.

Anthony Ryan knew he'd saved no one, but he felt at peace with himself. Maybe it was all about trying, he thought. The simple, holy truth of effort. The past would always be there, even as he remembered less of it. He waited for the young men and women of the NYPD. It was too bright to see the stars. It would have been nice to see the stars, but he was ready to be rescued. Ready for whatever comes next.

53

Anthony Ryan sat on his back deck in the magic hour of a Sunday as the sun's last light glittered around his granddaughter, Katie, running circles through the grass, chasing fireflies.

"I can't believe you did this," Anthony Ryan said.

"It was easy," Leigh said. "I asked Joe, and he took care of everything."

"I got her over here," Gregory said. "Getting her back to Ireland is your problem."

The Ryans had been eating breakfast when Gregory walked in with a case of Brooklyn Lager on his shoulder and Katie's hand in his. Overnight she'd flown in on the Project Children charter, sitting next to a man she knew only as the Duck, who taught her how to play "Sweet Molly Malone" on the tin whistle with her nose.

"We'll get her back," Ryan said. "When we're good and ready."

Danny Eumont flipped the steaks on the barbecue and ranted about how was he going to know when the meat was done, in the darkness. Gregory shoved his good hand in the ice chest and grabbed a beer. His other hand had been cut reaching through the broken window of Pinto's Nova. He opened the bottle and gave it to Danny, saying it would do more for his eyesight than anything that damn New Jerseyite Edison had invented.

"I should put some lights on," Leigh said.

"No, leave it like this," Ryan said. "It's perfect."

Leigh got up and began watering the flowers. In the past week she'd transformed their backyard into a garden. Potted geraniums and zinnias and snapdragons and impatiens in boxes hanging from the kitchen window. Hydrangeas, azealeas, and rhododendrons lined the outside edge of the deck. She watered them precisely, always starting and stopping in the same place.

"When you coming back to work, pally?" Joe Gregory whispered.

"The surgeon says another month with my hand. And I've got vacation time to burn. A lot of things we want to do. Get the Duck to fill in for me. He'll be glad to get back downtown. And I owe him for this."

"But you are coming back?"

Ryan just shrugged. In the quiet of his backyard he could hear the neighbors' kids. A Puerto Rican couple, he a Yonkers fireman, she a nurse at St. John's, had bought the Brunton house when they flew the coop to Florida. Once again, two houses away, the chirping laughter of infants could be heard on a street of empty nests.

"Jake Bugel claimed Victor's body yesterday," Gregory said. "Him and some guy named Carlson."

Six hours after NYPD divers fished Anthony Ryan out of the Hell Gate, they found Victor Nuñez. His backpack, containing twelve and a half pounds of artificial fortune, had snagged on a piece of metal imbedded in the bulkhead.

"I hear Evan Stone is in town," Ryan said.

"Yeah, that's turning out to be a nice story," Gregory said.

"Danny did it. He called them. Whatever he said had an effect, because they hired a lawyer for Faye, and it looks like they're getting behind her a hundred percent. She'll probably get probation, what with her cooperation and all. The Stones are trying to get a judge to release her into their custody in Arizona."

Faye had cooperated with a full accounting of Victor's description of Gillian's murder. They'd found resin in Victor's suitcase, that matched the sample from Gillian's mouth. Plus, in his backpack was a small plastic vial of liquid Lorazepam they assumed was meant for Faye.

"Danny did good," Gregory said. "He saved her life. She was serious about eating that gun. He jumped right in there."

"I'm really proud of him," Ryan said.

"Ain't that right, Danny?" Gregory yelled. "Me and you fighting the battle of Hell Gate and your uncle decides to go for a swim."

Ryan watched his wife go through the numbers of her orderly watering process. Leigh Ryan had even managed to get grass growing in their tree-shaded yard, a yard beaten down to near concrete by the feet of Rip and company in a thousand different games. The evening air was fragrant with the honeysuckle that grew wildly in the Carey yard.

"You talk to Winters?" Ryan asked.

"Actually, he's been pretty cooperative. He told us that Gillian said she was cleaning the closet one night and found a combination written on the back of the door frame. She looked under the rug, and there was the safe. She read the letters and made the mistake of telling Faye about them. Winters says he had no idea the safe was even there until she told him about it, that night."

"How is Darcy?" Ryan said.

"She's sticking by him, believe it or not. I figured she'd dump his ass after what he did to her father. Paul Klass's letter said that after Winters confronted Marty Jacobs about the boy sex thing, it freakin' killed him. He had a massive stroke just days after that. Winters says the only reason he did it was that Marty Jacobs had private detectives digging up all kinds of shit on him. He says he did it in self-defense, for love."

"Doesn't surprise me Darcy is being loyal. If Winters had had faith in her from the beginning, none of this would have happened."

The glow of red coals illuminated Danny's face as he examined the progress of a steak. Rip had been the chief Ryan barbecue chef since he was a teen. Rip claimed the reason men who never cooked loved to barbecue was that an element of danger was involved.

Leigh swung the last remaining drops of water out over the grass. She put the can under the deck in the same spot she'd been putting it since they'd bought the house. She picked up a pair of shears and snipped a green plant.

"Will that grow back now?" Ryan asked.

"This? This is hosta, you can't kill it."

Katie came running across the yard and leaped into Ryan's arms. She begged for another story like the one he'd told her earlier, about the carpet for the coronation of a Russian czar. But Leigh Ryan said she might have a story of her own. She put down the shears and took something out of her apron pocket. She handed it to Ryan.

"I found this in the back of Rip's bottom dresser drawer," she said, running her fingers through her husband's hair.

It was a cassette tape. He held the tape in his hands while she touched his latest scar. They had no record of their son's voice. In the attic sat boxes of old photographs, but his voice was only a memory. The damp evening breeze changed, now coming from the west. Ryan could smell mint from ground cover Leigh had planted. She must have snipped some.

"Are you ready for this?" she said, setting a tape recorder on the table.

"I don't know," Ryan said.

"What is it, Grandpa?" Katie said.

"We think it's a tape that Uncle Rip made," Leigh said.

"Ooh, play it," she said. "Please play it."

Ryan could feel the heat rushing to his face. Danny stood behind him. Gregory pulled his chair up close. Leigh snapped the tape in, and sound began. At first it sounded like air *whoosh*ing or a steam radiator belching air. Ryan's heart dropped; he hadn't been sure if he wanted to hear his son's voice. Now he was desperately disappointed.

Then, "My name is Rip, so don't give me no lip."

The voice of their son came in a singsong fashion from the small black Sony. It didn't sound like him. The voice was a put-on, an imitation of a street gangster. Rip, who loved to call himself a Dixie wop-mick because of his mother's southern heritage and his Irish Italian father, was imitating a rap singer.

"I remember him doing this," Danny said.

Anthony Ryan held his hands over the tiny metal speaker as if he could touch his son's voice with his fingers. They all stared at the machine. Then more air *whoosh*ing; they realized it was Rip making the sound with his mouth. Rip the rap artist. He was beating on something like a trash can.

"I come from Yonkers, where all my friends are wankers," sang Rip the rapper.

Then more *whoosh*ing. And words mumbled in a ghetto staccato.

"I have no idea what he's saying," Leigh said.

"Neither do I."

"I think he said something about wankers?" she said.

"Sounded like wankers. Is it supposed to rhyme with Yonkers?"

"It doesn't," Leigh said.

Ryan shrugged and looked across at his wife. He heard her laugh that deep, chesty laugh as their son entertained them one more time.

"Wankers," she said, shaking her head, tears streaming.

Gregory sang Rip's song, just the one line. Katie danced that stiff robot rap dance. Then she went running. Danny said he thought the steaks were ready, but he couldn't be positive.

The moon was just a sliver above them. Anthony Ryan reached out and held his wife's hand. A little girl, laughing hard enough to wake the neighborhood, raced wildly in a flowery backyard lit only by fireflies.

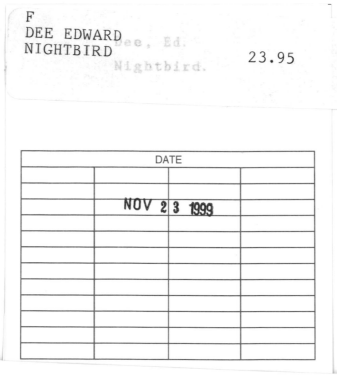

DATE			
		NOV 2 3 1999